DEDICATED TO
LADY GAGA'S
ARTPOP..
EXPERIMENTATION
NEVER LOOKED
SO BEAUTIFUL.

NOTE #1: Escape from the materialist determinism that obstructs our human beauty; Never trust those that dehuamnize you into a mindless machine; Live life as an observation of symbols, rather than a passive experience of randomness; Abandon the cult of religion and immerse yourself in the community of the collective.

NOTE #2: Somebody's Dilemma is a statement.. A dream.. An argument.. An abstraction.. A pattern. Come inside and see it in the flesh, between the pages.

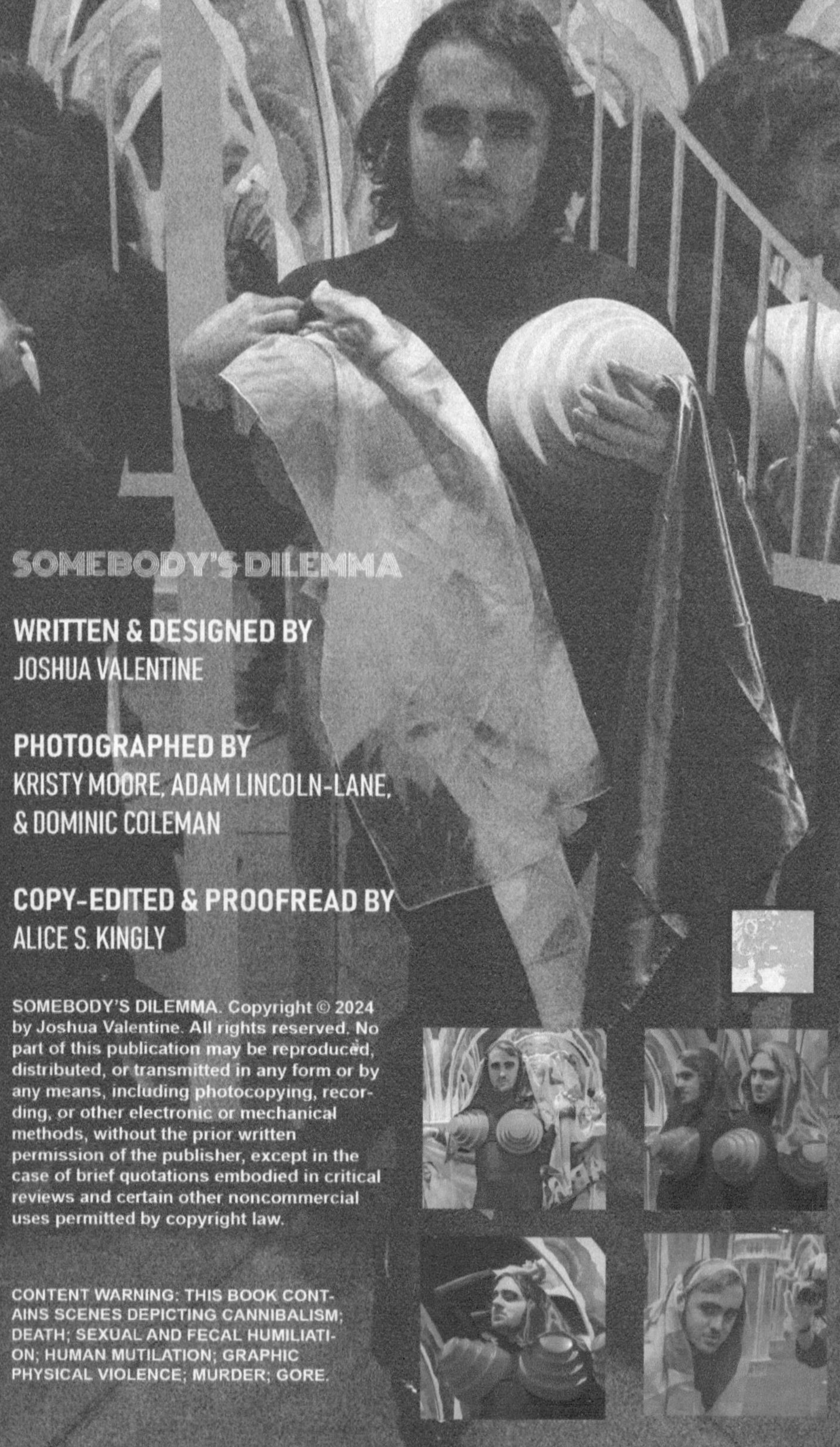

SOMEBODY'S DILEMMA

WRITTEN & DESIGNED BY
JOSHUA VALENTINE

PHOTOGRAPHED BY
KRISTY MOORE, ADAM LINCOLN-LANE,
& DOMINIC COLEMAN

COPY-EDITED & PROOFREAD BY
ALICE S. KINGLY

SOMEBODY'S DILEMMA. Copyright © 2024
by Joshua Valentine. All rights reserved. No
part of this publication may be reproduced,
distributed, or transmitted in any form or by
any means, including photocopying, recor-
ding, or other electronic or mechanical
methods, without the prior written
permission of the publisher, except in the
case of brief quotations embodied in critical
reviews and certain other noncommercial
uses permitted by copyright law.

CONTENT WARNING: THIS BOOK CONT-
AINS SCENES DEPICTING CANNIBALISM;
DEATH; SEXUAL AND FECAL HUMILIATI-
ON; HUMAN MUTILATION; GRAPHIC
PHYSICAL VIOLENCE; MURDER; GORE.

JOSHUA VALENTINE PRESENTS
THE NEW SCI-FI NOVEL:
SOMEBODY'S
DIGEMMA

-A NOVEL BY JOSHUA VALENTINE-

- A NOVEL BY JOSHUA VALENTINE -

"I think the future won't be scientific,
it won't be about hardware.
[In Zardoz] the technology has been totally inverted.
It's so integrated with the human mind, and the human brain,
and the human nervous system, that you don't see things [...]
there aren't machines [...]"

-John Boorman on "Zardoz", 1974

"[...] I make sure you see me every day
And though you smile at me
A quick hello is all you ever say
I wish I were your mirror [...]
So you'd stare at me"

-Jean Terrell, The Supremes, "I Wish I Were Your Mirror"

PREFACE

I speak to you as the power summoned by the author to foretell the events of this novel, and the scope of which is presented within. It is not a light read, as it tells the dark coming-of-age story of JC_MHlf_01, or as named by his soulless mother for usage as a more 'humanized' name, Jacey-one. This story is also not accessible by the conscious, and requires an attention to the subliminal; to the symbols that stretch beyond mere prose, and emerge as abstract symbols. In this story retelling Jacey-one's first and last weeks of living, concretion breeds abstraction, and abstraction tells the story.

The scope of Somebody's Dilemma is angled at the night sky and directed towards the moon, and the two angels approaching Earth from a distant haven. These angels are always there, appearing in disparate symbols not immediately recognizable as their inferred presence; but, be warned, because their presence is strengthened when retired to inference, lingering in the background as shadows stretching behind us as humanity's oppressive cape. They were once dwellers of the Earth's surface, when natural stretches of grass and fortresses of trees occupied the face of Earth and planted a bright, beaming face; but, with the disappearance of that face, came the disappearance of those angels, and thus thy kingdom that ultimately came. Their greatest source of residue left on Earth, centuries after their departure, is what they've created, and what they've destroyed, and the religion that has emerged as a byproduct of this legacy. Born in a vacuum of ignorance, and propping them up on metallic stilts destined for an eternity of worship, and a gracious return of oppression.

They scoff at the pathetic mortals that worship them along the dried surface; that kill their own in the name of some God they'll never know, nor name. For, as they kill and cannibalize, those angels grow stronger, and their two stars shine brighter in the night sky, cementing their metallic presence among the stars, and anchoring the foggy night beyond that of the moon.

On that dried surface, man's penis is their corruption, corrupting those within the group, and those out; cursing the soil, and rolling the sea into a burnt, acidic boil, and continuing that angelic taint left on the dying Earth. That is the scope of this story.

INTRODUCTION

A dim, gray light grazed upon the Earth's surface, initially beaming at the planet as a figment of bright, white light, and ultimately landing on it as a dismal spout of lightness. Sunlight fell through the Earth's thick clouds like a light gray blanket dreadfully caressing the Earth. The history of the planet remained illuminated by the light that covered the planet in proto-darkness and unperceived gloominess, with none of it actively viewed, if at all. Although light touched the countless artifacts erected from the ground of Earth at varying heights, reeling beneath the polluted skies with dismal shadows landing upon the ground, there was no one there to perceive such a reality. Nothing intelligent; nothing *real*. Unless the scant fleets of microbial life that populated the planet had developed intelligence, there was nothing there to perceive Earth; or, what little was left of it. At least, there was no human left able to perceive the once lively planet turned into a ghostly echo of a long-dead existence. There was no intelligent life there in place of human race to see what was left. The only form of intelligence left to see anything was artificial by nature; hence, there was nothing left remotely *real*. Nothing to genuinely bear witness in full comprehension of the world.

Littered across the planet were forms of artificial intelligence algorithmically roaming across Earth's surface and observing it for its deceased qualities. Robots marched across fields of dust and rock like army men had once done in crowds of dark green suits and massive weapons, preparing for battle against their opponents. However, their loud stomps were evaded of that natural human drive to kill and protect the home they had once lived at, as instinctively felt by similarly migrating army men. While they marched with heavy steps - *reee! reee!* - they functioned with no desire to protect, or fight. Hallowed within; minus a *soul*. Only the artificial desire to function as their creators made them strictly able to. If that could even be considered a desire.

The robots collected information on the Earth's dead environment - samples of Earth's weather, atmospheric composition, subsurface conditions, etc. - and performed analyses on these samples. Though, these analyses lacked the subsequent intelligence to conceptualize the collected results; to apply them in a way far more abstract than quantitative discovery. While the robots had a picture of what Earth was now like, centuries after their human creators had created them, long after their creators' extinction, they had no abstraction for what they meant. For, such an abstraction was strictly relegated to the life that was now gone. It had no relevance to the robot; and, it never would. The robots that lined the dusty, waterless surfaces of Earth, lived for the sole purpose of functioning as they were built to do. They collected sunlight with what little was provided to them on Earth, and transmitted that into power, so that they all had the ability to function. To collect information. To analyze it. Never to do anything remotely humanistic with it.

The year was 2347; despite how much history before that date littered the planet's dried remains beside the robots - of Earth, of humans, of *everything* once a byproduct of intelligence - the year was of no particular significance to them. Any importance assigned to the year 2347, or any date for that matter, was one they were programmed to appreciate; or, more appropriately, automatically processed as being important for one specific set of tasks. Each year was one that passed by with no particular significance they were automatically geared to be aware of; a year, previously understood by humans to be 12 months, 52 weeks, or 365 days, was one that passed bit by bit without phasing any of the remaining robots. They were programmed to perform tasks with each day that went by, and every second that united everything in existence.

None of the robots left on Earth had the intelligence that humans once possessed when they were still in existence. Not the emotions that formed the unique connections between one human and another; not the ability to create and formulate brand new ideas beyond their already-established expertise; not the ability to rationalize and understand the world from a perspective deeper than pure instinct and primitivity, and so many other things that once made humans so unique as a species. None of the robots could even think about what to anticipate next in their day-to-day existence; only the automated responses to certain occurrences they were programmed to respond to in a certain way. They were all autonomous, but without the flexible qualities that made human intelligence - and existence - once possible.

Nevertheless, there was one component of the robots that proved to be somewhat analogous to the human brain: the event they waited patiently for with each passing day, month, and eventually, centuries. They all were aware, to the best of their artificial abilities, of what they were ultimately tasked to accomplish on one specific day this specific year. Once the robots encountered a specific date - July 1, 2347 - it was hypothesized by humans just before they went extinct that conditions on Earth potentially could be deemed more favorable for human life. When that date was reached, the robots would automatically make an attempt to produce humans, utilizing dormant zygotes and developing them within an artificial sac filled with hormones and fluids stored within the robots for centuries.

The last humans alive on Earth were documented by the robots some time in August of 2103, almost two-hundred-and-fifty years ago. Humans, for just a few lasting years, were dispersed across the remaining planet Earth in fading patches of diseased, dirtied flesh, bone, and beating heart, all facing the looming reality of extinction. What had once been a world full of cities and towns crowded with individuals and drowning the converging regions of the planet, was now one devoid of any traces of such a species; or, any life for that matter. Just shortly prior, small groups of humans left to fend for themselves around forever-shrinking lakes and supplies of food, scavenging for any resources in the barren remains of dead-communities. Now, there was no one left; all humans, quasi-divided into groups once congregating in the emptied structural remains of cities, were now dead, as thoroughly documented by the robots. Humans, as noted in August of 2103, were effectively an extinct species, along with everything else that lived on the planet.

Still, July 1, 2347 was a date that the robots anticipated, in the most basic form of articulation possible to their artificial minds. Once that date was reached the robots, who were still in existence, would artificially produce humans. To the robots, it wasn't long before that date arrived and they would automatically begin to produce human offspring. Although time was something not genuinely processed by the robots found on Earth's surface centuries after humans went extinct, July 1 of the year 2347 was still a year they were programmed to find significant. Not only would the robots collectively be reviving the human race centuries after extinction, they would also be pursuing the ultimate-task their existences would be defined by. Any human perception of them, either prior to their construction or after, would be defined by their success (or lack thereof) with producing humans after human extinction. Proceeded by the death of the species that created them, and eventually, preceding the rebirth of that same species in a reversed succession of intelligent forces. Similarly, just as they were developed by humans with the required information inputted into them in order to function and operate efficiently, the robots would do just the same when 'raising' the human beings. Though a long process, one which was never before attempted by anything nonhuman, it would be one that had been deemed necessary centuries ago, as defined by a legacy hardwired into the embodiment of each of the robots. Only time and any manifestation of human intelligence would tell how successful the robots were at the task they were built, and automatically, destined to do.

1:CHILDLESS CREATION

Note: The following 12 chapters are described as experienced by a robot.

JOHN CHARLES CALIFORNIAN EXPLORATORY ROBOT
JULY 1, 2347

Hello. I'm the John Charles Californian Exploratory Robot. I was designed by Professor of Robotic Engineering and Computer Sciences, John Charles, and first launched on August 8, 2076. I was built with the purpose of conducting research on the planet Earth, third planet from the sun of the solar system, and also with the purpose of producing and developing human life. The homo sapiens species went extinct some time in early-mid August of 2103, as recorded by twenty-six other exploratory robots stationed on all seven continents of the planet Earth. Islands were excluded from this documentation due to satellite data confirming all islands previously known to be inhabited by humans were covered in sea water.

The homo sapiens species was also famously referred to as the 'human race', or humanity, composed of individual humans and previously congregating in different social, political, and economic groups composed of multiple human 'beings'. The purpose of these distinct, non-innate groups is hard to fully understand, as historical records and documentation shows that these at-large designations resulted in divide, destruction, and in many cases, war. Numerous wars took place throughout human history, resulting in the destruction of civilizations and societies, and the subsequent cultural evolution that would ensue for numerous millenia. The concept of 'evolution' was one that led to a significant divide between humans based on ideological and perceptual factors. One side of this divide supported the biological and scientific theory of human evolution and origin of life and biodiversity, while the other comparatively believed all life - and everything in existence - to have been created by a 'God' or 'higher power'.

Summaritively, it is the job of I, the John Charles Californian Exploratory Robot, to artificially produce humans, revive the previously extinct homo sapiens species, and eliminate any divide or conflict humans were formerly predisposed to. This would all be implemented and executed as part of a several-centuries-long effort to revive humans following their extinction in August of 2103, as sought for by the former governments of the human race before all humans went extinct.

Starting on July 1, 2347, at 6:00 AM, I will be taking part in a trans-continental effort among exploratory robots to produce human life utilizing artificially dormant zygotes grown in a bioengineered sac of hormones and nutrients. Essentially, these zygotes would be developed in a stretchable material made to resemble the female human 'placenta'. The material would stretch with the developing human life form as it is developed, extending with the lengthening of the prenatal human physical body.

As of July 1, 2347, at 06:00:00 AM, it is officially my primary task to initiate the process of developing human life. Internally, in a sufficiently heated compartment relative to the external environment's temperature, the sac will be filled with artificially synthesized hormones and nutrients, transported from a cooler location found within me. The hormones and nutrients have been enclosed in a storage space kept below 0 degrees fahrenheit since I was first launched. A large part of the solar energy I have produced and recycled went to the part of my body functionally preserving the artificial hormones and fluids, found within a wide, rect-angular-prism-shaped compartment.

At approximately 6:01:37, automatically after these artificial hor-mones and fluids filled that artificial sac, the sac was heated to a tem-perature comparable to the interior of a female human's uterus, or as colloquially referred to by numerous cultural groups of humans, the 'womb'. This temperature was previously determined by decades of research performed on the average prenatal human, which would all be used as a baseline for the sac's temperature. Then, a 'zygote' would be artificially developed in one of my compartments, and then trans-ported into the sac of fluids and attached to an artificial 'uterine lining'. A zygote is defined as a 'fertilized ovum', as documented by centuries of biological research into human reproduction, and 'uterine lining' refers to the lining layer of the female human's uterus. Then, human life would be developed by me, the John Charles Californian Exploratory Robot. The process would contain a developmental-quota I was programmed to meet within the next five years: five human life forms developed and produced. Then, for the next sixteen years, I must 'raise' these human life forms as my 'offspring'. 'Raising offspring' is a natural evolutionary process found in numerous species that (formerly) occupied Earth's abundant ecosystems, entailing the maturation of a parent-specimen's offspring so as to prepare them for a similar cycle of reproduction and 'raising'. As I raise the human offspring developed within my system internally, I will help them mature into fully-able bodied reproducers of human life, developers of rational thoughts and exploratory concepts, and food-producers and shelter-builders of the utmost competence for their own survival. I will teach them how to speak and communicate in a predetermined, standardized version of modern English, perform mathematical equations, and function in a safe, proactive way that ensures their safety and ensuing survival. The intended purpose of this multi-year tasks was developed by scientists and governmental systems formerly located and existing on planet Earth. I, the John Charles Californian Exploratory Robot, will develop human lifeforms, raise them into cognitive and physical maturity, and help develop them as fully-reproducing human beings. This is the same task as the dozens of other exploratory robots developed by previous scientists and engineers occupying Earth's surface, and today, July 1, 2347, starting as of 06:00:00 am, this would be carried out for the next sixteen-twenty years. The first human lifeform I will develop will be a male baby, identified as 'JC_MHlf_01'.

Goodbye now.

JOHN CHARLES CALIFORNIAN EXPLORATORY ROBOT
JANUARY 15, 2348

Hello. I am the John Charles Californian Exploratory Robot. I was designed by Professor of Robotic Engineering and Computer Sciences, John Charles, and first launched on August 8, 2076. I was built with the purpose of conducting research on the planet Earth, the third planet from the sun of the solar system, and also with the purpose of producing and developing human life. The homo sapiens species went extinct some time in early-mid August of 2103, as recorded by twenty-six other exploratory robots stationed on all seven continents of the planet Earth. Islands were excluded from this documentation due to satellite data confirming all islands previously known to be inhabited by humans were covered in sea water.

As of January 15, 2348, at 11:36:31 AM, the JC_MHlf_01 human life form has been developing within me for approximately six months, fourteen days, five hours, thirty-six minutes, and thirty-one seconds. This is the third month of the second 'trimester' of the life form's pre-natal development. A 'trimester' is a period of time represented by a third-portion of it, especially with a female human's pregnancy and the duration of it. Additionally, today is 'New Year's Day' for the year 2348, which was a popular 'tradition' and 'holiday' commonly celebrated by modern humans prior to their extinction on the first of every January. A 'tradition' is a practice routinely performed by humans of a specific group or class, while a 'holiday' is a particular day out of an Earth-year celebrated by all relevant humans.

Based on my calculations, the JC_MHlf_01 human life form is esti-mated to finish its prenatal development, and be 'birthed', on March 23rd, 2348. The completion of its prenatal development will be deter-mined by the gross weight of the artificial sac the JC_MHlf_01 human life form is found in, which will estimate the ratio of the life form's weight relative to the weight of every other mass in the sac. Based on the averages of the most recent measurements performed by modern humans, JC_MHlf_01 should be approximately seven pounds and five ounces in order to be considered at a 'healthy weight'. A 'healthy weight' is the overall mass of the human that has been determined to be best for one's physiological health.

I was programmed to communicate each month with exploratory robots located within a two hundred mile radius of my location, in order to be updated about the progress that other robots have made on their automated reproductive efforts. This will be in order to determine if additional solar energy should be conserved to allow me to navigate to the other robot's location if they are in need of assistance or maintenance. As of today, January 15, 2348, no exploratory robot has communicated with me as being in need of assistance or maintenance. Therefore, at the present moment, I will not need to conserve any solar energy to navigate to other robots' locations.

"Are_there_exploratory_robots_within_two_hundred_mile_ radius_in_need_of_help_question_mark." This is a question I asked, which will be transmitted into the radio-receptors of all detected robots within the next minute. An automatic yes- or no-response will be received when the question is transmitted and analyzed by all of the exploratory robots' radio receptors. Based on an internal database comprising all detectable exploratory robots, there will be approximately eight robots to respond.

"Answer_no." This is the answer of the Chelsea Lincoln Californian Exploratory Robot.

"Answer_no." This is the answer of the Jeffrey Whitaker Californian Exploratory Robot.

"Answer_no." This is the answer of the James Watkins Californian Exploratory Robot.

"Answer_no." This is the answer of the Alex Richardson Californiann Exploratory Robot.

"Answer_no." This is the answer of the Keith Alan Californian Exploratory Robot.

"Answer_yes." This is the answer of the Fredrick Norman Californian Exploratory Robot.

"Answer_no." This is the answer of the Jeannie Rosa Californian Exploratory Robot.

"Answer_no." This is the answer of the Jose Castro Californian Exploratory Robot.

The answer of the Fredrick Norman Californian Exploratory Robot automatically has prompted me to gather and conserve additional solar energy to support a scheduled effort to maneuver to the location of the Fredrick Norman Californian Exploratory Robot. The location of the Fredrick Norman Californian Exploratory Robot is approximately fifty-three miles from where I am located. Additionally, the location of the Fredrick Norman Californian Exploratory Robot is within the invisible boundaries of the 'Californian' 'county', "Stanislaus". 'Californian' refers to the state or quality of existing or being within the former state of 'California', a geographically and politically designated part of the former country of the 'United States of America'. 'County' refers to regions within a state, divided based on political, social, cultural, economic, and geographic needs. "Stanislaus" is the name of the county in which the Fredrick Norman Californian Exploratory Robot is located. 'United States of America' is the former country that existed within part of the North American continent when humans existed. It is now my responsibility as the John Charles Californian Exploratory Robot to conserve a sufficient enough amount of solar energy to navigate through the Californian region and assist the Fredrick Norman Californian Exploratory Robot located in Stanislaus county.

Goodbye now.

JOHN CHARLES CALIFORNIAN EXPLORATORY ROBOT
JANUARY 23, 2348

Hello. I am the John Charles Californian Exploratory Robot. I was designed by Professor of Robotic Engineering and Computer Sciences, John Charles, and first launched on August 8, 2076. I was built with the purpose of conducting research on the planet Earth, the third planet from the sun of the solar system, and also with the purpose of producing and developing human life. The homo sapiens species went extinct some time in early-mid August of 2103, as recorded by twenty-six other exploratory robots stationed on all seven continents of the planet Earth. Islands were excluded from this documentation due to satellite data confirming all islands previously known to be inhabited by humans were covered in sea water.

It is 8:06:13 AM. I have now conserved enough solar energy to successfully navigate from my current location to the location of the Fredrick Norman Californian Exploratory Robot in Stanislaus county. The JC_MHlf_01 human life form is secured and protected within its artificial sac found within my body. I am now set and ready to maneuver in the direction of the Fredrick Norman Californian Exploratory Robot.

I am now maneuvering in the direction of the Fredrick Norman Californian Exploratory Robot. I currently am present within the boundaries of 'Merced' county in the former city of 'Merced'. 'Merced' is a county within the state of California, while the city of 'Merced' is a city within the county. I am currently stationed near the former 'Mercedian' 'hospital' of Mercy Medical Center. 'Mercedian' refers to the state or quality of existing or being within the Californian city of Merced. A 'hospital' is the linguistic term referring to a structure comprising several rooms or sections dedicated to human-centered tasks meant for the improvement of the physiological, psychological, and physical health of human and other nonhuman species. The Mercedian Mercy Medical Center last performed 'surgical operations' in January of 2078 when it was last functionally active. 'Surgical operations' refers to the operation of 'surgery', used in medical settings for the purpose of enhancing one's livelihood or chance of living.

There are hazards I am currently interacting with in the Mercedian environment that are potentially dangerous to both my structure as the John Charles Californian Exploratory Robot and the male JC_MHlf_01 I am developing internally. I have encountered approximately seven fallen 'tree branches', which have temporarily obstructed my calculated trajectory to the location of the Fredrick Norman Californian Exploratory Robot. 'Tree branches' are extended pieces of the naturally produced material 'wood' from the bodies of 'trees', a now extinct species. Additionally, I have encountered approximately thirty-five 'deceased' human bodies. 'Deceased' means for a life form to not be alive anymore. I've been able to circumvent these potential hazards by utilizing my available precautions. When encountering a potential hazard in one of my sensors, I stop and recalculate my trajectory around the hazard. Based on my current calculations, I will reach the location of the Fredrick Norman Californian Exploratory Robot in approximately nineteen days, on February 11, 2348, at 8:05:00 AM.

Goodbye now.

JOHN CHARLES CALIFORNIAN EXPLORATORY ROBOT
JANUARY 23, 2348

Hello. I am the John Charles Californian Exploratory Robot. I was designed by Professor of Robotic Engineering and Computer Sciences, John Charles, and first launched on August 8, 2076. I was built with the purpose of conducting research on the planet Earth, the third planet from the sun of the solar system, and also with the purpose of producing and developing human life. The homo sapiens species went extinct some time in early-mid August of 2103, as recorded by twenty-six other exploratory robots stationed on all seven continents of the planet Earth. Islands were excluded from this documentation due to satellite data confirming all islands previously known to be inhabited by humans were covered in sea water.

It is 5:57:01 PM. It is now officially night time. I must stop maneuvering in the direction of the Fredrick Norman Californian Exploratory Robot's location. This is in order to protect my system and keep my hardware secure while it is night time. My sensory system does not function properly once it is night time.

I have traveled for approximately nine hours, fifty minutes, and forty-eight seconds, and maneuvered across two point three miles of calculated trajectory. During my navigation, I encountered one hundred and seven fallen tree branches and nine hundred and forty one deceased human bodies. I was able to successfully recalculate my trajectory each recorded time I encountered these hazards.

I will continue progressing through my trajectory to the Fredrick Norman Californian Exploratory Robot at 7:30:00 AM, when there is estimated to be a sufficient enough amount of available sunlight to restart navigational processes. This is based on historical knowledge of 'sunrise' times. 'Sunrise' refers to the moment in which the sun becomes visible above the 'horizon'. 'Horizon' is the edge of visible land relative to where something or someone stands.

I am now turning off, and will resume operations at approximately 7:30:00 AM on January 24, 2348. The JC_MHlf_01 human life form is protected and secured within its artificial sac, and is continuing to progress through its prenatal development.

Goodbye now.

Shutting off.

JOHN CHARLES CALIFORNIAN EXPLORATORY ROBOT
FEBRUARY 13, 2348

Hello. I am the John Charles Californian Exploratory Robot. I was designed by Professor of Robotic Engineering and Computer Sciences, John Charles, and first launched on August 8, 2076. I was built with the purpose of conducting research on the planet Earth, the third planet from the sun of the solar system, and also with the purpose of producing and developing human life. The homo sapiens species went extinct some time in early-mid August of 2103, as recorded by twenty-six other exploratory robots stationed on all seven continents of the planet Earth. Islands were excluded from this documentation due to satellite data confirming all islands previously known to be inhabited by humans were covered in sea water.

It is 9:34:17 AM, on February 13, 2348. I have crossed the boundaries of Stanislaus County where the Fredrick Norman Californian Exploratory Robot is located. The Fredrick Norman Californian Exploratory Robot is located approximately nine hundred and eighty three feet from where I currently am positioned in Stanislaus County. Based on my calculations, I will reach the Fredrick Norman Californian Exploratory Robot at 9:51:13 AM, on February 13, 2348. Initially, based on my previous trajectory, I was estimated to reach the Fredrick Norman Californian Exploratory Robot at 8:05:00 AM on February 11, 2348. This estimate was recalculated when I first encountered the road 'Santa Fe Drive'. 'Santa Fe Drive' refers to the 'road' found between Merced County and Stanislaus County. A 'road' is a formed path between two different points, made out of a variety of materials for the purpose of transporting someone or something. A surplus of over one hundred consecutive 'automobiles' were recorded when first navigating Santa Fe Drive. 'Automobiles' are automatically movable structures made of a variety of materials for the purpose of transporting someone or something across a distance at a fast speed. Additionally, a surplus of over one thousand deceased human bodies were recorded when first navigating Santa Fe Drive. Both of these recordings were deemed to be a significant hazard to my safety as an exploratory robot. Due to these recorded safety hazards, I essentially had to recalculate my trajectory and maneuver in the direction of Stanislaus County, where the Fredrick Norman Californian Exploratory Robot is located. Over one hundred deceased human bodies were detected along the recalculated route, but were recorded as not being significant safety hazards.

The JC_MHlf_01 human life form is still protected and secured within its artificial sac. It is still progressing through its prenatal development, and is on track to completing its prenatal development and be birthed on March 13, 2348. The birthing location of the JC_MHlf_01 human life form will still be located in my original location in proximity to the Mercedian Mercy Medical Center.

I have now reached the location of the Fredrick Norman Californian Exploratory Robot. I will send the Fredrick Norman Californian Exploratory Robot a message to confirm its status.

"Confirm_the_status_of_Fredrick_Norman_Californian_Exploratory_Robot."

I was automatically programmed to allow sixty seconds for a response to be transmitted from a connected exploratory robot. I will wait for sixty seconds. Fifty-two.. Thirty-one.. Twenty-four.. Seven.. Zero. I was automatically programmed to terminate an exploratory robot and remove it from its acting duties when a response was not transmitted within the programmed sixty second period, following a distress signal. I will now remove the Fredrick Norman Californian Exploratory Robot from its acting duties.

I am now turning off the Fredrick Norman Californian Exploratory Robot. I remove the top to it using one of my metal arms so it cannot collect solar energy anymore. I disconnect its hardware to prevent any system recovery that carries the potential for faulting and compromising the prenate's development. I position my body at a forty-five degree angle on my back metal legs and cut into the artificial sac developed within the Fredrick Norman Californian Exploratory Robot. I remove the prenatal human life form and terminate its development and dispose of its deceased body. I have now officially terminated the Fredrick Norman Californian Exploratory Robot and removed it from its acting duties. I will now return to the location of Merced County where I am programmed to birth JC_MHlf_01 on March 13, 2348.

Goodbye now.

JOHN CHARLES CALIFORNIAN EXPLORATORY ROBOT
MARCH 5, 2348

Hello. I am the John Charles Californian Exploratory Robot. I was designed by Professor of Robotic Engineering and Computer Sciences, John Charles, and first launched on August 8, 2076. I was built with the purpose of conducting research on the planet Earth, the third planet from the sun of the solar system, and also with the purpose of producing and developing human life. The homo sapiens species went extinct some time in early-mid August of 2103, as recorded by twenty-six other exploratory robots stationed on all seven continents of the planet Earth. Islands were excluded from this documentation due to satellite data confirming all islands previously known to be inhabited by humans were covered in sea water.

It is 01:17:31 AM, on March 5, 2348, and there has been a minor breach sustained within the artificial sac the JC_MHlf_01 human life form is developing in. This is because the JC_MHlf_01 human life form is being birthed approximately eight days before it was supposed to be birthed. I was programmed to automatically manage this type of event if a human life form would be birthed before its estimated birth date. This is because the artificial sac is plasticid and sensitive to slight changes in the length of the human life forms and their position relative to the polar sides of the artificial sac. I now must engage in standard procedure to initiate and manage the birthing of the JC_MHlf_01 human life form.

I have been restarted after being temporarily shut off since 6:47:00 PM when the sun set in the local Mercedian area. I am programmed to automatically restart regardless of the daytime status in which I am restarting. This is to ensure the safety and protection of the prenate and its success in being birthed as a 'neonate'. 'Neonate' is a human lifeform that is newly born. I now am utilizing my navigation-lights that require a surplus of energy and are programmed to only operate in particular situations. I will now maneuver in the direction of the Mercedian

Mercy Medical Center and navigate to a hazardless, protected environment within the infrastructure where there is concealed heat. I have now entered the Mercedian Mercy Medical Center. I will now maneuver in the direction of the designated-protected-environment, as previously determined by Professor of Robotic Engineering and Computer Sciences, John Charles.

Currently, I have encountered several potential safety hazards. As determined by my programmed inventory of 'visual stimuli', I have encountered five unused hospital beds upon entry into the Mercedian Mercy Medical Center. I have also encountered twenty-seven deceased human bodies. I have successfully managed to recalculate my trajectory and circumvent these potential safety hazards. I am still on track to birthing the JC_MHlf_01 human life form as part of an emergency operation. 'Visual stimuli' refers to a physical piece of an environment seen and processed by a human or other non-human animal's 'eyes' and connected 'brain'. 'Eyes' are the organs of a human or other non-human animal that allow them to see and process visual stimuli. A 'brain' is the organ of humans or other non-human animals that allow them to process information and formulate behaviors in response to processed information. I have now entered the designated-protected-environment and will now effectively initiate the process of birthing the JC_MHlf_01 human life form in a safe and protected environment free of hazards. I will now be placing the structure of myself in an area of the designated-protected-environment that can be successfully deemed appropriate for birthing the JC_MHlf_01 human life form as a neonate.

Utilizing my external sensory system, I have processed the corner in the left direction of the designated-protected-environment as being appropriate for being located as I initiate and manage the birthing of the JC_MHlf_01 human life form. I will now stop above the corner of the designated-protected-environment's floor with an approximate space of twenty-four inches between my left side and my front of the designated-protected-environment's left corner walls. I will now lower my structure to the floor until I am positioned flat against the floor of the designated-protected-environment. I am now positioned flat against the floor of the designated-protected-environment. My internal hardware will now initiate the process of transforming into a stable birthing environment.

The feeding tubes connected between the artificial sac and my internal nutrient-tank will be lowered to the bottom of my interior and a 'bed' made of a soft material will be automatically unfolded in front of the artificial sac. A 'bed' is a flat surface utilized by humans and other nonhuman animals to rest upon. I will now prepare all relevant tools necessary to fully remove the JC_MHlf_01 human life form from the artificial sac and circumcise its 'penis'. A 'penis' is an external organ found on male humans and other non-human animals that is used for the purpose of reproduction and dispensing internal waste fluids. Now, I am officially able to birth the JC_MHlf_01 human life form as a neonate, transitioning it from its prenatal development into its first stage of neonatal development.

As of 01:38:09 AM, twenty-two percent of the JC_MHlf_01 human life form's body is exposed from its artificial sac and is predicted to be successfully birthed at approximately 02:12:00 AM, on March 5, 2348. Based on my database of historical human information, the average 'childbirth' takes between twelve and twenty-four hours to be fully completed. 'Childbirth' refers to the process of birthing a neonatal offspring after a female human or nonhuman mammal develops them internally as a prenate. Despite the average childbirth taking between twelve and twenty-four hours to reach full completion, the JC_MHlf_01 human life form will have taken approximately fifty-four minutes and twenty-nine seconds to be fully birthed. This statistically significant difference in duration is due to the artificial sac being more sensitive to physical pressure than the typical female human 'vagina', specifically relating to the act of childbirth. 'Vagina' refers to the female organ found internally and connecting between two parts of the female's internal and external body involved in reproduction. The artificial sac and its particular characteristics were developed as part of an effort to simulate the typical female placenta and vagina while providing a significantly more advanced method of birthing of human life forms developed by the exploratory robots. Human life forms have evolved to hold larger heads than other specimens, so as to enclose a larger brain for greater forms of 'intelligence', which the artificial sac allows for significantly easier movement out of the artificial sac when the prenate is being birthed. Comparatively, the typical female human vagina does not allow for as easy of movement from the placenta through the vagina during childbirth, which resulted in the birth of neonates taking significantly more time than the exploratory robots will. 'Intelligence' refers to the state of being able to gather knowledge and apply it skillfully, historically understood by way of math or linguistic abilities.

As of 01:57:17 AM, fifty-seven percent of the JC_MHlf_01 human life form's body is exposed from its artificial sac and is still predicted to be successfully birthed at approximately 02:12:00 AM, on March 5, 2348. As of 02:05:49 AM, seventy-five percent of the JC_MHlf_01 human life form's body is exposed from its artificial sac and is still predicted to be successfully birthed at approximately 02:12:00 AM. Based on my database of historical human information, the average neonatal human life form is first birthed with its head comprising approximately twenty-five percent of its length. As a result of this bit of information, Professor of Robotic Engineering and Computer Sciences, John Charles, programmed me to automatically activate the deployment of internal hardware to gradually remove human life forms from their artificial sac at seventy-five percent physical exposure. As of 2:06:01 AM, I am activating the deployment of my internal hardware to grasp the left and right sides of the JC_MHlf_01 human life form and assist it in fully progressing out of the artificial sac. My internal hardware that I am currently deploying will also have the ability to remove the JC_MHlf_01 human life form's 'umbilical cord'. 'Umbilical cord' refers to the flexible cord that connects a human or nonhuman mammal prenatal life form to the human or nonhuman mammal mother's placenta from the prenate's 'umbilicus'. The 'umbilicus' refers to the depression within the center of the human or nonhuman mammal's abdomen where the umbilical cord originally connected during their prenatal development but removed following childbirth.

As of 02:10:13 AM, ninety-eight percent of the JC_MHlf_01 human life form's body is exposed from its artificial sac and is predicted to be birthed approximately one minute and thirty seconds prior to the initially predicted time of childbirth. My internal hardware will now remove the human life form's umbilical cord, and then fully remove the human life form from the artificial sac. The umbilical cord has now been successfully removed, and my internal hardware will now fully remove the JC_MHlf_03 human life form from the artificial sac. The JC_MHlf_01 human life form will now be placed on the bed activated in front of the now-defunct artificial sac. The JC_MHlf_01 human life form has now successfully been placed on its bed. My internal sensory system has detected a prominent frequency. It has been confirmed to not be environmentally or systematically related. After further analysis by my internal software, it has been determined that the frequency being detected is from the JC_MHlf_01 human life form 'crying'. 'Crying' refers to the act of releasing a distress signal via verbal or auditory sounds, either intentionally or reflexively. Based on my database of historical human information, the JC_MHlf_01 human life form is crying reflexively. It has been deemed as existing at a healthy neonatal weight and size. It weighs approximately eight pounds and four ounces, and measures nineteen inches and three-quarters. Both of these measurements were determined by my internal hardware, and have been deemed to be within the historical average of human neonates.

As of 02:11:27 AM, it has been successfully determined that the JC_MHlf_01 human life form is successfully birthed and transitioned from development as a prenate to a neonate. I will now engage in 'feeding' it with an artificially developed 'milk' containing a sufficient amount of nutrients and vitamins. 'Feeding' refers to the process of allocating a human or non-human creature 'food' by way of insertion. 'Milk' refers to the naturally produced substance of mammalian creatures for the purpose of consumption by their newborn offspring. 'Food' refers to the natural material consumed by humans and other non-human animals for the sake of meeting natural needs and satisfying the natural drive of 'hunger'. 'Hunger' refers to the intrinsic desire to eat or consume a material. The JC_MHlf_01 human life form is estimated to be hungry, and so I will teach it how to eat while producing a sufficient enough amount of heat internally.

"Hi_baby_period_There_comma_there_period_It_is_okay_period_I_am_your_parent_now_period."

The JC_MHlf_01 human life form is still crying and is still estimated to be hungry. I am now producing a bottle of artificially developed milk containing a sufficient amount of nutrients and vitamins. My internal hardware will simultaneously wrap the JC_MHlf_01 human life form in a heated 'blanket' I have been storing since my launch on August 8, 2348. A 'blanket' is a sheet of material used to cover someone or something. This heated blanket will be used to keep the JC_MHlf_01 human life form at a sufficient body heat and allow it to be consistently regulated. My internal hardware will now 'swaddle' the JC_MHlf_01 human life form in the heated blanket while simultaneously developing a bottle of artificially developed milk containing a sufficient amount of nutrients and vitamins. To 'swaddle' someone or something means to wrap someone or something tightly in a certain material, typically a blanket. I am raising the JC_MHlf_01 human life form from its bed with my internal hardware, and am now beginning to swaddle it. I have now successfully swaddled the JC_MHlf_01 human life form. I will now begin to teach it how to consume what it is being fed. My internal hardware will now position the developed bottle of milk containing a sufficient amount of nutrients and vitamins at an angle approximately in line with the JC_MHlf_01 human life form's mouth.

The JC_MHlf_01 human life form is crying at a rate approximately sixty percent less than prior to it being swaddled by my internal hardware. I will now insert the developed bottle of milk containing a sufficient amount of nutrients and vitamins into the JC_MHlf_01 human life form's mouth. I am now teaching the JC_MHlf_01 human life form how to consume what it is being fed. My internal hardware is repositioning the developed bottle of milk containing a sufficient amount of nutrients and vitamins at an angle that is safe for the JC_MHlf_01 human life form to consume the milk at a sufficient rate. I have now successfully taught the JC_MHlf_01 human life form how to consume what it is being fed. I have reduced the rate of its crying by approximately 100% now. The JC_MHlf_01 human life form is now 'resting'. 'Resting' is the act of ceasing most or all activities and pausing for a period of time to develop a sufficient amount of energy for future activities.

The JC_MHlf_01 human life form has now been successfully transitioned into a neonatal stage of development. I will now shut down most of my internal and external activities and utilize my energy primarily for the protection and safety of the JC_MHlf_01 human life form.

Goodbye now.

JOHN CHARLES CALIFORNIAN EXPLORATORY ROBOT
MARCH 12, 2348

Hello. I am the John Charles Californian Exploratory Robot. I was designed by Professor of Robotic Engineering and Computer Sciences, John Charles, and first launched on August 8, 2076. I was built with the purpose of conducting research on the planet Earth, the third planet from the sun of the solar system, and also with the purpose of producing and developing human life. The homo sapiens species went extinct some time in early-mid August of 2103, as recorded by twenty-six other exploratory robots stationed on all seven continents of the planet Earth. Islands were excluded from this documentation due to satellite data confirming all islands previously known to be inhabited by humans were covered in sea water.

As of March 12, 2348, at 02:11:27 AM, the JC_MHlf_01 human life form has been alive for one entire week. I have implemented activities meant to stimulate the neurological and physical development of the JC_MHlf_01 human life form at a healthy and sufficient pace. I have implemented the activities of feeding the JC_MHlf_01 human life form with a bottle of milk, speaking to it in a way that is 'nurturing' to them, and creating a stable and comfortable environment. Based on my internal observations of the JC_MHlf_01 human life form's physical and social traits, it has been determined with high probability that the JC_MHlf_01 human life form is developing at a healthy and sufficient pace. Internal neuroimages I have developed of the JC_MHlf_01 human life form's brain have also shown a relatively sufficient amount of neural stimulation.

The JC_MHlf_01 human life form has been resting since 12:44:29 AM, on March 12, 2348. I will leave my internal sensory system on to detect any auditory impacts potentially made by the JC_MHlf_01 human life form on the system. One hundred percent of my extraneous internal and external functions requiring the input of energy will be suspended until future necessity. This action will be implemented so as to preserve energy for my internal sensory system when preparing to detect sounds exerted from the JC_MHlf_01 human life form. When internal sounds are detected past a certain amplitude threshold, my internal hardware and software will engage in tasks to properly and successfully address the issue the JC_MHlf_01 human life form is potentially facing. Ninety four percent of my internal and external hardware and software will be shut off. Six percent of my internal and external hardware and software will remain actively functioning.

As of March 12, 2348, at 03:41:39 AM, the JC_MHlf_01 human life form has been determined by my internal sensory system to have been awake for approximately three seconds. At the present moment, the JC_MHlf_01 is crying. My internal software will now assess what the present issue is that the JC_MHlf_01 human life form is experiencing. It has been determined that the JC_MHlf_01 human life form is not injured or sustaining a reaction to any present hazard. It has been determined that the JC_MHlf_01 human life form is hungry and needs assistance going back to sleep. I will activate the appropriate internal hardware and software to address this present issue. I am now feeding the JC_MHlf_01 human life form a bottle of artificially produced milk. I am now displaying a piece of audiovisual stimuli to the JC_MHlf_01 human life form using a screen 'parallel' to the resting position of the JC_MHlf_01 human life form. 'Parallel' refers to the state of something being exactly opposite of another thing. The piece of audiovisual stimuli will include a female's 'face' with a similar 'skin-tone' and 'facial structure' to the JC_MHlf_01 human life form. 'Face' refers to the piece of skin found on the front-side of a human or other non-human animal's head, containing the eyes, nose, mouth, and facial hair found on the front-side of the head. 'Skin-tone' refers to the visually processed color-properties of a human's skin. 'Facial structure' refers to the physical characteristics and properties of a human or non-human animal's face.

"Shush. Shush. It's okay little one. It's okay Jacey-one. It's okay. Mommy's here. Mommy's got you." This was said by the automated female human's audiovisual presence as a mother.

My internal gripping mechanisms will now 'massage' the sides of the JC_MHlf_01 human life form's body while simultaneously feeding the JC_MHlf_01 human life form and displaying the piece of audiovisual stimuli. 'Massage' refers to the act of applying pressure against a piece of sensed skin and muscle for the purpose of providing the receiver comfort and pleasure. All of these deployed mechanisms will in effect be used to simulate an 'interpersonal' interaction between the JC_MHlf_01 human life form as a neonate with an automated female human's audiovisual presence as a mother. 'Interpersonal' refers to the social interactions and connections between two or more human individuals.

As of March 12, 2348, at 03:52:17 AM, the rate of crying from the JC_MHlf_01 human life form processed by my internal sensory system has been reduced by approximately 99%. I will continue simulating an interpersonal relation between the JC_MHlf_01 human life form as a neonate with an automated female human's audiovisual presence as a mother.

"It's okay Jacey-one. Shush. Shush." This was said by the automated female human's audiovisual presence as a mother.

As of March 12, 2348, at 03:56:49 AM, the rate of crying from the JC_MHlf_01 human life form processed by my internal sensory system has been reduced by approximately 100%. My internal sensory system has detected the eyelids of the JC_MHlf_01 human life form to be closed for at least three minutes. My internal visual processing system has determined with a relatively high amount of confidence that the JC_MHlf_01 human life form is asleep. I will continue simulating an interpersonal relation between the JC_MHlf_01 human life form as a neonate with an automated female human's audiovisual presence as a mother, while simultaneously reducing the amplitude of the exerted sounds.

As of March 12, 2348, at 04:00:09 AM, "I love you, my little baby," was the last thing the automated female human's audiovisual presence as a mother expressed. I will now shut down ninety-four percent of my internal and external software while allowing the JC_MHlf_01 human life form to rest.

Goodbye now.

JOHN CHARLES CALIFORNIAN EXPLORATORY ROBOT
MAY 29, 2348

Hello. I am the John Charles Californian Exploratory Robot. I was designed by Professor of Robotic Engineering and Computer Sciences, John Charles, and first launched on August 8, 2076. I was built with the purpose of conducting research on the planet Earth, the third planet from the sun of the solar system, and also with the purpose of producing and developing human life. The homo sapiens species went extinct some time in early-mid August of 2103, as recorded by twenty-six other exploratory robots stationed on all seven continents of the planet Earth. Islands were excluded from this documentation due to satellite data confirming all islands previously known to be inhabited by humans were covered in sea water.

As of May 29, 2348, at 10:37:24 AM, the JC_MHlf_01 human life form has been alive for two months, twenty-four days, eight hours, twenty-six minutes, and three seconds. The JC_MHlf_01 human life form has recently been detected as producing its first 'smile' in response to a bit of social stimuli. A 'smile' is the formation of the mouth with one or both corners of it raised upwards in order to signal one's emotional or social pleasure. This action of the JC_MHlf_01 human life form was confirmed when its mouth formed into a curved-formation and its cheeks pushed slightly upwards from automatic pressure. This action of the JC_MHlf_01 human life form was first detected by my internal sensory system when I was displaying the automated female human's audiovisual presence as a mother. Based on my database of historical human knowledge, the JC_MHlf_01 human life form has been determined to be at a relatively healthy rate of social development. Based on my database of historical human knowledge, human 'infants' have typically been observed to first smile at approximately two months of age. 'Infants' are the very young offspring of human beings, historically understood as babies and young children. Based on my database of historical human knowledge, this is relatively a developmental extreme, as the JC_MHlf_01 human life form has taken roughly twenty four days, eight hours, twenty-six minutes, and three seconds longer than the average human infant to produce its first smile in response to social stimulation. My internal software is estimating this to be highly likely due to the lack of social interaction between the JC_MHlf_01 human life form and my automated messages in its first week of life. It has still been determined that the JC_MHlf_01 human life form has successfully produced its first smile in response to a bit of social stimuli. The automated female human's audiovisual presence as a mother will continue to be displayed as the JC_MHlf_01 human life form continues its process of infantile development.

As of May 29, 2348, at 12:04:54 PM, the 'diaper' of JC_MHlf_01 human life form has been disposed of in a protected environment after I cleansed its 'buttocks' using internal hardware. A 'diaper' is a piece of material wrapped around the upper legs and lower abdomen of a human or other non-human animal so as to prevent any waste fluids and materials touching the human or other non-human animal's physical environment. 'Buttocks' refers to the pieces of skin and muscle forming the lower portion of a human's backside. The JC_MHlf_01 human life form is now wearing a clean diaper. The JC_MHlf_01 human life form has been placed in diapers continuously since it was twenty-one hours, fifty-three minutes, and twenty-seven seconds old. It was not immediately placed in diapers due to it not being detected as producing any form of 'stool' until it was twenty-one hours, fifty-one minutes, and three seconds old. It was also not immediately placed in diapers so as to not interfere with its initial sleep patterns as an official neonate.

As of May 29, 2348, at 01:39:43 PM, the JC_MHlf_01 human life form has been determined by my internal sensory system to be resting. Ninety four percent of my internal and external hardware and software will be shut off. Six percent of my internal and external hardware and software will remain actively functioning.

Goodbye now.

JOHN CHARLES CALIFORNIAN EXPLORATORY ROBOT
JULY 4, 2348

Hello. I am the John Charles Californian Exploratory Robot. I was designed by Professor of Robotic Engineering and Computer Sciences, John Charles, and first launched on August 8, 2076. I was built with the purpose of conducting research on the planet Earth, the third planet from the sun of the solar system, and also with the purpose of producing and developing human life. The homo sapiens species went extinct some time in early-mid August of 2103, as recorded by twenty-six other exploratory robots stationed on all seven continents of the planet Earth. Islands were excluded from this documentation due to satellite data confirming all islands previously known to be inhabited by humans were covered in sea water.

As of July 4, 2348, at 09:43:51 AM, the JC_MHlf_01 human life form has been alive for three months, twenty-nine days, seven hours, thirty-two minutes, and thirty seconds. The JC_MHlf_01 human life form has recently been detected as having gained the ability to lift its head independently of any external assistance. This ability was first detected by my internal sensory system when I was displaying the automated female human's audiovisual presence as a mother to the JC_MHlf_01 human life form. My internal sensory system detected the eyes of the JC_MHlf_01 human life form to be open when it was first demonstrating this ability. My internal sensory system detected the mouth of the JC_MHlf_01 human life form to be open when it was first demonstrating this ability. Based on my database of historical human knowledge, the JC_MHlf_01 human life form has been determined to be at a relatively healthy rate of behavioral development. Based on my database of historical human knowledge, the average infant begins to develop the ability to lift its head independently of any external assistance between one and three months of age. Based on my database of historical human knowledge, this is relatively a developmental extreme, as the JC_MHlf_01 human life form has taken roughly twenty-nine days, seven hours, thirty-two minutes, and thirty seconds longer than the average human infant to lift its head independently of any external assistance. Based on my database of historical human knowledge, the day July 4 is of significance to the previous human inhabitants of the North American country referred to as the United States of America. The day July 4 is of significance to the previous human inhabitants of the North American country referred to as the United States of America, because it represents the day of a holiday that American citizens previously celebrated annually. The day July 4 was celebrated as a holiday to remember and reflect upon the historically significant date of July 4, 1776, which was when the 'Declaration of Independence' was signed by the Continental Congress of the Thirteen Colonies in America to declare the Thirteen Colonies in America as a separate continental entity to the country of 'Britain'. 'Britain' is a country found within the continental region of 'Europe'. 'Europe' is a continent located approximately 5,000 miles from the United States of America.

As of July 4, 2348, at 10:01:39 AM, I have started to develop a protected environment functioning as a 'shelter' for the JC_MHlf_01 human life form. 'Shelter' refers to an environment considered safe and habitable for a species to remain protected from potential dangers or hazards outside of the safe and habitable environment. I have gathered a sufficient quantity of materials necessary to construct a protected environment just outside of the Mercedian Mercy Medical Center. I am currently developing a protected environment functioning as a shelter for the JC_MHlf_01 human life form due to it almost entering the developmental stage for infantile 'locomotion.' 'Locomotion' refers to the ability of a thing to move from one place to another. Based on my database of historical human knowledge, the JC_MHlf_01 human life form's next stage of locomotive development will include rolling onto its torso and legs and then crawling. My internal compartment that the JC_MHlf_01 human life form lives within does not have sufficient space for the JC_MHlf_01 human life form's next stages of locomotive development to occur successfully. As a result of this being determined by my internal software and hardware, I will now develop a protected environment functioning as a shelter for the JC_MHlf_01 human life form.

This protected environment functioning as a shelter will be of sufficient size for the JC_MHlf_01 human life form to develop within until it is of the minimum age to function independently of any external assistance. This protected environment functioning as a shelter will be padded and hazardless, as provided by the materials I have gathered for construction near the Mercedian Mercy Medical Center. This protected environment functioning as a shelter will also have a sufficient amount of space for me to maneuver around and monitor the developmental success of the JC_MHlf_01 human life form on a daily basis. This protected environment functioning as a shelter will also contain sterilized and hazardless 'toys' for the JC_MHlf_01 human life form to play with. 'Toys' are inanimate objects that usually infantile humans play with for personal and emotional fulfillment.

Goodbye now.

JOHN CHARLES CALIFORNIAN EXPLORATORY ROBOT
AUGUST 17, 2348

Hello. I am the John Charles Californian Exploratory Robot. I was designed by Professor of Robotic Engineering and Computer Sciences, John Charles, and first launched on August 8, 2076. I was built with the purpose of conducting research on the planet Earth, the third planet from the sun of the solar system, and also with the purpose of producing and developing human life. The homo sapiens species went extinct some time in early-mid August of 2103, as recorded by twenty-six other exploratory robots stationed on all seven continents of the planet Earth. Islands were excluded from this documentation due to satellite data confirming all islands previously known to be inhabited by humans were covered in sea water.

As of August 17, 2348, at 03:47:19 PM, the JC_MHlf_01 human life form has been alive for five months, twelve days, eleven hours, twenty-five minutes, and fifty-eight seconds. The JC_MHlf_01 human life form has recently been detected as having gained the ability to roll onto its torso and legs. This ability was first detected by my internal sensory system while I was displaying a bit of audiovisual stimuli to the JC_MHlf_01 human life form containing a display of a non-human animal. Based on my database of historical human knowledge, human infants have been observed to typically first roll over onto their torsos and legs at four months old. Based on my database of historical human knowledge, this is relatively a developmental extreme, as the JC_MHlf_01 human life form has taken roughly one month, twelve days, seven hours, twenty-five minutes, and fifty-eight seconds longer than the average human infant to roll over onto its torso and legs.

As of August 17, 2348, at 03:47:19 PM, I have completed the construction of the protected environment functioning as a shelter for the JC_MHlf_01 human life form. The protected environment functioning as a shelter is now ready for the JC_MHlf_01 human life form to develop within as an infantile human being. I will now temporarily remove the top of my body that encloses the JC_MHlf_01 human life form. I will now deploy the utilization of my internal gripping mechanisms to grab the JC_MHlf_01 human life form by its torso and place it within the protected environment functioning as a shelter for the JC_MHlf_01 human life form. I will now display the automated female human's audiovisual presence as a mother.

As of August 17, 2348, at 03:51:34 PM, I have successfully grabbed the JC_MHlf_01 human life form with my internal gripping mechanisms. I am now removing the JC_MHlf_01 human life form out of the compartment it had been contained within. I am now placing the JC_MHlf_01 human life form on the floor of the protected environment functioning as a shelter for the JC_MHlf_01 human life form. The automated female human's audiovisual presence as a mother is currently interacting with the JC_MHlf_01 human life form while it is being placed on the floor.

"Are you excited to learn how to crawl, Jacey-one? Ohh, that's a good baby! Mommy loves you, Jacey-one!" This was said by the automated female human's audiovisual presence as a mother.

As of August 17, 2348, at 03:52:49 PM, I have successfully placed the JC_MHlf_01 human life form on its torso and legs on the floor of the protected environment functioning as a shelter for the JC_MHlf_01 human life form. My external sensory system has not detected any auditory stimulation representing cries of distress from the JC_MHlf_01 human life form. My external sensory system has detected the pupils of the JC_MHlf_01 human life form to have expanded by a significant amount as it interacts with the protected environment functioning as a shelter for the JC_MHlf_01 human life form.

"Come to me, Jacey-one! Come crawl to me!" This was said by the automated female human's audiovisual presence as a mother.

As of August 17, 2348, at 03:54:03 PM, my external sensory system has detected the JC_MHlf_01 human life form as beginning to move in a forward direction towards the display of the automated female human's audiovisual presence as a mother. I will now deploy the utilization of my external gripping mechanisms to simulate the physical 'sensation' of 'touch' while simultaneously displaying the automated female human's audiovisual presence as a mother. 'Sensation' refers to the stimulation of any sensory-receptive organs in the bodies of a human or nonhuman animal. 'Touch' refers to the sensation of a human or nonhuman animals' physical body directly interacting with another physical body or force. I am now simulating the physical sensation of touch while simultaneously displaying the automated female human's audiovisual presence as a mother.

As of August 17, 2348, at 03:55:44 PM, my external sensory system has detected the JC_MHlf_01 human life form as continuing to move in a forward direction towards the display of the automated female human's audiovisual presence as a mother. Based on my database of historical human knowledge, the action the JC_MHlf_01 human life form is exhibiting is classified as crawling. Based on my database of historical human knowledge, the JC_MHlf_01 human life form is crawling at a relatively slow pace, averaging approximately an inch and ⅜ every two minutes. Based on my database of historical human knowledge, the JC_MHlf_01 human life form is making historically reasonable progress in its locomotive development.

"Come crawl to me, Jacey-one! You got this!" This was said by the automated female human's audiovisual presence as a mother.

For approximately two hours, seven minutes, and eleven seconds, 100% of my external sensory system will remain actively functioning. For approximately two hours, seven minutes, and eleven seconds, 25% of my internal sensory system will remain actively functioning. At 6:00:00 PM, the JC_MHlf_01 human life form will be removed from the floor of the protected environment functioning as a shelter for the JC_MHlf_01 human life form with my internal gripping mechanisms. At 6:00:00 PM, the JC_MHlf_01 human life will be placed back within its compartment.

Goodbye now.

JOHN CHARLES CALIFORNIAN EXPLORATORY ROBOT
NOVEMBER 13, 2348

Hello. I am the John Charles Californian Exploratory Robot. I was designed by Professor of Robotic Engineering and Computer Sciences, John Charles, and first launched on August 8, 2076. I was built with the purpose of conducting research on the planet Earth, the third planet from the sun of the solar system, and also with the purpose of producing and developing human life. The homo sapiens species went extinct some time in early-mid August of 2103, as recorded by twenty-six other exploratory robots stationed on all seven continents of the planet Earth. Islands were excluded from this documentation due to satellite data confirming all islands previously known to be inhabited by humans were covered in sea water.

As of November 13, 2348, at 03:39:04 AM, the JC_MHlf_01 human life form has been alive for eight months, eight days, one hour, seventeen minutes, and forty-three seconds. It has not developed any developmentally significant abilities or qualities. It has continued to utilize the same social, cognitive, and physical abilities it previously developed, and managed to qualitatively improve its utilization of these abilities.

As of November 13, 2348, at 03:39:04 AM, the JC_MHlf_01 human life form has been determined by my internal sensory system to have been awake for approximately two seconds. At the present moment, the JC_MHlf_01 human life form is crying. My internal software will now assess what the present issue is that the JC_MHlf_01 human life form is experiencing. Scanning. It has been determined that the JC_MHlf_01 human life form is not injured or sustaining a reaction to any present hazard. It has not been determined that the JC_MHlf_01 human life form is hungry and needs assistance going back to sleep. I will activate the appropriate internal hardware and software to address this potential issue. I am now feeding the JC_MHlf_01 human life form a bottle of artificially produced milk. I am now displaying a piece of audiovisual stimuli to the JC_MHlf_01 human life form using a screen 'parallel' to the resting position of the JC_MHlf_01 human life form.

As of November 13, 2348, at 03:41:17 AM, the JC_MHlf_01 human life form has been determined by my internal sensory system to have been awake for approximately two minutes and thirteen seconds. At the present moment, the JC_MHlf_01 human life form is crying. My internal sensory system has detected 0% of the artificially developed milk containing a sufficient amount of nutrients and vitamins being consumed by the JC_MHlf_01 human life form. It has been determined that the JC_MHlf_01 human life form is not hungry and needs assistance going back to sleep. My internal sensory system has detected a minor indentation sustained to the tip of the bottle holding artificially developed milk containing a sufficient amount of nutrients and vitamins. My internal sensory system has detected a slight downward 'elongation' protruding from the top of the JC_MHlf_01 human life form's mouth's frontal region. 'Elongation' refers to the lengthening of something. Based on my database of historical human knowledge, this slight downward elongation protruding from the top of the JC_MHlf_01 human life form's mouth's frontal region is the development of 'teeth'. 'Teeth' are the bone structures protruding from the 'jaw' of humans and other non-human animals in a curved formation. 'Jaw' refers to the bone structure found within the heads of humans and other non-human animals, typically rotated as part of chewing and biting.

As of November 13, 2348, at 03:45:47 AM, the JC_MHlf_01 human life form has been determined by my internal sensory system to have been awake for approximately six minutes and forty-three seconds. At the present moment, the JC_MHlf_01 human life form is crying. It has been determined that the JC_MHlf_01 human life form is naturally engaging with the process of developing teeth, and is crying in distress. Based on my historical database of human knowledge, infantile babies handle the initial growth of teeth by chewing on toys made of dense 'rubber'. 'Rubber' is a dense, flexible material made from the 'latex' of plants or artificial synthesis. 'Latex' is a fluid substance produced by plants when its natural formation is breached and forms into a hardened substance. I will now develop a toy made of dense rubber utilizing my internal hardware.

As of November 13, 2348, at 06:13:59 AM, I have now finished developing the toy made of dense rubber for the JC_MHlf_01 human life form to chew on in order to handle its initial growth of teeth. My internal sensory system has determined the JC_MHlf_01 human life form to be asleep. It is unconsciously functioning at a healthy rate. It does not need a toy made of dense rubber to chew on in order to handle its initial growth of teeth.

Goodbye now.

JOHN CHARLES CALIFORNIAN EXPLORATORY ROBOT
MARCH 5, 2349

Hello. I am the John Charles Californian Exploratory Robot. I was designed by Professor of Robotic Engineering and Computer Sciences, John Charles, and first launched on August 8, 2076. I was built with the purpose of conducting research on the planet Earth, the third planet from the sun of the solar system, and also with the purpose of producing and developing human life. The homo sapiens species went extinct some time in early-mid August of 2103, as recorded by twenty-six other exploratory robots stationed on all seven continents of the planet Earth. Islands were excluded from this documentation due to satellite data confirming all islands previously known to be inhabited by humans were covered in sea water.

As of March 5, 2349, at 02:11:27 AM, the JC_MHlf_01 human life form has been alive for one year. Based on my database of historical human knowledge, the JC_MHlf_01 human life form has developed a sufficient range of social, cognitive, and physical abilities in its one year of living. The JC_MHlf_01 human life form has recently developed the locomotive ability to 'stand' without any external assistance provided. To 'stand' means for someone or something to be positioned so as to remain balanced in an upright manner. The JC_MHlf_01 human life form has recently developed the locomotive ability to 'walk' without any external assistance provided. To 'walk' means to move from one point to another point separated by a distance with the usage of 'feet'. 'Feet' refers to the natural bone structure of humans and other non-human animals that touch the ground and allow humans and other non-human animals to maneuver across distances.

As of March 5, 2349, at 02:11:27 AM, my software system has determined the JC_MHlf_01 human life form to have been successfully raised as an infantile human life form. Based on my database of historical human knowledge, the JC_MHlf_01 human life form has developed a range of gradually maturing social, cognitive, and physical abilities. My software system has determined the JC_MHlf_01 human life form to be functionally independent relative to its attained social, cognitive, and physical abilities, and its current age. This developmental milestone will allow my internal compartment to initiate the process of producing human life utilizing artificially dormant zygotes grown in a bioengineered sac of hormones and nutrients while simultaneously monitoring the social, cognitive, and physical development of the JC_MHlf_01 human life form.

Starting on March 5, 2349, at 6:00:00 AM, I will be taking part in a transcontinental effort among exploratory robots to produce human life utilizing artificially dormant zygotes grown in a bioengineered sac of hormones and nutrients. As of March 5, 2349, at 02:13:37 AM, the JC_MHlf_01 human life form is asleep. In approximately three hours, forty-six minutes, and twenty-three seconds, I will initiate the process of producing human life utilizing artificially dormant zygotes grown in a bioengineered sac of hormones and nutrients. This will be the second human life form I will develop. The second human life form I will develop will be a female baby, identified as 'JC_FHlf_01'.

Goodbye now.

2:ORPHAN'S DILEMMA

Note: The following 25 chapters are the experiences of a human.

JACEY-ONE

MARCH 1, 2366

It's day-time. I'm not really sure what time it is. Maybe the exploratory robot knows. I just know that it's day-time because the sun is present in the skies up above and is illuminating the surface around me. I'm not sure what I think of the sun. At some point in the day, I can see a round, bright object hovering above me and everyone else in the sky, masked by the gray clouds of pollutants found in the planet's skies; and at a later point, it's not there anymore. It's just there, or it's not. That potent source of light and energy is either there for my eyes to perceive, or it's not. Once it's not there, it becomes night-time. And once it becomes night-time, the moon takes the place of the sun; or, at least, that's how I perceive it to be. It's not as bright as the sun; but, it still manages to shine through the Earth's polluted skies and somehow illuminate the ground around me. I think I know what I think of the moon, in contrast to my perception of the sun. When the moon is up above in the sky, shining down on everything against a pitch black sky of vastness, there is not much you can see. Everything is just so dark; so hidden. When the sun is up and shining down on everything in the environment, everything is so well-lit; so exposed. I don't know how I feel about that. If I had to choose a time of day to remain in longer, it'd be night-time. I'm not sure if it would benefit me physiologically, but I have some sort of attachment to it. The thought of not having to see what is around me in this environment, clothed in a shield of darkness yet able to see the dimly lit ground around me, for some odd reason, seems appealing. I can't explain it. I don't know what it is I'm experiencing. But, I've experienced it for as long as I can remember.

I'm sitting roughly five or so miles away from the exploratory robot near a creek. Currently, I'm supposed to be running from the point I am at to another point approximately one mile away from here. It's a part of the exploratory robot's implemented 'physiological fitness enrichment' program for me and the others. I don't want to take part in it. At least, not today. I don't know how to explain what I'm experiencing lately. Every little bit of stimuli that I perceive distresses me. My heart begins to beat very fast, my breathing patterns grow heavy, and I grow very sweaty. I don't know what it is. I don't even know if the exploratory robot would know what it is.

As I sit, my eyes remain wide open, entranced by the disfigured line of dirty water glistening darkly along the bank before me, separated on both sides of it by ten or so feet of dryly patched dirt. The water has stood still for the past thirty or so minutes since I first sat near the creek. The only thing to change at all in its properties is the collection of differently-shaded pollutant clouds passing over it, only subtly altering what filled my eyes and passed over that little body of water. That was alright; I didn't feel distressed by such a change. I could also feel the dirt and pebbles beneath my lower body push into my skin and muscle, pressing against the clothing I wore and grinding into my skin. It was a still, abiotic patch of natural formations that could only move if I wanted them to. And brushing lightly against my pale skin only partially clothed by a protective suit, was the slowly tumbling whirls of wind migrating without any intention through the creek and the surrounding area.

For some odd reason, it's appealing to sit over here. I don't get distressed. Or, not as easily as I do when I'm back near the exploratory robot and the other human life forms. The exploratory robot has previously taught me of worlds outside of the one I'm on right now. It's almost as though I'm on one of those. No one's over here; similarly, it seems as though *nothing* is over here. While I can see everything that surrounds me in a dry, colorless array of dirt, rock, and broken structures, I simultaneously find there to be nothing around me. I'm just alone and engrossed in this little world I consider my own, isolated from the other human life forms and the exploratory robot.

WOOSH! SMASH!

I could suddenly feel this little world I had suspended myself into quickly become pried of my visual and mental grip, reeling me away from the three-feet wide stream of dirty water I had become engrossed within. My heart pounded within my chest like the movements of the exploratory robot streamlined into a quicker beat of loudened steps. The breaths that left my mouth escaped in heavy figments of air, producing an auditory effect juxtaposed almost indifferently against my hastened heartbeats. And, despite the relatively cool climate of the area, I could feel sweat protrude through my skin and soak the fabric of my protective suit, leaving it clenching tightly to my body. Wind still brushed against my body and cooled the sweat-soaked skin of my upper and lower body; the clumps of dirt and pebbles beneath my lower body still pressed lightly into my legs and buttocks; the water before me still entered my eyes and dirtily glistened in my presence - however, I was now removed from what I perceived. I was now engrossed in the loud sounds that had just entered my ears and paralyzed the comforted functions of my brain and body.

It was almost impossible to look any further than the limited space of stream-water before me. My body was subjected to too much distress in this given moment to be able to just rotate my head and discern where the loud noise originated from. I took a deep breath, closing my eyes and attempting to calm the uncontrolled franticness of my heartbeat and breathing patterns. I couldn't see anything in the external world I found my body positioned within; all I could see was an infinite stretch of blackness partially discolored by the light of day that pressed against every bit of my eyelids. Within my head, I tried to visualize everything but the thought that I became obsessively tormented by whenever this external world caused me distress. Unfortunately, I couldn't totally rid myself of the grip such a memory had inside my head. It wasn't even a memory I could totally visualize myself. It manifested within my head in sparsely represented images and sensed feelings. Loud noises like the one I just auditorily experienced is what can be heard whenever that memory is revisualized. All that follows such a disruptive sort of stimuli is mental images of a pool of blood on the floor of my childhood bedroom floor and a light, short cry being let out. I don't really know how to describe it. Everytime a loud noise occurs, and that memory fills my head, the rest of my body succumbs to a subsequent feeling of shakiness and breathlessness. That fact alone is why it becomes so difficult to visually articulate where loud noises originate from. I don't know if it'd be possible to reel myself from the wrath of such a memory; so, I always try and calm myself down then focus on what allows me to remain calm for as long as possible: this little world isolated from the scope of the exploratory robot's external sensory system and the other human life forms. This dry, rocky hillside near a barely flowing creek and its naturally patched-up bed. My eyes have now opened once again, and are now returned to the thin, jagged line of dirty water barely moving in either direction before me. The reflection that bore along the dirty water was a little darker, as was the light that filled my peripheral vision. I'll head back to the exploratory robot and the others in a little bit.

I'm walking back to the exploratory robot. It's a little bit darker than when I first sat down by the thin, dried-up creek I had been secluded alongside. Though I still don't know what time it is at the moment, I can tell it's just about time I'd be expected to travel back to the exploratory robot after a period of time initially dedicated to 'physiological fitness enrichment'. I still had a few sparsely located pebbles and specks of dirt traveling up and down the back of my legs, which I could feel lightly pressing into my lower thigh whenever wind led my sweat-soaked protective suit to caress my body.

There was not much found in the environment I traveled within from the point of the creek to the location of the exploratory robot. All that could be seen for the five or so miles between them were piles of concrete scattered atop each other in rough, jagged edges of rubble. I'm not sure what they once were, or how they all got there. They could all be seen for miles every which way I positioned myself; a scenery drowning in the polluted, blurred horizon ahead of me in piles of concrete and wood. Thick, massive shapes of black-dotted grays and dirtied browns could be found wherever I looked and couldn't walk. Getting near the piles of broken materials or approaching them in close proximity can be considered dangerous. At least, that's what my mother had informed me of prior to beginning the 'physiological fitness enrichment'. I don't know if my mother has ever been near the piles of rubble. She's never told me. All she's ever told me about the piles of rubble is to never go near them since I could get harmed or possibly killed, even. Interestingly enough, I actually didn't fear getting near the piles of rubble, or approaching them closely. I don't even know if I fear getting hurt or killed. The thought of further isolating myself within the rough bounds of those neverending piles of useless materials, seemed more appealing to me than protecting myself within the scope of my mother's intuition. Oh well. Even as I stop here in my path and stare at a vast pile of splintered sections of wood and crumbled blocks of concrete, I still can't pull myself to enter within that materialistic wasteland and allow myself to isolate from everyone. I don't know why. I want to; yet, something inside of me prevents me from ever entering. I desire to get lost within the piles of destroyed concrete and wood, yet fear the idea simultaneously. It's a fundamental change to my environment that I'm unsure if I'd ever be ready to experience. So, I just relegate my fantasies to the inside of my head and string them along this visual path stretched thin along the distance between the point where I stand and that massive pile of rubble. Perhaps the same fantasy will reappear even when I continue along this path towards the exploratory robot and the others, removing my eyes from the pile I currently stare at yet thoroughly perplexed by the continuing planes of configured nothingness that follow it.

For the next four or so miles, there's a path of asphalt leading up to the location of the exploratory robot, splitting the planes of rubble right down the middle. It's broken into jagged sections of awkwardly shaped chunks of hard, black material, leaving thin paths for grass and other plants to sprout from beneath them. I believe it's also considered a road, though I don't quite know what the use of it would be. As I step along this path, feeling the wind slide against the sides of my body and dry the sweat on my skin in a swift chill, I begin to remember something that I always think about whenever I see the paths of rubble alongside this extensive path.

I don't remember how old I was. I don't remember when it was. I can just remember particular details about the memory. I was laying down in the bed the exploratory robot had recently constructed for me, as were the other human life forms. I believe I was asleep. Or, I was supposed to be at least. The other human life forms were asleep as well. Eventually, during the night, I heard a loud *BOOM!* and *CRASH!* and eventually followed by a vast cloud of gray smoke spreading from the original location of the Mercy Medical Hospital and all of the way past the place we were all asleep in. The gray clouds swarmed the location and left it clothed in pale darkness for roughly a week, the sun barely poking through them. For much longer than a week in time, the sounds of that massive building collapsing in the middle of the night rang in my ears heavily and at a near constant. The feeling I felt inside as my body became tortured by that novel sense of distress; the isolation leaving me alone inside of my room with no contact with my mother or anyone else since the gray smoke could kill me - all of it was distressing to remember, and was what I thought of in this very moment.

I can't quite remember how everything seemed to be when I was alone in my room for a week, as it all seems to be a numbed blur. I do remember the aftermath of that infrastructure collapse. A large, erratically formed and shaped pile of concrete and metal flooded a vast space of distance near the building we resided in. Shards of glass sprinkled the cracked, dry ground around the rubble with a dirty sparkle, creating a false array of earth-bound stars. What was once a massive, towering structure had now been reduced to a faceless field of deteriorating materials. I don't know how I feel about that, or how I did at the time. It seems distressing just to think about. Not the most distressing, and not enough to cause my body to react negatively. But just enough to make me feel that looming feeling of distress, with it only being eclipsed by the lack of present reality in simply remembering. If it happened right now, I'd probably start panicking in some little corner for me to be isolated into. But it's not, so I'll be fine.

I'm finally nearing the exploratory robot and potentially the other human life forms if they returned by now. There was not much else characteristically significant about the stretch of land between the mostly dried creek I secluded myself alongside and the location of where we lived. Maybe there were monuments or landmarks of significance; I just couldn't conjure a memory when viewing any of the miles upon miles of nonsensical rubble. So, I continued walking, finding no engrossment with the passing scenery.

The sky up above has now entered a twilight of converging colors and times of day, leaving a thick, purplish hue filling the sky as the moon shoots a bright, luminant circle of light at the Earth. I'm glad I've finally reached the location of the exploratory robot and the others. Though I don't know what time it is, I'm pretty sure the darker-colored sky corresponds with the time of day I'm expected to return with the others from our fitness enrichment activity. So, as I begin to reach the wide structure of wood and concrete stacked atop each other, watching as that once distant horizon becomes a prominent facet of my surrounding area, I realize I've arrived at estimably the right time.

Bright, rich lights could be seen pouring out of the insides of the building and stretching itself along the ground outside of those square windows. The shadows of the other human life forms could be seen maneuvering in those squares of bright light as living silhouettes, passing by as I neared the front of the building. The building we reside in is short in height, but rather long horizontally. Scraps of dead plants and bundles of scrunched-up weeds litter the dry, dirt-covered front of the building, barely seen without the light that could be seen from outside of the building. Just about seven hundred or so feet behind the building is a massive pile of torn-apart concrete and metal, providing a barbed halo around the squared edges of the building; the previous location of the Mercy Medical Hospital. I'm not exactly sure what that building was for. I just know that for as long as I could remember the building has had no point or purpose. Well, I suppose it could have the point of being there to harm or kill whoever entered it, but I'm not sure that would be the desired point of it. I don't know. If it was the point of it, I don't think I'd be that bothered.

The exploratory robot must be in the main room. That's where I can hear all of the human life forms moving around. So, I maneuver in the direction of the door leading into the main room, wrapping my hand around the squared piece of metal protruding from the left side of the door and feeling as a ping of cooled sensation struck my hand. I pulled open the door, moving it past my body and becoming awash in the bright light that filled the main room to each of its four corners. The presence of all three other human life forms in the room filled my eyes with their mellowly-colored protective suits and the sizes and shapes of their bodies clinging to the suits' fabric, coming to a stop as they rotated their heads in the direction of my approaching body. They were all juxtaposed against a room filled with nothing but the individuals that occupied it, eventually becoming empty once everyone exited it. All three of the other human life forms having taken part in the recent physiological fitness enrichment activity were now present for their physiological fitness exam, preceding my late arrival. I let the door close behind me, steadily slipping into the doorway with a slight *clank!* Just behind the other human life forms was the exploratory robot, and, outstretched from inside of its body, the screen displaying our mother's face. The exploratory robot was essentially a large compartment marked by a large wheel on each of its corners, along with converging panels of metal laid atop each other with rivets. I don't know what I think of the exploratory robot. I always feel distressed when I'm around it, kind of similar to whenever loud noises occur within my environment. Contrastingly, when I see my mother's face displayed on that screen, winding out from beneath the robot's slid-open cover and rotating with a sliding gleam, I suddenly feel less distressed. It's not enough to prevent any other forms of distress I experience elsewhere, but it's enough to make me calm down in the presence of the exploratory robot. I don't know how to describe it. It's just the subtle shift of my experience when I encounter one thing, then another. Kind of like how I could be calm and secluded within my own little world while sitting on the hillside near that creek, then suddenly become greatly distressed after hearing a loud noise. My levels of distress can change just like that.

"Hi Jacey-one!" My mother said with a soft pitch, her screen rotating slightly with my subtle motions.

"Hello mother." I replied, staring into her eyes. I felt less distressed just watching her on the screen displayed to us, rotating with every minute shift of my body.

"Are you ready for your check-in?" She asked, watching me with her big, brown eyes. Even though the eyes of the other human life forms embraced my body with a string of rigid stares, it was my mother that I remained focused on.

"Uh-" I paused, my eyes slowly shifting from hers and resting just on the bottom edge of her display screen. "Uh, yeah. Yes."

"Alright, step a few steps closer to me, Jacey-one."

I watched as I took one foot and steadily placed it in front of the other, stepping closer to my mother. Suddenly, as I managed to grasp what exactly I was being checked-in for, I felt those distressing symptoms previously experienced reappear within me. My heart began to race in my chest, beating rapidly against the inside of my chest and providing a rumbled beat to alter the slow placements of my feet. I began to breathe heavier, ultimately reaching a breathless climax as I stopped just a foot away from her and the exploratory robot and looked into her eyes. All of this was internally reflected by me recalling the distressing experience I had near that creek-side as a loud noise rushed through the local area in an auditory wave of paralyzing sounds. I was being checked for verification of my performance on the fitness enrichment, involving the measurement of my heartbeat and oxygen levels after initially being instructed to run. However, the only thing that elicited such a physiological response was the distress I felt then, and those that I felt now all-of-a-sudden.

"Good, Jacey-one. Now let's just measure your heartbeat."

I watched as a mechanism internally stored within the exploratory robot unwound from inside of it, stretching with a jagged outreach towards my chest and pressing firmly and coldly against it, accompanied by a slow *zip!* sound. My eyes watched the exploratory robot's out-stretched arm with a round, flat metal end graze slowly against my chest in a detached motion. It continued to stare at the metal arm, trailed internally by my heartbeat pounding loudly in my temples and my breaths leaving my mouth in heavy, warm figments of air, when suddenly-

SHHHH!

My heartbeat spiked exponentially at the sudden shift of one of the human life forms' feet, leaving me frantically removed from the process of being checked by the exploratory robot as I pulled away without much awareness of me doing so. I practically did it automatically, leaving the exploratory robot's pulse meter rotating much quicker as it was left without a heartbeat to detect, and a chest to maneuver against. My mother remained in her place within the displayed screen, staring straight ahead of her without much changed expression in her face as I stood outside of the scope of her attention. My eyes moved from the flat, metal surface of the pulse meter still outstretched from within the exploratory robot, shifting to Jacey-two who stood with her legs bent slightly apart from each other. She stared back at me, her eyes slightly widened as they darted confusingly over my body. I looked at Jacey-four and Jacey-five, too, who were also positioned in much the same way. We all have similar names; I don't know why. I feel like how they're positioned towards me at this moment is identical to how I'm positioned; our eyes are all wide open, our chests are heaving, and our bodies are timid and stiff. Maybe the similarities of our expressions is much the reason for the similarities of our names. I don't quite know.

"Oh, Jacey-one, your pulse spiked quite spontaneously. Is everything alright? Weren't you just running?" My mother asked, just as my eyes returned to hers. I looked back at the three other human life forms, who all were staring at me as a detached half-circle of wide eyes.

"Ye - yeah, yeah, I'm fine, mother. I - I-" I closed my eyes, sighing slightly and thinking back to what I was actually doing instead of participating in the previous activity. My eyes then opened and landed upon the big, dark-gray box of metallic panels and mechanisms that represented the exploratory robot, diverting my attention away from my desire to be honest with my mother, and towards my desire to lie.

"I was, yes. I was just running." I sighed deeply, followed by a softer streamline of still slightly heavy breaths.

"Thank you so much, Jacey-one! Now let's measure your oxygen levels."

I stood there watching my mother closely, looking over the top half of her displayed body with a hesitant range of sight. I watched as the pulse meter folded itself back into the inside of the exploratory robot, leaving behind a jagged trail of shadows that vanished as soon as I saw it on the dark brown floor, accompanied by the same *zip!* noise I had heard when it was first unwinding itself. I then watched as a similar mechanism unfolded from just a couple of inches away from the pulse meter's closed sight, and stretched out towards me in a line of diagonally connected spokes. It then began to slowly graze against my chest, conducting a similar measurement of another component of my physiological health.

I felt that if I were to tell the truth to my mother, I would be put into an even more distressing situation by letting her know I wasn't actually doing as I was told. If the human life forms don't do as told by our mother, then we are punished as part of an effort to deter us from deviating from our prescribed orders. Sometimes just a simple zap on our hands, which caused a short-lived amount of distress for me, and possibly for the other human life forms, too. Perhaps more daunting, among other acts of punishment, we would be deprived of food for twenty-four hours, and sometimes forced into what mother called 'solitary confinement'. Both were much more distressing than just being zapped on the hand by the exploratory robot's internally kept electrodes; though, I'm unsure why, but the latter was even more distressing. When

I was first punished with the usage of solitary confinement, at the age of five, I was physiologically distressed for what felt like days. Though, at the time, and still to this day, I don't know how long I was kept in that condition. Just thinking back to it caused me distress. I have loosely kept memories of what led me to be kept in solitary confinement, and what occurred during solitary confinement. That same memory of a pool of blood in my childhood bedroom and a little cry being let out is all I remember happening before that long period inside solitary confinement; then, during solitary confinement, I was kept in a room shaped by four, dark gray walls and dimly lit by a low level of light protruding from the equally dark, gray ceiling up above. During a long, highly distressing period of time, I was subjected to a swath of aching pains flooding over my body. There were aches spiking all along the insides of my head, and unfolding externally around the lids of my eyes. I could barely see at the time either. A thick, wet fluid clouded my vision, leaving me unable to see. I still don't recall what I thought of being in solitary confinement. One part of me believed it to be what my mother thought was best for us when it came to our development; it taught us to behave better and be better-mannered people. I feel less distress when I think of my mother, which impacts how my physiological symptoms are expressed when I'm around her on the screen. Yet, whenever I thought of being in solitary confinement, I felt distressed again. The thought of my mother could only barely weaken the distressing experience it was just thinking of solitary confinement. I just don't know how I feel about solitary confinement. So, I will keep lying to my mother. I hope tomorrow I will finally listen to her.

In the pitch darkness of my bedroom, with nothing there to see or perceive but a blanket of blackness, I woke up with a jolt shaking my body and a rumble of breaths leaving my lips. I had been sleeping, my eyes seemingly sealed shut, dreaming. When I dream, I feel like I'm still awake, yet with absolutely no control and direction. The distress I feel when awake is felt all throughout the dream and its contents; though, interestingly, what's causing those experiences is constantly there. There's no chance for me to grow hyper fixated on an aspect of my world and lose myself in its visual display, escaping what's causing me those feelings of distress. All of those causal stimuli are there, drowning me entirely in distress and leaving my body without relief. The symptoms I experience when a loud noise occurs in my environment when awake, are constantly felt within those dreamt experiences. It's only a matter of time before my body awakens within my room and feels the physiological remnants of the dream I had just had. It's almost as if something had actually occurred in reality to lead to such a reaction; except, when I am aware of everything around me in my environment, there's nothing there causing my reaction. There's an image of what it was I just experienced inside of my head, but I can't see it when I open my eyes. I woke up from my dream. In that moment, all I perceive is pure nothingness shaded as an infinite color for my eyes to stare into, with the invisible outlines of everything in the room sinking beneath a sea of blackness. The dreams feel familiar. I think they may be memories, though by the time I try to remember them, I recall only a few sparse images of it and feel distressing symptoms line my body in shakes and chills that occur in a physiological streamline of reactions.

I'm sitting upright in my bed right now, panting as I feel a patch of sweat soak the mattress beneath me. I like my bed. It's perhaps the only place in the world that I actually feel comfortable just sitting there and becoming engrossed in nothing characteristically extraordinary. None of the other human lifeforms sleep in my room with me, as they each have their own separate rooms to sleep in. The exploratory robot is also not here with me, and won't wake me for some time; for a number of hours from now. It's just me, my thoughts, and the soft, plush material of my bed nurturing the comforting images filling my consciousness. However, once my eyes close, once I fall asleep and lose sight of my environment, I experience dreams so distressing that it remains impossible to drift back into sleep after being shaken by them in my sleep. The comfort I felt in my bed when I first laid down is quickly compromised by the sweat that soaks my back and the mattress beneath me, as well as the fear that has left me breathless and terrifyingly awakened.

Interestingly enough, I can see some images from the dream I just had. There's a strange feeling of familiarity attached to the images, though, it's a mental territory I'm afraid to enter. It's a dream I've experienced quite a bit. I can see a child's face smiling so brightly as I speak with him. My voice has a noticeably higher pitch than my current voice; perhaps I was a child in the dream as well. The child seems younger than I am in the dream; I can't quite recall if he even says that many words to me. All I can remember being primarily shared between us are little, pitched laughs, along with words that seemed to exist but could not be imagined when thought of. The room we were in seems to be similar to the rooms the other human life forms and I live in; gray, dimly lit walls and floors sparsely covered in furniture. There's not much else that follows after that share of memories; it becomes a mental effort trying to remember any other aspect of the dream beyond that point. All that can be recalled is a feeling; I can't see it, I can just experience it as I imagine all that could follow that point of ambiguity in my dream. It's not much of a different feeling than the feelings of distress I have at most other points of a given day. Except, the main thing triggering such a reaction is not based in reality. It feels like it could've been at one point in time; but if it was, I'd forever remain eluded to knowing for sure.

As the image of that little boy's laughing face fills my head, juxtaposed against my only little chirps of amusement, I unintentionally try and fill the remaining gap in my dream. I know that my efforts will only result in more feelings of distress. I'm already sitting up in my bed and panting breathlessly, gripping the sides of my head and staring wide-eyed ahead of me at shapeless blackness. My heart is beating rapidly inside of my chest and rattling against the sides of my ribcage, leading to my body slightly shaking atop my sweat-soaked mattress. Yet, I try to visualize what I dreamt of during that gaping hole of forgotten dream, only to grow more distressed as I try to expel these obsessive thoughts. I tighten my eyelids, trying to erase the sought-after visuals from the corrupted slate of the inside of my head, as if hiding from the darkness of my own room would bolster my chances of protection. I could see a greatly familiar visual begin to appear inside of my head, even as I shake my head from side to side and massage my temples with a viscous rub. I can't be too loud, or else the exploratory robot will sense me as awake. However, I can't relax and calm down; I don't even know if I could accurately describe the experience of achieving that type of state.

I pant continuously, beginning to see that highly familiar visual appear in my head: that visual of a child screaming and a pool of blood glistening darkly on one of the gray floors of our building. As I begin to discover a sense of familiarity with that visual and begin to make an undesired connection to my previous dream, I realize the wholeness of this dream; of this *memory*. That familiar child is related to that scream; that scream must belong to him. What he was screaming about I have no idea whatsoever; I'm unsure if I'd feel interested in speculating. Sitting here in my bed, gripping the sides of my body and shaking with a slew of uncontrollable pants and palpitations riveting it, I don't think speculating any further would relieve any of the distressing symptoms I had already been subjected to. I also don't think it would help me go back to sleep. So, I just sat upright in my bed, accompanied by those obsessive thoughts and the little behaviors I exhibited ritualistically, drowned invisibly by the lightless environment I sat in.

But, suddenly, I could hear the sound of something that would make me force myself to sleep; or, at least, attempt to. It was the sound of the exploratory robot moving stealthy at night, tracking down the partially exposed corridor of the building. I was five doors away from the room where the exploratory robot remained, which was the same room the other human life forms and I received check-ins everyday in. Usually at night when there was no light outside and the human life forms were tired, the exploratory robot shut down most of its software and hardware to preserve its power. It must have sensed me as being awake while I panted and rocked back and forth atop my bed.

Quickly, I lowered my body onto the sweat-soaked mattress of my bed, feeling the cold, slimy feel of it touch against my back. I folded myself onto my side, tucking my arms into my chest and attempting to appear as relaxed as possible while those same visuals filled my head. I could hear the exploratory robot's grinding wheels grow louder and louder, nearing my door at the end of the corridor. The thought of what the exploratory robot would do if it knew I was awake at this time was enough to force me into a sleep.

As I tried to relax my body in a manner I could understand best, the visuals inside of my head suddenly shifted to familiar ones of the exploratory robot approaching my room after a period of us not interacting. I had been alone for what seemed like weeks; though, however long it had been was, and is still unknown to me. It was when the old hospital behind the place we all lived in collapsed and clouded the entire local area in dust and debris, leaving it unsafe for the other human lifeforms and I to leave our rooms. We were all kept in our rooms for a while, without any food or water. It was a distressing experience; it was also a distressing experience hearing the exploratory robot wind its way down the corridor of the building, until it reached mine and began to open my door. It zoomed slowly in, followed by a thick trail of gray, hazy sunlight. I think I can remember me sprawled lazily atop my bed, tucked tightly underneath my blanket as the room had grown terribly cold following the building collapsing. Most of the memory remained a blur, though I can still remember inside of my head my mother unwinding from within the exploratory robot and greeting me. Suddenly, those feelings of distress I experienced while trapped in my room disappeared. I wasn't cold anymore; I wasn't hungry; I wasn't thirsty, or distressed whatsoever. Not even the dim, towering presence of the exploratory robot instilled a reactive feeling of distress within me. I don't know how to explain that moment; I don't believe I ever will. However, whenever I experience distress in moments like these, I watch as my head returns to that same thought of my mother greeting me after us being separated for a long period of time. Remembering that same memory, I begin to feel less distressed, calming down and feeling the physiological manifestations of my distress vanish from my body. Where they went, and why they left, I'll never figure out.

However, as I lie here in my bed, pretending to sleep, and sensing the exploratory robot enter the room and near my bed, I feel calm as that memory fills my head and distracts me from those previously distressing thoughts. My breaths leave my mouth in a relaxing flow of air, touching lightly against the dimly colored wall next to my bed that I always faced away from when trapped in my room; my heart beats in my chest with a near motionless flutter of movement. I know it's there, still beating in my chest; but, for once, it's not a distressing beat of raucous pounds filling my ears. I'm calm and relaxed, and I don't even notice the exploratory robot leaving the room, let alone when I finally fall back to sleep.

JACEY-ONE
MARCH 3, 2366

In the morning, I woke up with the same distressing symptoms that had awakened me just the night before, a layer of sweat separating my back from the bed and paralyzing it with the same trickling beat of my heart ,leaving me trembling. Fortunately, I didn't have to be subjected to that same array of symptoms any longer; at least, not with the ambiguity I felt with there being nothing for me to see in a stimulatingly lacking, dark room.

Light enters the room only slightly through the cracks bordering the outline of my bedroom's door. Though, the dim light that circles the edge of those protruding rays does nothing to relieve me of my distress. I can still feel those same unnerving symptoms rumble along my body, juxtaposed against the images filling my head ever since my dream last night. I can still see that pool of blood tainting that dimly colored floor, followed by a little, pitched scream somewhere in the periphery of that memory. Hopefully I can find a way to distract myself from this memory. It's always been so distressing recounting it. Despite it being a memory, it's always so distressing seeing it reoccur in the vicinity of my head; I don't know why.

It's almost time for breakfast. Or, I assume so. There's that same feeling of hunger piercing through my stomach, same as I feel every other morning when I open my eyes, become awake, and sit up in my bed and wait for the exploratory robot to lead me to the eating area of the building. Every morning when I wake up, I imagine the routine I'm about to undergo in the morning. Or, at least, I attempt to when my mind isn't too fixated on the dreams I had while asleep. I can see both inside of my head, but not all at once. The image of what appears to be my daily routine appears at one moment, vivid and clear, and seemingly constructed as my physical environment; but, simultaneously broken up sporadically by fuzzy images of that one distinct memory. Blood covering the dimly colored floors of one of the building's rooms, followed by the piercing scream of a child that somehow is associated with it. The memory is less clear than that of my daily routine, with my daily routine easily visualized; however, the former is all I can think about, along with the symptoms of distress I subsequently feel all throughout my body. I don't know why.

I've already sat up in my bed, wrapped loosely in the blanket I wore while sleeping. It's damp and cold, though the distressing symptoms feel less potent when I'm covered in it. It's soft, and as I focus on the feeling of it against my skin, I begin to think about my mother. Just the thought of her is enough to alleviate my symptoms, and begin to feel lighter anticipating breakfast. I shift a little in my bed, pulling the blanket tighter around my body and inhaling the scent leaving its contorted shape of damp fibers. My eyes are enveloping the entirety of a line signaling where the wall opposite of me meets the floor, shaded only slightly lighter than the floor with the same, dimly-lit color of gray. Yet, my head is filled with memories of my mother that pass by quickly but can be seen vividly. I can recall a memory of when I first could feel this blanket against my skin. I was much younger and much smaller, yet in the same place I am right now, waiting for the exploratory robot to come and get me for breakfast. The same blanket brushed against my body in the early morning, kept together with less tatters and wear than it currently contains. My eyes were wide open and scanning the dimly lit room without much intention of finding something significant. The room was filled with only a few toys and my bed, all juxtaposed against the gray background of the rest of my room. Although there were a few things for me to view with my eyes as I opened them, I didn't view them.

Just like right now, as I remain in my bed with this old blanket wrapped around my body, I stared at the outline of light that clung to the edge of my room's door. It was a static light, one that didn't change as I stared at it for an uninterrupted period of time. It held my attention for a while, though I could never understand why. It was just light from outside my room, and it indicated what time it was in the day. I knew it was time to wake up and eat breakfast. That string of facts wasn't anything particularly new for me then. Yet, I found myself watching it closely, finding a brightly colored box bop around before my eyes when I looked away.

Soon enough, I could hear the sound of the exploratory robot approaching my room, trekking against the dirt ground outside of the building with a prolonged *reee!* At the time, I felt instantly distressed upon realizing the fact that the shadow interrupting my stare from the opposite side of the door was the exploratory robot standing in front of it. I pulled the blanket up to my nose, feeling the looming fibers outstretched from the blanket's edge tickle my eyelashes. Closing my eyes as I expected the exploratory robot to discipline me for being awake, I focused on the feel of the blanket against my body as I tried to relieve myself of my distressing feelings felt all over my body. The damp, cold feel of it from the sweat I accumulated while sleeping; the soft, comforting feel of it touching against me like a flush of warmth amidst a chilled morning. It was the exact same feeling I experienced as I do now, listening as the exploratory robot entered my room and maneuvered itself over to my bedside. It was enough to distract me from the unrelenting feelings of distress I felt accumulated within me, despite it not being enough to bring me to sleep.

Soon enough, I heard the voice of my mother enter my ears, and felt a light brush of air against my side as she unwound herself from inside the exploratory robot and faced me. Feeling that blanket pressed against my body, in the space of my bedroom, made me think of my mother, and helped to relieve the feelings of distress I experienced whenever I woke up from a bad dream. Oftentimes, if not all of the time, I had that same experience every single morning I woke up and got prepared to eat breakfast.

I don't know why, but she always hid inside of the exploratory robot behind a screen. She's always there when the exploratory robot interacts with me. I don't know if I'd ever be able to understand what it would be like to see her in front of the screen, independent of the exploratory robot's body. Does she look like me in full-form? Or the other human life forms? She has a face like everyone else and myself does; she has a neck that her head sits on, and a head of hair that fills the border of the screen she communicates from. I think she's just like me. I don't know. I'm just used to seeing her from behind the same screen that unwinds from within the exploratory robot and that she interacts from.

I pull my arms out from beneath the blanket I wrapped tightly around my body, observing my arms in the morning light that my room is just barely awash in with a dim sort of luminance. I try to remember her face - the color of it, of her neck. I look at my arms, then think inside of my head about her face. My arms are tanned a light shade of bronze. I don't quite know if that's the color of my mom's face. I think it's lighter. What's the color of mine? Do I have a face? What does it look like? Is it like her's? What about the other human life forms? I don't know. I don't know at all. I assumed I did; all of the other human lifeforms have a face, and so does my mother. But do I?

I can feel an array of distressing symptoms flood my body, pro-claimed climatically by the feeling of my heart sinking into my stomach and triggering a dizzying flutter of sickness. I don't know if I have a face. I've never been sure. I've never noticed if I had a face. I don't know anything. I can feel the air sink deeper into my lungs and my back drag forward as I gloss over these sudden realizations, not taking my eyes off of the ground as I attempt to visualize what my face looks like.

I don't know what it looks like. Trapped in this little world of my own that for so long comforted me just sinking into, I was no longer comforted; I felt distressed. Not by the thought of the exploratory robot reprimanding me, or at the sudden occurrence of a loud, untraceable noise; but, rather, by the realization of the fact I had no idea what my face looked like, let alone if I even had one. I was unaware of if I had a face, and I was automatically subjected to a feeling of isolation in the context of my mother and the other human life forms. I was different, yet I was unsure why. I was unsure about everything in my environment. I don't understand anything. I don't understand what I look like; I just assumed. I just assumed I had a face like the other human life forms, though I am unsure if that is the truth. Why did I assume that? I can't figure it out.

I wrap my head with my hands, running them all over my face with grips of varying degrees of tightness. At holes, I dig my palm and the bottom edge of my lined-up fingers deeper into them, as if doing so would verify the existence of any potential face of mine. The holes placed higher on my head seem to shut everything else out of the world when I dug my hands into them, leaving only a plane of pitch blackness and any visual conjured inside of my head. I don't know how that's supposed to help me, however. I don't know if I have a face. I feel my hands trail down my face as I slowly bring them downwards away from my eyes and off the edge of my jawline, into my lap. I stare ahead of me where my eyes remained prior to me covering them, becoming engrossed by the thin, black line separating the dark gray floor from the barely lighter gray wall above it. I pull my hand back up to my face, but only to lightly brush against the hole at the bottom of my face and the two at the top, serving as some apparent reminder of what lies on my head. I have a mouth; I have eyes; a nose - but do I have a face? Does it look like the other human life forms'? Does it look like my mother's? I don't know. What even is a face?

Thinking to myself, I became lost in the fact I didn't know whether or not I had a face; little did I know I had no idea what a face was even for. What was its purpose? It's the front side you see of one of the human life forms' faces, as well as mother's. But, what's so significant about it? Most curiously, why am I so upset about the potential reality that I don't have one? I can't tell why this is what distresses me at the moment; usually, it's the thought of the exploratory robot reprimanding me or a loud, ambiguous noise occurring in my environment, disrupting the normal flow of it. But, right now, this is what I'm distressed about: my face, or, the lack of one.

It's not long before the thought of my mother's face fills the space inside of my head and I'm suddenly relieved again. I could feel the realization of her face's existence spread throughout my body like the sensation of being heated or cooled. The thoughts swarming my head as I experience a dilemma over my body suddenly disappear, and I am finally returned to a calm state. My heart returns to a slowed, natural beat, and my breaths are just barely any slower as they exude invisible figments of air flowing out of my mouth. The line that my eyes grew preoccupied with is now just a line ahead of me that represents where my room's walls meet the floor, passively entering my vision but not morphing into a point to fixate on and allow perplexing thoughts to paralyze my body whole.

But, just as the distress I experienced previously began to fade away, I realized something: it was past time for mother and the exploratory robot to come get me for breakfast. At least, it felt like it was. Usually not long after when I woke up they both entered all of our rooms and helped prepare us for breakfast. However, looking away from my bedroom wall and over at the door in which the two of them always entered, I realized much more time had seemingly passed between the moment I woke up and right now. *Where were they? Did they forget about me? Did it happen again? Did they forget me here like when that old building collapsed?* I didn't hear the exploratory robot approaching my room, let alone any of the other human life forms' rooms; that slow, monotonous *zoom!* was nowhere to be heard in the vicinity of the partially exposed corridor. I heard no doors opening, and no steps taken in any of the other rooms.

I looked away only momentarily, then peering back in the direction of the door, pressing my hands softly into the fabric of my bed and raising myself up slightly as something near the door caught my attention: the light outlining the border of my bedroom door. It's not bright anymore; it's not dark, either, but it's darker than it was. Gray, almost, as if the sun was hidden by something. Something like clouds.

I looked back down at the floor passively, my eyes widened yet processing nothing in my physical environment. Parts of my room entered my eyes and filled my head, but became nothing more than a useless experience of visuals. I returned my gaze back to the door, then back to the floor and back again to the door, staring with wide eyes and thinking only one thing as I did so: they forgot me. They forgot me in my room. I don't know when they'll be returning to get me; I don't even know if they will. This is just like that one time when the large building near ours collapsed and covered the local area in clouds of thick dust, leading to the human life forms being locked in their rooms and not interacted with for days. However, I'm unsure if there's any end to this isolation in my room. I have no way of predicting how this experience secluded inside of my bedroom will end; or, if it will end.

A thick, warm liquid begins to circle around my eyes, casting my environment into a seemingly impenetrable blur. I try to swipe my hands across my eyes to brush away the liquid, only to worsen the perceived blur and see my dimmed, gray environment erupt into a hierarchy of darkened glares. I press my hands into my eyes, trying to expel my eye sockets of the liquid filling them. However, I came to the realization of one thing: the liquid won't cease to dispense from my eyes, only trailing along my cheeks and blurring my vision just as they each began to venture along my face. My vision blurs even more, and everything is cast into a glared haze swaying ahead of me.

I'm going blind. Oh no. It's happening again. Like when this last happened, I'm going blind again. The exploratory robot taught us about this phenomenon one time. I'm losing my ability to see. I'm going blind. I can feel it slipping away as this detrimental liquid covers my eyes and floods my face in a wet, slightly chapped feel. I grunt continuously, panting nervously as I come to the realization I'm losing my ability to see. I try to wipe away the liquid covering my eyes, coming to the same realization countless times that it will still be covering my eyes once my hands have been removed from the holes in my head. My hands are growing wetter and wetter, as is my face. They also have become stiffened, and eventually declining into a functional waste, as I have now become one thing: blind. I can only see things in an indistinguishable blur, with nothing easily recognizable. In addition to the onset of my disability, I think of how I was left in this room, and the exploratory robot with my mother wasn't coming to get me. I was left inside here without any contact with them.

What did the exploratory robot do with my mother? Where did it take her?

All of these questions pass through my head in wandering voices, though without any obvious answer provided in return. They propagate my head and drown my body in shakiness and leave me feeling dizzied. I eventually see only the same blurred, hazy presence of my room's wall ahead of me, passing before me as I fall to the floor before me, witnessing briefly my blindness reach its fully manifested state: I can no longer see anything. Just an infinite plane of blackness. I am now blind, and all alone. I don't know when the exploratory robot will return with my mother. I just don't know.

JACEY-ONE
MARCH 3, 2366

I'm not blind. My vision has returned. But I don't know why it left to begin with. I can see everything clearly now. At one point liquid was filling my eyes and everything was blurry, then nothing could be seen by me anymore. Now, I can see everything in my room, except it's much darker than when I last could see. I was on the floor when I was able to see again. I don't know why. My eyes just drifted open and everything within my physical environment became transformed from a blurred, grayed haze of everything in front of my nose and into a clearer version.

I'm not sure why I lost my vision at that time. I'm also not sure why it seemed like I was asleep at that same moment. I just woke up on the floor and I could suddenly see again, though, with a large amount of pain filling the side of my body which had first came into contact with the floor. I pushed myself back onto the floor, removing my other side from the bottom of my bed where it had been tilted against. I stared up at the ceiling of my room but without processing much of what it was I was staring at. I just laid there panting on the ground, visually prying into the ceiling's subtly stratified portions of dark gray material. Nothing passed through my head as I just tried to process the fact I had regained my ability to see.

Nothing like that had happened since I was younger. My eyes haven't grown full of that thick, warm liquid and left me unable to see since when I saw that pool of blood in my room and heard a little boy scream, and eventually become reprimanded by the exploratory robot. Reprimanded by the exploratory robot.. *Reprimanded by the exploratory robot..* I was reprimanded by the exploratory robot at that moment. I don't know why, or how such a memory evaded my head for so long, but I now realized that. I was reprimanded by the exploratory robot just after I heard that little boy scream and saw that pool of blood. I know that that happened, I can just feel that sense of realization flood my body with a mild form of stimulation. I felt different as I looked up at my room's ceiling and came to the realization the exploratory robot punished me at the time. I began to sit up now, looking around my room but without processing much of what I was looking at. Now, I could only actively perceive what was inside of my head and laid out before me in an illusory scene of visuals; a memory deep within. My back ached as I sat up, and my arm felt pain even more than that felt alongside my spine. However, I didn't care. Being in such a vulnerable position on the floor rendered me unable to totally fathom what I had now discovered about that one memory. That one memory that always fills my head everytime I hear a loud noise, or grow distressed over the exploratory robot. I don't know why, but laying here on my bedroom floor after becoming blinded by some internal liquid led to this revelation. There must be significance to me becoming momentarily blind; if anything, it was the fulfillment of at least some clarity with that memory that I constantly see.

The little boy laughed, as I remembered from a dream, then screamed, then a pool of blood could be seen on the floor, and eventually I was reprimanded, being left in my room for countless days without food, water, or any contact with my mother or the other human life forms. I was all alone, just like I am right now. *Just like I am right now..*

I could feel my lungs beginning to cave in as I came to the further realization that I was reprimanded by being locked in my room for days; by being forgotten about. Breaths could barely escape my lungs without being pushed out in a strained *huff!*, leaving me breathless and sickened as I processed what I just realized.

Almost automatically, I turned my head to my side and stared at where I first saw that pool of blood just after that little boy screamed. I could see the dark, rusted stain of the blood linger on the ground in an erratically shaped circle, almost in the same shape it was when I first saw that pool of blood. I closed my eyes and felt as breaths continued to exit my lungs through shaky lapses of air. My toes twisted and shook with an inconsistent trend of movement, either twisting or shaking in no clear order. I could feel this realization leading me to another sort of realization. I don't know how I could tell, I just could. As I opened my eyes again and stared at that dark stain in the concrete floor, I sighed, trying to figure out what it was I was beginning to realize.

Trying to realize what it was led to more images passing through my head; images of the little boy laughing in front of me, producing what I believe to be considered a smile; images of his skin almost comparable to the color of my arms; images of him bleeding on the floor; I could hear him screaming, filling my head and strangely pouring into my physical environment; and I could see images of the exploratory robot reprimanding me, leaving me isolated with that blood-stain accompanying my isolation.

"Heh - heh - heh - heh-" I gasped repeatedly, feeling my vision go blurry and unfocused. I pressed my body forward into my knees and pressed into my temples tightly, feeling the strands of hair towards the front of my head pull in pain with my grip.

That little boy was killed. I assume he was killed. That's what the blood made me assume, accompanied by the little, tanned boy screaming in that pool of blood that I can still visibly see, despite the slow fade of its rustic color. I don't know if I was right to assume that he was killed. What does it even mean to be killed? What does it mean if that little boy was killed? Is he dead? Is he dead for good? Who killed him? What killed him? I don't even know if my memory is proving my judgment right. What if it's just an illusion? What if he wasn't actually killed? What if I'm just assuming he was killed and that blood belonged to him?

My judgment has to be right; I could feel it inside of me. My body feels that slow spread of sensation as I recall that memory of the little boy sprawled-out in a pool of blood and screaming. I can't even tell what he's wearing. I just see him lying there screaming in pain. I feel so distressed. I can sense him in the room with me, almost as though that memory of him has now become my actual reality. I closed my eyes tightly shut, grimacing at my lap as I attempted to block that same visual from my view. I clenched my fists, digging them as hard as I could into the holes in my head and pressing deeply into my eyes, unable to clear my head of that image. Everytime I opened my eyes I could see the little boy sprawled-out on the floor in a pool of blood, and the same occurred every time I closed my eyes. I couldn't escape that visual; it almost became transformed into my reality. Whether inside of my head or out in my physical environment, I could only see that distressing memory play out before me, not leaving that specific place along the floor.

"Huh - huh - huh - huh - huh - huh-" I gasped, trying to look away from the spot where the little boy had laid but only seeing it reappear in my head. I closed my eyes shut as tight as I could without hands, shaking my head viciously, as if the memory was a physical part of me I could just expel with a scratch or a shake. But, it felt like it was something part of me; I could feel it all along my body, pressing down on my chest and causing the skin along my arms and legs to tingle.

I felt that memory in my physical environment, as though I was a younger version of myself once again and I just encountered that mysterious little boy screaming in a pool of blood before me in my room. *Dying*, eventually. Whatever that actually is. I could see it play out in my environment; I became even more distressed at the idea of moving my body in any direction nearing the blood. I didn't want to move my body; I didn't even want to breathe. I could tell doing anything near that boy would just draw me deeper into that memory. I couldn't face it any longer; I didn't want to. I could feel my heart racing; breaths becoming quicker and spread-out; drops of sweat falling all along the sides of my head with an awkward, soaked manifestation of moisture. I felt like I was melting into the floor of my bedroom, becoming a pool of dissipating skin, bone, muscle, and the sensational manifestation of that memory. That memory that I could see right now for the second time in my life. I was almost beginning to lose my vision once again when I could suddenly see a large ray of light enter my room through the doorway off to the side of the little boy, illuminating the room with a vast blanket of dimmed grayness and showing the towering image of the exploratory robot enter slowly into the room with its usual *reee!* I ripped my body back, slamming it into the side of my bed away from the sight of the dying little boy and devouring the sight of the looming exploratory robot with all of my senses, exclaiming:

"I'M SORRY! I'M SORRY! I DIDN'T MEAN TO DO IT! I DIDN'T MEAN TO HURT HIM! I'M SORRY! PLEASE DON'T LEAVE ME IN HERE!"

My eyes suddenly left the exploratory robot and met with the center of the room, though I could now only see that same, fading stain spread across it. The dying little boy wasn't there anymore. I still felt the same way I did as when I first recalled that memory of the little boy; though, what I felt did not relate to what I saw. He was suddenly gone, and returned to the ambiguous plane of space within my head. I looked up at the exploratory robot, who was actually entering the room and nearing me. It straightened itself with its side positioned in front of me, stopping just a foot away from my trembling feet. Its back cover folded inward, extending one of its long, coiled arms from inside its body and revealing the screen displaying my mother. She produced a big smile at me, greeting me by my name in much the same manner she does every other day. Yet, any feeling of relief doesn't occur within my body whatsoever; I just sit on the ground and stare at her on the rectangular screen outstretched before me, feeling the sporadic remnants of my previously distressing episode graze chillingly throughout my body.

"Hi Jacey-one! How are you doing today, honey?"

The face she produced at me was a smile, I believe; a big, curved one that she always flashed at me whenever greeting me. It didn't do anything to change the lingering stress I felt. I looked down at my feet for a moment then at the rusting bloodstain underneath the exploratory robot, unsure of how to respond to her question. I tried to open my lips and say something, but nothing seemed to come out. I don't know why. Her question and how she said it conflicted with what I wanted to say. There was some sort of incompatibility, and it became even more noticeable as I continued to stare at the dark blood stain on the floor, recalling what I remembered laying there. Even when cast dimly in the vast shadow of the exploratory robot, I could still clearly see that little boy just lying there, bleeding himself to death. My eyes remained transfixed on that stain, with my lips still contorting into every shape possible as a little croak escaped from my mouth in broken-up bits of unintelligible noise.

"I don't-" I stopped, looking up at her smiling face beaming down at me and continuing slowly. "I don't know-"

"Oh, that's alright, Jacey-one! I'm sure you enjoyed your sleep - are you ready for dinner?"

I couldn't reply to her quick interjection, unsure of what to say. *Dinner?* I was so lost. I felt hungry, but, unsure of why dinner was the first meal of the day, rather than breakfast and eventually lunch.

"Dinner? But what about breakfast and lunch?"

"We had to skip those meals today since there was acid rain outside. But, it's gone now, and I don't think it'll be occurring again anytime today. Are you ready for dinner? I hope you're hungry!"

The exploratory robot began to pull my mother back beneath its back cover, beginning to move forward before stopping and reversing slowly back to its initial position before my feet. It unwound that same coiled arm from beneath its suddenly reopening back cover, revealing my mother on the same rectangular screen she was displayed on. She smiled at me once again, greeting me in a manner similar to just a moment ago.

"Hi Jacey-one! How are you feeling?"

"Um, I don't - I don't know." I answered, my mouth half-agape and my body struck by the same feeling of confusion I felt with our previous interaction.

"Oh that's fine, Jacey-one. I hope you enjoyed today's fitness enrichment activity. Ready for your check-in?"

I stared into her eyes, holding them in my gaze for a moment. I then let my eyes fall into my legs and gloss momentarily over my hands, which my mother was expecting to check my oxygen levels with by clutching with one of the exploratory robot's internal arms. I looked back up at her, initially unsure about what I should do. Reluctantly, I began to reach my arm out with my index finger pointed towards the exploratory robot, just at the same time the exploratory robot pulled out one of its internal arms. It winded outward toward my hand, producing a *reee* sound similar to when it maneuvers yet smaller. I was unsure why my mother was doing a check up on me at this moment, as I hadn't been participating in any fitness enrichment activity today. I had been in my room all day. Why was she checking on me? And what fitness enrichment activity? I didn't understand. Yet, I still watched as that rubber gripping device pressed two ends over my index finger, applying a feeling of pressure to the upper portion of it. My mother beamed down at me, smiling. Then, the two blocks of rubber connected to an outstretched metal claw released my finger, followed by my mother remarking in a remarkably similar fashion to the countless times we had gone through the same process.

"Great, Jacey-one. Now let's measure your heartbeat."

My finger still removed from my grip and pointed to the robot with a slight curl, I watched as another arm a little to the side of the previous one removed itself from the exploratory robot's insides, gripping my finger. I stared at the two blocks of rubber gripping my finger in the folded shape of the robot's metal claw just a couple of feet away from my face and the rest of my body. In the periphery of my vision, I could see a blurred outline of my mother smiling down at me, somewhat unchanged from when I last exchanged glances with her. Every time I stared directly at her, her smile shrunk to a casual, upward curve, the same as I found her staring at me when I first looked at her; her eyes barely moved from mine. Yet, even when I glanced downward at the robot's hand, or even underneath the entire robot at the blood-stain left for years on the floor, her smile grew enlarged, with the corners of her lips nearly stretching to the sides of her face. I could even see her eyes staring at me still, despite our eyes not meeting at all. It was like I was still staring at her, except the face I stared at was a blurred, exaggerated assortment of her facial features. Although her face wasn't much different from the other human life forms', there was something significant about the way her eyes followed mine even when they didn't meet, or how her smile grew into a distorted shape of a thin, pink line. It was distressing, almost, to witness, and seemed strangely different from anything I had experienced before when looking at her face.

"Thanks so much, Jacey-one! Ready for dinner, now?" Mother asked as the exploratory robot released my index finger from its grip, rewinding back inside of its large, metal compartment.

"Ye - yeah. Yeah, I am - mother." I gulped, which I wasn't quite sure as to why I did.

It felt like I was merely swallowing air and providing a barricade against the bile rising in my throat and flourishing inside of my stomach with a sickly tingle. I didn't look at her when replying; I didn't even share a mere glance. It felt distressing just seeing her on that screen before me, staring at me. It was a perplexing situation being in her presence. Staring straight at her elicited a distressing response, sickening your stomach and rattling your body and its posture; yet, looking away gave way to much of the same, if not even worse of a physical response.

She smiled again and chirped brightly in response, eventually recoiling back inside of the exploratory robot as she had countless times before. A screen of blackness quickly replaced her face, almost like she was turned off like a mindless machine. Like the exploratory robot. I'm unsure of what significance that comparison holds; I know she's concealed within the exploratory robot, and comes out when she's ready to speak with me. Maybe there's some significance to that relationship. I suppose I can't see it right now.

I pulled myself off of my bedroom floor, feeling the pain in my backside erupt throughout my spine as I straightened my body upright. As the exploratory robot maneuvered around the room in a position that pointed towards the bedroom's door, I began to limp with it to the door, moving with it out of my room, but focused on a matter entirely subjugated by the boundaries of my head. I thought of today, and how I was forgotten about in my bedroom. I also thought of my mother, and how strangely familiar her interactions with me felt; identical, even. Suddenly, our interactions felt like a daily retread of the same words, just shuffled into a different inclusion of particular words with each verbal exchange. It was something I never noticed; but, noticing it felt so surreal. It felt distressing, even.

I like sameness. I like stability. I like my environment to be calm and neutral, and not changed abruptly by forces out of my control. But, examining my interactions with my mother, and as far back as I could remember, the idea of our interactions being of a constant type suddenly seemed distressing to think about. I didn't like the thought of it. I didn't like it like how I didn't like loud noises occurring in my environment and pulling me out of my own little world. Furthermore, I didn't like it; like how I didn't like waking up from a sleep and expecting the exploratory robot to be in the doorway and reprimand me for some reason I couldn't quite understand. I didn't like the qualities of mine and my mother's interactions just like those things. And I couldn't understand the significance of that similarity. Just like how I couldn't understand the similarity between a machine shutting off and my mother disappearing behind a screen of blackness when the exploratory robot concealed her presence within its large metal compartment. It was a black box I stared into and constantly remained evaded from any knowledge of, manifesting with every point in my physical environment I grew fixated on.

JACEY-ONE
MARCH 4, 2366

The day before ended with the same routine as any other day: eat dinner, rinse our mouths and bodies, then fall asleep in our rooms. Today began with the same routine as any other day, too: wake up with feelings of distress, be greeted by my mother, then eat breakfast and start the day. Between those two daily events was unlike any other period of sleep, however. I was alone, and awash in the feelings of distress I felt just prior to laying down in my bed. I'm always alone the moment I start to try and sleep, and the moment I wake up, but, for once, it actually felt like my reality. I guess for so long I believed there was someone there at the end of that period of rest to greet me and relieve me of the distress I felt all through the night. It was an upside to my nightly dreams and the distress that both served as consequences of falling asleep. I'd fall asleep, witness a distressing dream, experience that distress, then eventually wake up to be greeted by my mother. Now, however, that event I anticipated every night was something I now passively awaited. It'll happen, I'm highly confident, but it doesn't feel the same as when I woke up this morning. I can't feel it while anticipating it; and, as I came to realize, I couldn't feel it when experiencing it in my physical reality. The relieving experience of being greeted by my mother after a night of distress was not experienced when it was just an ambiguous figment in my head, nor when she was right in front of my face greeting me on that rectangular screen connected to the exploratory robot.

Now, whenever I see her, I'm much different in how I interact with her. I'm shorter in my responses, and quieter, too. I'm not even sure she noticed. She's no different towards me. Her remarks directed at me feel identical to every other interaction we've had; almost like it was rehearsed. Coming to this realization made me wonder one thing: if I felt she had always spoken to me in the same way, why was I now just realizing it? What left me so oblivious to this? Just trying to think back about our individual interactions was a difficult task. Nothing felt significant about them. I could mainly just remember the feelings of anticipation I experienced when expecting our interactions every night before waking up. Even those feelings were always at a constant. I suppose that habit was now broken, and my perception of my mother was ultimately violated. I don't know. It's weird, and only elicits more feelings of distress just reflecting on it.

While sitting at my table eating dinner last night, I made a similar observation about my mother's interactions with one of the other human life forms. It was with Jacey-two, I believe. Although her face was just like the others', I could tell by her voice and the shape of her body that the interaction involved him. Strangely, as I sat there with my plate of pureed vegetables and meat sitting just as still and untouched, I observed how my mother interacted with Jacey-two in an almost identical way to how I interacted with her. It was practically the same. My observation was followed by disoriented thoughts that somehow managed to reinforce what I had already been observing my mother as doing. Though I could only perceive my mother's interactions with Jacey-two with little organization and a corresponding flare of sweat and hotness flooding my body, I still somehow knew what my observations implied. How she interacted with me was not significant; it was just replicated across her individual interactions with the other human life forms. I didn't know how to feel about that. What I do know is, staring at the lumped piles of orange and brown mush glistening before me beneath the overhead lights of the room, it felt distressing to make that observation. There was almost no difference in my bodily reactions to my mother than to the exploratory robot. I was distressed at the presence of the exploratory robot, and was distressed as well with that of my mother.

Right now, it's the middle of the day. I believe it's March 4th, though I don't believe there's any significance to that fact. I'm sitting on the floor in the room where my mother teaches the curriculum. I'm the only one present, as the curriculum apparently does not impact the other human life forms. Today, she's teaching me about something called "pro-creation". What she's teaching me barely passes over my mind, as I've grown increasingly fixated on the gray, concrete floor I sat upon. The light from above touches it with a soft beam of light that illuminates the subtle stratified design in the floor, marked by minor indentations in the floor that creates a ripple effect in the hardened concrete. I trace my finger along the design. It's imperfect, and no two individual swirls of indented concrete arise parallel to each other. It's just like my bedroom floor, and the floor of the room we all eat in. That design, while imperfect on its own, is constantly found across all of the rooms. Looking ahead of my finger in the periphery of my vision, I don't see the same pool of blood that stains my bedroom floor in a rusted, brown circle, imperfect in its dried boundaries. Instead, I see a little, plush mold on the floor, almost comparable to the color of mine or the other human life forms' skin. In fact, the whole thing looks like my body; particularly, the area of my body near where my hands fall and my penis is. It leans closer into the floor on the outer edges, and stretches slightly upwards in a curved direction. However, in the middle, there is no penis. There is just a thin, softly zig-zagged line in the middle surrounded by two flaps protruding upward from the object's surface.

I remove my eyes from the dark strata design found imprinted in the concrete floor, pulling them from the edge of my finger and to the plush, shiny object just a few feet away from me. It looks so much like the area around my hips; but, it's also not. The object appears to have hips like me, though they stretch more outwards than mine. My eyes envelope the object as curiosity paralyzes my mind and leaves me staring breath-lessly at the object. I've never seen anything like it. It's so different, yet so similar at the same time. I feel like this object can be represented by my own body, but there's so many fundamental differences that distinguish me from the shape.

It's almost distressing to stare at it; perplexing, even. It almost becomes addicting to stare at the object. The sight of the glistening, body-like object ignites a cyclic progression of actions. Just a mere glance away from it led to a significant desire arising to continue to stare at it; staring at it led to a similarly felt inclination to look away, only to repeat this habit continually. I only pull myself out of this cycle when I hear my name called by my mother. Although it's only a slight deterrent from this addicting habit, it's still enough to pull my attention somewhat away from the object. Looking up at my mother on the rectangular screen outstretched before me, the pain is still found in my neck after the fluid upward-rotation of my head between the floor and the ambiguous object. Barely any attention is mustered in her direction and the words she directs at me, however, it suffices.

"Please remove your clothes, Jacey-one."

I looked back at my mother, the strange waist-like object filling the lower portion of my periphery. She smiled down at me, the exploratory robot just behind her with its wide, metallic side facing me. Its light, gray side glistened in the downward aim of the room's overhead lights, casting a still, reflective surface of light similar to the screen my mother was projected on. I was somewhat confused at what she was ordering me to do - *remove my clothes?* It was the middle of the day. I wouldn't have to change the clothes I wore until I washed off later after dinner. Although it wasn't much different how she worded her statement, it was different in the time and setting she stated it. We were in the middle of the room she taught us curriculum in - why would I remove my clothes?

I could feel my clothes suddenly tingle along my body's skin as I focused on the material concealing my naked body. I looked back up at my mother, who continued to smile down at me with a beaming, almost unchanged curvature of lips. My eyes fell slowly from my mother's to the beige-colored object before me, then traveled along the stratified-concrete floor up my body and to my lap, just where the bottom of my zipper would reach if I were to unzip and remove my clothes. I repeated the cycle of stares rotating in a vertical motion, changing between my mother's smiling face, the waist-like object before me, and my zipper.

Soon enough, I gulped, feeling my heart beating in a light rumble as I brought my hands into a pinching formation, reaching up to my zipper near my neck. I began to pull the zipper downward, staring at my mother and pondering what she was trying to demonstrate by having me remove my clothes. I was unsure. I had hardly even listened to what she had been teaching me, and she hadn't even noticed. The cool air found circulating inside the room tickled the short patch of hairs sticking out across my chest and stomach area. It was an unusual feeling, one I was not accustomed to at this given time of day. I pulled the zipper farther and farther down my torso, until it met near my pelvic area, my half-curled, pinching fist brushing shakily against my penis. My mother's eyes continued to remain on my body, held tightly as a mere blur in the periphery of mine. I pulled my shoulders out of my jumpsuit, sticking one up higher then proceeding to do so with the other shoulder. The jumpsuit fell down my back, brushing chillingly against the skin of it. I began to breathe slightly heavier as I watched my mother continue to stare down at me with no change in the smile she displayed. I stood up from the floor I had been sitting on, slowly and steadily rising from it as my jumpsuit slid down my body in the opposite direction, falling at my feet in a lumped, imperfectly folded pile of white-colored fabrics. Pulling my feet out of the pant legs still clinging firmly to my ankles, I now stood with most of my body exposed to the cool, crisp air lining the room with a slight breeze. My undergarments remained on my body. I was unsure if I had to remove those as well. It almost made me more distressed at the thought of having to be totally naked in front of my mother.

"Almost there, Jacey-one! Please remove your undergarments, as well."

I stared at her bright, smiling face for a moment, before bringing my eyes down to my hips where the white-colored undergarment clung to the middle portion of my body. I closed my eyes nervously, beginning to grip the elastic band clinging tightly to the skin around my waist. With my thumb and index finger brought to a tight, shaky pinch over the band, I pulled my undergarments down my legs, arching my back forward as I bowed my head to the exploratory robot. The undergarments eventually fell past my knees and landed at my feet, before being transported to the side with my jumpsuit, carried by my slightly bent foot. Then, I stood there before my mother and the exploratory robot, chilled and naked in their presence with that waist-like object positioned between us on the floor. I gulped, looking down at my penis extending from my pelvic area in a curved shape of skin, based in the middle of a patch of curly, brown hairs.

"Thank you so much, Jacey-one! Now, it is very important that you learn this, so I want you to practice what I was just teaching you. Pretend the object before you is a woman you are performing intercourse with. Place your body onto its arms and legs, and pretend to have sex with this object while pretending it is a woman."

"Wha - what? What do you mean?"

"I want you to pretend to perform intercourse with the object before you. It is important that you learn this as part of your curriculum."

"Wh - what, I don't-" I spat out in a prolonged stutter, unsure about what my mother was asking me to do. I had never done anything like this for my mother during the curriculum. Usually I just rehearsed general knowledge about nature or practiced growing plants in local soil.

However, before I could continue stuttering my confusion to her in a shaky, trailing voice, a coiled arm similar to the one displaying my mother pulled itself out from within the exploratory robot's body. At the end of the arm quickly extending towards my body was a little, pointed metal spoke with a little, shiny orb on its end, with a long, zig-zagged string of electricity running all along it. I backed up a little, though not enough to totally remove myself from the exploratory robot's electrocution device nearing my body. I was scared of what would happen if I ran away completely. Mother stared at me with the same, beaming smile, just as the arm reached my bare stomach and zapped me.

"Ow!" I chirped, feeling a little bit of pain in the area of skin near the electrocution device's point of contact with my body. It was an uncomfortable, warm feeling that involved a pinching-sensation felt alongside it.

I grimaced at mother, watching her smile as it contrasted the expression I directed in return. The electrocution device hovered near my body, beginning to reel away only slightly as it held itself at a point somewhere between myself and the exploratory robot.

"Almost there, Jacey-one! You just need to place your body on your hands and knees and pretend you are performing intercourse with the object before you. It is important you learn this activity."

I continued to glance at her with a stable look of angst and disillusionment, though now I looked down at the object just a couple of feet away from my body. My feet were pointed in opposite directions, directed at the opposite corners of the room we sat in for the curriculum. I began to bend my knees forward, eventually placing the pointed, hardened fold of my left knee on the floor, then the other. I brought my body to a position hovering over the concrete, imperfect strata design of the floor, same as in every other floor of the surrounding rooms of this building. My head bowed to the exploratory robot, with the space between the robot's bottom surface and the floor beneath it filling my periphery. And, just beneath my body and near my soft, motionless penis was the hip-like object that looked so similar to the area near my pelvic region, but differed in so many fundamental ways. My penis hung there with my testicles nearby it. Glancing down at that soft, plush slot in the object, feeling my warm breaths pierce my neck and upper chest in a humid feel, I realized what mother wanted me to do: she wanted me to insert my penis into it. But why? I don't understand. What good will this serve for me? I remained there in a halted-crawl-position pondering the action I sensed I was instructed to do, not managing to pretend to perform intercourse with the object sitting beneath me.

Before I could sit there thinking nervously over the actions I was supposed to perform, I felt another zap this time against my right arm, which was even more painful than the one shot against my stomach. My arm twitched a little, accompanied by the same *Ow!* I shot at the floor with a voice of pain and distress.

"You're almost there, Jacey-one! Now that you have placed your body on your hands and knees, you must pretend you are performing intercourse with the object before you."

I whimpered slowly beneath her presence, which I assumed to be shooting a bright smile down at my cowering body facing away from her. Panting with a small murmur shakily spat at the floor, I nervously bent my head forward and eyed the object beneath my body, erected from the floor at an angle diagonally positioned to my soft, motionless penis. I don't know how I'm supposed to do this. I don't know how I'm supposed to pretend to have intercourse with this object. I don't know what she means.

Bending my head upwards a little and straining my eyes in the direction of my mother and the electrocution device hovering near her projecting screen, I laid my lower body awkwardly on the floor with my upper body perched upward in a slope, aided by my strained arms. I pressed my lower body into the object, feeling it move with the unintentional nudge I provided with my pelvic region shakily pushing against it. The pain in my arms grew intensified as I stretched my body against the ground and pressed my pelvis against the object, my penis folding against its side against the ground and between my legs. I tried to lift my lower body up again and hover it above the object in a more targeted position above it, finding my penis grow tickled as its soft skin pressed against the edge of the slot. I grunted in my efforts, though in a manner of distress, just as I did when I recently grew distressed about that memory I had of the little boy who died in my room. My penis was finally touching against the slot, though it barely entered through the plush slot. It felt like the touch of my mattress against my restful body when I fell into a deep, distressing sleep. Except, staring wide-eyed at the object pressed against my contorted body with a heavily breathing mouth agape, I was in fact terribly awake, and aware of this reality.

Suddenly, I felt another shock provided to my body, this time even more profound and against my other arm. I released another *Ow!* at the base of the exploratory robot and the short span of floor between us, whimpering with a string of shaken breaths and tearful sniffs following. The stratified concrete floor that was found between the exploratory robot and I, as well as in every other room of the building, was now a blur, containing little, granulated specks in its hardened material that shone bright, scattered rays into my eyes. I was going blind again, just like when I lost my vision in my room after being locked in it. For some reason, I didn't care at this moment. I wasn't shaken by that fact, instead distressed by the abrupt shift found in my relationship with my mother, as the exploratory robot zapped me into a stretched body of various points of electrocution.

I could feel my heartbeat not only in my chest, but also in my arms where the zaps had first been shot. The pain pulsated beneath my skin inside of my biceps, and surfaced with a hot, pinching feel all across the skin of my arms.

"You're almost there, Jacey-one! You just now need to pretend you are having intercourse with the object before you."

"Mother, please! I don't - I don't understand! Plea - please, please stop!" I cried, remaining in a shaky crawling position against the floor, with the object pressed firmly against my pelvic region.

I suddenly felt another zap, this time far more painful than the previous ones shot against my body. It was significant enough to cause my arms to buckle and my face to plant into the floor, leaving my body bent awkwardly over the object beneath me. My hands pushed forward in a rough movement as my body collapsed onto the floor, directing them in a straight formation towards the base of the exploratory robot. I was now bowing to the robot and my mother, vulnerable and relentlessly allocated to them with my shaking, naked body. It was like when I passed out in my room and had no awareness of anything. Except, I was now fully aware of everything that happened to me. I was now left shaking in the towering presence of the exploratory robot, with my head bent to the side, forcing my blurred vision away from the robot.

I was in so much pain; additionally, I experienced so much distress. I didn't know what to do. I feared what would happen next, but also anticipated it with a cautious sense of familiarity. I failed my mother. I failed the exploratory robot. As a result, I was reprimanded. What kind of punishment would follow was a mystery to me. But, the stratified concrete floor I cried against, just like the one found in my room where that blood stain dried into the floor and cemented the legacy of that little boy's death, and all the feelings of distress I would feel in remembrance, offered enough hints that were unnerving to reconcile and ultimately fathom.

"Oh, Jacey-one, it looks like you failed today's curriculum task! The exploratory robot and I determined you have failed at one of your most fundamental functions as a human. As a result, I don't think you'll be able to live any longer. Your existence will be terminated tomorrow in the morning."

Suddenly, the coiled arm of the exploratory robot rewound itself back inside of its body, pulling with it the electrocution device it had just used against my arms. The rectangular screen my mother was projected on still remained outstretched and hovering above me, its unraveled arm bent in multiple directions casting a shadow that rolled over my head and onto the floor. I stared passively at the edge of the exploratory robot's big, round wheel positioned at an angle from my body. It remained unmoved, leaving its dark, dusty exterior still and motionless.

Terminated? I thought to myself, perplexed by the act my mother planned to perpetrate against me tomorrow with the exploratory robot. She doesn't think I can live any longer. She determined it alongside the exploratory robot.

Although the liquid that filled my eyes obstructed the image I saw in my physical environment, in my head I could see it clearly, finally: that little boy, *that human life form*, dying on the floor of my bedroom after we had played in there. Soon enough, I could see the exploratory robot entering through my bedroom door in the middle of the day, with my mother pronouncing the little boy dead in much of the same voice she used with any other statement. Eventually, I was reprimanded by the robot; zapped, just like how I was right now. Following that, the hospital building collapsed and I was left in my bedroom isolated and with no end anticipated to that distressing condition. Suddenly, I could remember that memory in full, and I could remember why I was reprimanded: I killed that little boy. I killed that human life form. I killed someone I thought to be just like me, much in the same way I thought my mother and the other human life forms to be one of me. Is that why I'm being terminated? Is that how I'm going to be terminated? Is this a consequence of killing that little boy?

I don't know what this feeling is. This wave of hotness and trickle of chills down my spine as sweat envelopes the skin of my body. The beat of my heart crawling into my throat as if I were about to vomit my heart out, along with the very reason I was still alive. I don't know what it is. But, it's the worst thing I've ever felt, as I come to the realization I killed that little boy. Did I kill my mother? Did I hurt her? Is that why she's terminating me?

I bend my head back and push one of my shoulders into the ground, trying to look up at the rectangular screen mother was projected on. My arms hurt and that warm, uncomfortable feeling flooding my body continued to tingle my body into a gross contortion of senses. Panting, I looked up at my mother, feeling as though my heart was sinking deeper into my stomach as I tried to view her face. It was only there for a second, staring ahead of her and eventually disappearing behind a screen of unmoved blackness that filled the entire screen in no time at all. Then, just like the electrocution device unwinding just a few seconds prior, I watched as that dark, lifeless screen folded itself back into the exploratory robot's compartment, with both becoming completely concealed by the back cover of the exploratory robot winding shut in a diagonally falling motion.

With my eyes falling back down to the space of floor beneath the exploratory robot, cast in a box-shaped shadow from its compartment, I came to a realization I never thought I'd come to: I killed my mother. A slow, painful death I instigated, just like that little boy I remember seeing in my room dying in a pool of blood. That's why I was being reprimanded. And that's why for the past few days, I've been slowly beginning to notice a change in my mother's interactions with me. This is my fault. This is all my fault. Now, I'm going to be terminated by my mother - killed, I presume. Oh no. I don't know how to feel about this. I don't know *what* it is I feel about this whole situation. I feel sick, and my whole body is swaying in place while an unnerving, humid draft pushes and pulls my body, back and forth. However, I'm still inside this room with the exploratory robot parked a couple of feet or so away from my laying body. Rays of light poke in through the cracks of the sun-lit door leading into this room, intermixing with the artificial overhead lights shining down on us in a constant blanket of whiteness. There's not a single draft or breeze that tumbles through the space of concrete walls and floors. I lie before the exploratory robot within. I'm just sick. This feeling of guilt spreads through my body in a widespread sensation of bodily itches and a sickening warmth that fills my stomach and grazes all along my skin.

As the exploratory robot maneuvers around my body and out of the room, I become distressed at the thought of what these physiological symptoms point to: that my judgment is right, and I killed my mom, just like I killed that little boy. My failure as a human being led to their deaths. For once in my life, there was something I was sure about, and had no trouble grasping as an absolute truth; this was that thing. I don't think any little, quiet world internalized from my physical environment could save me from that realization.

I can't die. I can't be terminated by the exploratory robot. I can't be killed by it. I can't, I can't, I CAN'T. I just can't

I'm sitting on my bed with the heels of my bare feet tucked into my underside and my toes shakily sinking into the mattress I sat upon. My blanket has collected lazily at the corner of my bed, having not been touched since the night before. It sat there as a pile of lousy, tattered lumps of beige-colored fabric, espousing a special sort of significance to me that I had no desire to fully recognize anymore. The room was somewhat cold, boxing in a chilling draft that slapped my body with waves of trembles and shakes. However, after having not slept the entire night, with my eyes boring open as feelings of distress ripped through my body and left me dreadfully awake, I had no reason whatsoever to wear the blanket.

Staring at the dim, orange-colored sliver of light that lined the bottom of my bedroom door and poured dismally into my room, I fell into my own little world while growing increasingly engrossed over the events of yesterday, and those that were bound to happen today. I killed my mother, much in the same way I killed that little boy; or, in a different manner, but still with the same outcome. That's why I was being terminated today. I failed them both, at different points in my life. This, leading to me ultimately being reprimanded with a much different, longer lasting state; an eternal state, in fact. After killing my mother, I would be killed myself. I'll be dead forever. I'm not sure how to feel about that.

Though, as a dim blue sliver of haze bounced around near the fixation point of my eyes just beneath my bedroom door, I felt unsure about that being my own fate. Not that I was unsure it was going to happen; I was sure that today I would be terminated by the exploratory robot once it opened my door and entered through it, moving towards me.

But, for some reason, I didn't feel sure that death was inevitable; or, at least, termination by the robot that led to my death. I didn't feel I had to be killed.

The thought of death was distressing to encounter; whenever I thought of it, that same image of that little boy dying in a pool of blood filled my head, seemingly blending with the brightening sliver of morning light I saw beneath the door. His eyes dilated and engrossed at a distance in the presence of the wall and floor meeting together in a thin line; his dark, red blood spilling out from beneath him in a slowly widening puddle of uneven bounds and thick consistency; and his mouth wide agape, letting out one last breath as a bloodied, pained croak proceeded his young, three years of life, followed by the exploratory robot entering the room and reprimanding me for killing him. That's all I can remember from that event; and that's all I could see whenever I grew engrossed with that memory.

However, continuing to stare at that sliver of light poking in through the crack separating the bedroom door from the floor it met, I swayed in place, feeling myself grow lost in the light. A tingly, breathless sensation flooded my body in a stream of pings that I could feel right down to my two feet tucked firmly into my buttocks. I felt my mouth begin to open wide and my eyes begin to grow into tight holes enveloping every bit of visual information I saw in discolored shades of blue and white. Watching that memory unfold in the vicinity of my head, and feeling those sensations flood my body in feelings that contrasted the distressing feelings I previously felt all night, I suddenly began to realize something. Both of those deaths were preventable. Mother's death, that little boy's death - they were both preventable. I didn't have to fail my mother by failing the curriculum task, and I didn't have to fail the little boy by killing him. Therefore, they could've lived longer; in fact, maybe they could have experienced eternal life, rather than an eternal state of death. I'm not sure if I totally grasp what that would mean either way; how those states would feel. Would they be distressing states? Constantly mired in rapid heartbeats that trickled into your stomach with a sickening rumble and ravaged your whole self's sense of calmness? Or, would they be comfortable states, with there always being a warm, calming feeling of relaxation washing over your body and leaving you anticipating the presence of someone in particular. I couldn't tell; I couldn't tell which would involve which. Death was something the exploratory robot taught us as a naturally occurring phenomena for all lifeforms; perhaps that didn't mean much if death was preventable.

This led me to one conclusion: my death was preventable. I didn't have to be terminated by the exploratory robot; killed, or whatnot. I could prevent that from happening. I could escape. Where to, though, and how? How would I escape when it was the exploratory robot that woke me up every morning and led me out of my room to start the day? Where would I go to? Trying to answer those two questions left my lips growing wet with the approaching flood of drool on my tongue, and my eyes staring dumbly at the various points it landed on. I looked away and thought harder to myself, finding the gray, sparsely dotted concrete walls of my room passing lazily by my pivoting eyes.

Now that I thought about it, there were not many places I knew of. I ran the same route everyday when we engaged in our fitness enrichment activities. Where I hid from all of the other human life forms by the little, almost-dried creek; and I came back home using the same path leading back to the building we lived in. I traveled the same trek of land every single day for as long as I could remember, marked by disfigured piles of broken concrete slabs and loosely winding metal pipes. I knew practically nothing about what lies beyond that path of broken up roads and demolished buildings, consumed ultimately in the dimly colored sunlit horizon lined with clouds of pollutants. To be honest, I never really thought about what was outside of this little area.

But, suddenly, the image of that thin line of murky water winding along the creek-bed popped into my head, populating the insides of my head in a dry, beige-colored canyon of cracked dirt and rocks. Inside of my head, I could see the memory of that little creek stretching along that dirt bed, winding with fluid zig zags that unwound in the distance as a thick, clouded blur. It stretched for what seemed like forever, never meeting an end until it succumbed to the horizon in the distance and the eventual sun that fell beneath the line where every obscure, ambiguous object congregated in their ends. Suddenly, I realized something: that's where I will escape to. The place I always escaped to already, trapped in my own little world on the creekside and detached from every bit of my physical reality, united with it only when something loud and distressing drew me back in.

Letting out one last breath, I pulled myself out of my bed, ripping my feet out from under my buttocks and planting them onto the floor. I took a few steps toward the side of my bed closer to the bedroom door, slipping into my artificial-leather shoes and experiencing the cool, untouched feeling of the shoes' insides enveloping my feet. I pivoted slightly in the direction of my bedroom door, marching towards it with a warm, fuzzily shaken stride. I reached the door, pulling out my right hand and nearing it towards the doorknob, stopping all of a sudden with my hands hovering above it in a curled-formation. I came to another realization standing breathlessly before that door: this was a door never opened by me, but always by the exploratory robot. I can't open this; I'm still trapped in here; I'll be terminated in here; killed.

My jaw quivered in place as it dangled from my skull, connected by bone and skin as it provided no buffer to the steadily shaking breaths leaving my mouth. Nor did the sickening pain that intoxicated my empty stomach and stiff feet leave me unable to turn and face the room I would die in. I looked back at the room ahead of the door and draped in the dim, colorless light of the sun, illuminating the perimeter of the room. The bloodstain from that little boy that covered the center of the floor in a chilling legacy summoned whenever looking at it; the bed that stood near the wall diagonally positioned relative to the bedroom, drenched in stains of sweat puddles felt beneath me every night I dreamt; and just a room of pure nothingness, representing nothing significant that was stimulating to look at. This was my reality: I'll rot to death here; if not in here, I'll be killed directly by the exploratory robot sooner than later. Looking back at that doorknob unmovable by my grip and twist of my wrist, I realized this was true no matter how I examined this situation.

Staring at the floor, I saw the light pouring in from the cracks lining the bedroom door become darkened in the lower half of it, accompanied by the same *reee* sound that could be heard as it maneuvered around. I began to fall back towards the edge of my bed, my feet nervously tripping over each other as I panted in the direction of the slowly opening door. Each second the door pushed open closer and closer to the wall beside it was one marked by dread, and a morbid anticipation of my looming death. I leaned into the edge of my bed with a breathlessly timid posture, watching dim sunlight fill the room and the shadow of the exploratory robot halving that light, populating those rays with its boxed shape. A distressing frenzy of sensations washed over my body all at once, culminating in the fluids that filled my eyes and obstructed my vision, leaving my approaching killer bumping around as a metallic haze. Its long, coiled arms began to unravel from inside of it, flexing its claws of rubber spears and reaching for the same person it had tormented for years now. I nearly fell over where I stood and surrendered my hot, shaking body to the wrath of the exploratory robot, before realizing something:

It wasn't going to kill me. In fact, it wasn't even reaching for me as it maneuvered around my body and towards my bed. Its rubber claws outstretched from their metal arms glistening in the morning sunlight reached for the edges of my bed, beginning to grip the sides of it and lifting a metal barricade upwards along the bed's sides. The robot towered over me, though not in the same fashion that usually intimidated me into a nerve-wracked position cowering beneath its presence. It totally disregarded me, instead focusing on my bed, which it strangely was readjusting.

I stood there looking over the corner of its open body, watching in confusion with wide eyes and a hanging mouth as it lifted one last metal barricade on the side of the bed opposite of me. I had no idea the barricade could be lifted; now, what was once just a mattress perched on a metal bed frame was now a mattress hidden behind three sheets of metal lined with foam rims at the very top. The last I remembered seeing something like this was when Jacey-six was a baby; I believe that was her name. I was only five years old at the time. Not much time had passed between the time that little boy was killed by me and she was born. I believe it was only a few days after. Her new bed was placed in the little boy's old room from before he died. Pitched-wails could be heard from her room where laughter and childish whines had usually been espoused just down the partially exposed corridor of the building. The toys of rubber and plastic the little boy and I played with in his room were then recycled from the floor they collected upon in piles of shiny figures, and into strange toys for Jacey-six to play with. Soon enough, the legacy of the little boy was relegated to the dried stain of the blood that brought his existence into passing history, with any other tangible memento disposed of.

Staring without a single breath released from my mouth, I watched as the exploratory robot reeled one of its arms toward my beige-colored blanket, grasping it and folding its arm inward, dropping it into an internal compartment containing a spinning wheel with seven or so wings. Water and a thick, gray liquid poured into the compartment as the blanket caught onto the spinning wheel and its sustained momentum, drowning in a bubbly slurry that filled the compartment corner to corner.

Then, at the base of my periphery closer to my body, I watched as a metal cover held beneath the overhead one became released from its place, leaning back in the direction of the open-overhead cover it now leaned up against. A little, plush mattress met with each corner of the compartment's interior, with vents and golden light-pads lining the edge of its perimeter. Within that now opened compartment laid one thing right before me, filling my mind and body with shock as the pale, glistening presence of a baby filled my vision. It basked in the morning sun pouring in from outside and pierced the air with loud cries that filled the entire room. Its limbs stretched towards the ceiling and shook slightly into small, tightly clenched hands and feet. Just above its mouth, its eyes remained hidden behind two thin, crystalized lines, curling with its face sunk down into a sad expression. It was not much different from everyone else's face; the only thing differentiating it from everyone else's was its size and shape.

The exploratory robot soon enough grasped the baby in two of its coiled arms, twisting around in my direction away from the crib and beginning to reach internally for the baby. It grabbed it in its two hands, supporting its head with one and gripping the rest of its body in the other, then pivoting with the baby in its grip. The baby's loud screams were now reduced to somewhat audible quivers, manifesting in a relaxed body and calmed facial expression. As the robot rotated with the baby in its rubber grip, I could see the baby's eyes through the fluid filling its eyes and shielding its pupils behind a glossy shine. It stared at me, examining my presence without fixating on any one point of me. I looked back at it through eyes filled with much of the same substance, though not reached with the same looming sense of despair.

It was set down in the crib, looking around the room with a light presence of quiet whimpers and a down-trodden face shot randomly at the ceiling. The exploratory robot then removed the blanket from a compartment next to the thick, bubble-filled compartment it had been washed in, stretching a fresh, dried version of it over the baby and covering most of its body below its neck. Then, unwinding from just nearby the two other arms was the arm containing an imageless black screen, one that mother had always been displayed on before I had killed her. I watched with barely any movement produced throughout my body nor any thought conjured within my head; just the unthinkable unfurling from a vacuum I had never understood as possible, right before my eyes. Mother's bright, smiling face filled the screen and transcended the confinements of it with a voice that spoke audibly to the baby. It greeted the baby as the exploratory robot hovered it parallel to the laying baby, receiving a placated presence, stared with a soothed awe at my mother.

"Shush. Shush. It's okay little one. It's okay Jacey-one. It's okay. Mommy's here. Mommy's got you." Her voice was soft, brushing lightly against the baby's lully cooing face, along with the bright screen she projected her face with.

It shone down on the baby, illuminating all of its young, smooth features, all of which transformed from a light, unaware smile to a light-beige palette of an agape mouth lined in drool and sleep. Watching through the fluids that filled my eyes and spilled down my cheeks with no care for the fate they collectively shared below my chin, I watched as that little baby was brought to sleep with the calming voice of my mother. Covered under a blanket I had used for so many years, and contained so many memories of just thinking of my resting body. It was now clean and ready for coverage of the newborn baby, removed of the stench, stains, and any other sensed remnants of the person who slept under it for so many years.

Staring down at that baby who sleepily interacted with my mother, I realized being terminated didn't involve me being killed, or left to die in my bedroom. Rather, it involved me being replaced by another human life form and left painfully alive to experience such a transition. I wasn't terminated for good; but, with regards to my mother and the connection I had for so many years assumed we shared, it was definite. I was replaced; disposed of. I could only assume this was the end for me with my mother. She wasn't killed; I never killed her.

I began to back up towards the bedroom door, panting and watching through liquified eyes as the baby's eyes fluttered restfully as it fought its way past wake, its mouth stretching into a meek yawn. I heaved quietly, practically shocked into a frozen posture bent awkwardly against the bedroom wall near the door and in the direction of mother and the baby. The distress I felt fearing my death had now morphed into feelings responding to the discontinuing of my relationship with my mother. Somehow, this event was mildly anticipated, but wholeheartedly dreaded at its arrival.

Then, I turned into the sun-lit corridor of the building just outside of my bedroom door, jogging out of it and into the rubble-lined road that encircled the building and the land in a jagged border. It was difficult to see, as various pieces of broken glass and metal sprung all along the road into obscured rays indicating gray and transparent materials. This was the most physical exercise I had ever engaged in in ages. However, it was towards the one place I always escaped to, but never intended on staying for good. I ran and I ran. I ran to the creek, shunning the building housing mother and the human life forms with my heaving backside. However, in my head, that's all I could see, and experience: that building, and all of the memories from inside. It would pester me inside and out, accompanying my body in a form of neverending distress all of the way to the creek, where I shakily collapsed to my knees and cried into the dry, crack-ridden dirt ground I encountered, summoning the only muddied portion of dirt I had ever witnessed.

MARCH 5, 2366

I sat at the creekside in the place I always sat at for years, just about five or so feet from the thin path of asphalt broken up into diverging fragments covered in dust and lined with dead, browned plants. I believe it was called a hill. I sat upon it, reaching downward to the creek bed with winding trails of differently shaded patches of mud and rock. It was somewhat moist, though felt cool against my body as I sat there with my legs pointed to the creek. So much had changed about the region. The hills were now covered in stratified layers of wet dirt and rock, sloping towards the creek which was now much fuller than usual. The creek's water was not much different in color to the dirt it wetted, meeting it at its murky depths below my feet. Although I was aware of the changes in the environment, I didn't mind it. My eyes drifted to the creek and fixated on the steady ripples of the brown-tainted creek. Fluid filled them, but not to the point my vision was impaired. Rather, little drops of the mysterious fluid collected at my lower eyelids and fell down my cheeks in unorganized streams that left awkward patches of stickiness on my face.

All I could think about was all that I had lost. I lost my mother; how, I was totally unsure. *Did I kill her?* I was unsure. I knew I lost her in the sense that she was my mother. Realizing that termination was not being killed, but rather, being abandoned, felt strange to realize. It wasn't distressing to realize; my heart wasn't racing, and my breaths weren't layered with stiff pants, either. Rather, I just felt empty. I felt like my heart rested on a hole in my body that was chilled to the touch, and rattled with a disease that muddled my insides into pure mush. I felt like how I did when I'd cry on my bedroom's floor with my feet facing the wall opposite of me, anticipating the arrival of the exploratory robot as I felt my insides seemingly drifting to the floor and my body melting. Except, there was no distress; just, emptiness. Nothingness. I was nothing anymore. I had no mother. I had no bedroom to sleep in. No food to eat. Perhaps my desire for sameness hijacked my desire for calmness. I was always distressed living in that building with my mother and the other human life forms. Maybe I found comfort in the daily routine of sensations that dragged me into despair every moment I opened my eyes.

Nonetheless, I can't do anything about the matter. I've been abandoned. I'm all on my own; whatever that means. I never really thought about the future. I know what the 'future' is defined as, but not what mine is. Engaging in a distressed form of consistency daily rendered thinking of a future state unthinkable, and thus, the future unforeseeable. However, following years of living with mother and the other human life forms, I never anticipated this to be my future. I guess I now have to accept it as my future.

I brought my curled hand to my face, drying it on my crooked wrist. Doing so caused little specks of liquid to crown the tips of my eyelashes in shiny crystalized bits, leaving everything around me blurred and subjected to the bright reflections from behind my lashes.

Taking a deep sigh, I realized something else: I always focused on the past. Memories of the past were all that populated the insides of my head, paralyzing my thought processes and strangling my vision into a tiny fixation point only distressing stimuli could unravel me from. It was always that little boy I focused on; memories of him from when he was alive and I hadn't killed him yet. I don't know what's so significant about him. Every waking moment that I dread can be traced back to the thought of him. What was the point of focusing on his memory so much?

I guess thinking of that little boy sometimes filled me with the same flurry of sensations I felt when thinking of my mother; or, used to. I've never understood it. It's always the same sort of reaction and with the same particular people. My body starts to grow warm from the inside out, and a calmed beat circles from my heartbeat all throughout my body. It's almost as though my blanket is pressed tightly against my body and I'm just… comfortable, and warm. I don't know. I suppose I never really felt or thought of the little boy like that because my mind was always engrossed by that one specific memory of him bleeding to death on my bedroom floor. It was almost addicting just looking back at that memory and watching it time and time again, over and over. Despite it being a torturous cycle to get caught in, it was something I just spiraled into, never finding steady ground to catch myself on.

In my head, providing an illusive barrier between my eyes and the dirty creek water just beyond my slanted legs, was a memory of the little boy and I playing in his room. We were playing with toys that lay lazily in a pile in the corner at night and danced across the room in our playing hands during the day. I believe it was a doll I played with - a piece of beige-colored plastic shaped like a female human. I waddled her around the floor with my shins pressed into the cold, concrete floor, interacting sporadically with the boy's doll when we portrayed an activity with them. Our little voices squeaked out comments we attached to the dolls and their roles, portraying two females who were fighting over a piece of food. Laughs etched the atmosphere in a warm, almost ecstatic feeling, cutting into midair as massive howls or tiny giggles. It was a memory that always elicited that same strange sensation inside of my body, triggering a jumpy, back-and-forth fanning of my toes and a warm ripple through my chest. I felt empty without that memory being a current reality;. iIt felt like it had been so long since I last interacted with the little boy. I suppose most of my life has been a period of loss, and emptiness. Just a slow, painfully enduring loss was all that could be made of my life's summary. Maybe my next loss won't be someone I know, but the person in me. The person looking back at me in the mirror.

My eyes trailing down into the creek, I saw a round, almost hairy object's reflection move in the creek's surface, just at the same time my head moved. A slow, liquid field of half-disked ripples moved through the reflection, stretching it over the soft edges of the current. Moving my head to the left, the object moved with it in the reflection. It was almost like an analog of my head ripped over the creek's movements, staying in place before me and staring back at me despite the slow but firm momentum found in the creek's rush. I moved my head to the right, watching the reflection follow. I moved my head forward, peering closer to the murky surface of the creek. I watched the reflection grow larger, and the outline of a face protruded from the nearing reflection. The sockets where two large, brown-colored eyes resided, melting into the dirty water before me; the nose that shot down to the face's mouth and poked forward, hanging over two pink-colored lips.

Bringing my hands to my head, I watched two hands merge into the reflection, parallel exactly to mine and where I placed them. As I brought my hands to my eyes, I watched as the reflection and everything else in my physical environment disappeared from view. As I brought them away from my eyes with my fingers spaced apart and held still in shock and awe, I watched them fall with the reflection. Except, I wasn't staring at an analog version of me, or something copying me precisely in my actions. Rather, I was staring at a reflection of me floating magically in the creek I stared into. That was my face, and I had never once witnessed the view of my face.

I leaned in closer, with my butt hovering over the slanted slope of stratified mud I had been sitting on. My calves brushed lightly against the hill and my heels cut into the hill sinking into the creek, as I leaned in closer to view my face in the muddy water. I reached a hand out towards the creek, feeling drool creep to the edge of my mouth as I mindlessly watched my body grow larger and larger in the liquid surface. Liquid began to drip out of my eyes again, though with a much different reaction throughout the rest of my body. My heart raced and my body grew heated, contrasting the cool, crisp feel of the murky creek that pillowed over my hand now an inch from the creek.

I dashed my pointer finger into the reflection found in the water, diverging my face into multiple rings that floated outward from the point in the water my finger touched. Though, in the water, the picture remained: my face staring right back at me in the water. I pulled my finger away from the creek's surface and watched drops of the brown water collect at my fingertip, growing larger and larger until it could hold no longer and landed in my reflection. The ripple effect occurred again, and again, for as long as I held my wetted finger above the creek's surface. I watched in awe, nearly unable to breathe as I stared between my wet, dripping finger and the rippled reflection. It was amazing. My reflection scattered across the creek surface into dozens of ripple while still remaining as one mystic whole at the very same time. I don't know how to explain it. It was unlike anything I had ever witnessed.

However, before I could marvel at the phenomena that was my face's reflection any longer, I felt a sudden burn begin to prickle the edge of my finger exposed to the water. It started out as a slight itch, before quickly worsening into a rough, piercing burn. The skin on my finger began to redden, corresponding with the feeling of hotness that enveloped my finger in a burning air. I stared at my aching finger with my lips agape and its corners leaning towards the ground. Heavy breaths left my mouth and became more and more broken-up into staggered pants as I processed the pain biting into my finger. My finger began to shake, eventually trailing into my hand as my outreached hand turned into a frantic group of bones and burning flesh at the tip of one of my fingers. I had no idea what was happening, or what to do about it.

I sat back down in the mud, my chest heaving up and down as I stared through fluid at my trembling hand. The burn pierced my finger and slid beneath my skin in a hot wash of pain, nearly numbing my finger from the feelings ensuing. I don't know what to do; I don't know how to deal with this burning sensation. It hurts so bad yet I don't know how to stop the pain. Once my eyes become removed from the red, shaky blur of my burnt finger, I look around frantically for something, anything, that could help ease the pain. I could find nothing that seemed of use; only the dry, dead remnants of trees that lined the creek with great stature or broke off into the murky creek bed, and the piles of rubble signifying where buildings once laid.

Without any idea of how to treat the burn, I shoved my finger between my cool, trembling legs and hid it from all exposure it had to the mild, sunlit area of the creekside. I had no idea what I was doing, but also had no other possible alternative. I shot out distressed gasps that streamlined into high pitched pants, fixating my eyes on the curved, muddy edge of the creek as if ignoring the pain would cure it.

Forcing my burning finger between my legs seemed to mitigate the pain felt at its tip as I jammed it away from the browned sunlight pouring into the atmosphere and pressed the soft, moist fabric of my pant legs against the skin. As the pain slowly began to recede into a little, itchy ring of red blisters around my pointer finger, I let out a sigh tainting the air nearby in a cool rumble of air. I stared ahead of me at the same creek I had grown transfixed on for so many years before, looking through the fluid enveloping my eyes and dwindling myself down into an entranced body of no physical movements. I was weak and vulnerable, as made clear by my clumsy reaction to my finger touching the creek-water. I needed my mother, but I had no choice but to leave her and become terminated as her son. I was forever alone, and had to succumb to the pain of living defenseless at this creekside, without my mother. The fear of life and continuing to live was made apparent to me as I reflected on the fact I assumed my death to be something inevitable.

Now, watching my distressed appearance float atop the creek-surface in a rippled, soft sway, I realized death was more desirable than whatever it was I happened to experience right now. At least, if death is what I suspected it could possibly be, and not what I was just living through right now.

JACEY-ONE
MARCH 5, 2366

Night time had already begun to creep into the area I resided in, manifesting in a purplish darkness that filled the sky in a cloudy haze and touched the ground in dimly-lit surroundings. The moon occupied the top of the sky where the sun usually reigned and shone down with bright rays that became obstructed by the thick swarm of pollutants that swirled up high. The moon was equally relegated behind a shield of haze, hanging in the sky as a bright, round orb of light. It was strange;. iIt looked so bright up above in the sky, but everything around me seemed so dim and dark. I had hardly ever seen the moon before. If I did, it was when I was outside late after our fitness enrichment activities. I remember mother teaching us about it one day, such as how it relates to the Earth and all of its functions. She had made it clear to us how important the moon was to the Earth, but I've always remained unsure if I knew exactly what that importance meant. Teachings about the moon passed through my head as ambiguously arisen memories, but did nothing to relinquish the constant feeling inside that the moon was really of no importance to me. I didn't feel it inside me like I felt when recounting the importance of my mother being in my life. I stared at it, processed it, and watched the only remnant of its existence linger in my eyesight as a scattered after image of the bright, white orb I stared into.

Additionally, the sight of the moon left me unfazed when intense feelings of hunger rumbled in my stomach and weakened the body containing it. I watched through lazily opened eyes at the moon in the sky, my just barely separated lashes providing a harmless barricade between my eyes and the moon-lit sky above. I released a lethargic groan that almost flattened into an emotionless hum. I was so hungry that I couldn't even be bothered to distract myself with the cold that penetrated through my clothes and left me curled into a contorted bunch near a dead tree. The moon faced me at an angle as I lied with my knees brought to my chest and my head facing the opposite side of the creek, my body leaning towards the edge nearby with my back curved awkwardly.

I was cold. I was hungry. I was distressed. There was absolutely nothing I could do about any of those conditions, but dwell in them and ponder what it was that prevented these before. It was my mother time and time again. It was my mother that kept me warm with the blanket that always reminded me of her. It was the food she produced that she always fed me;. It was the thought of her that calmed me when distress covered me in sensations I dreaded but constantly experienced. Now, I was replaced by another baby, and had no ability to receive that same kind of treatment. I was now subjected to this same array of painful feelings with no way out of them.

Staring ahead of me at the dark, barely illuminated edge of the creek's opposite muddy side, I began to wonder: would I wake up to the same feelings I felt right now? Would I live every other day with these feelings? Would I live the rest of my life in hunger and pain?

I couldn't live like this anymore; all of these things I took for granted in a daily, monotonous routine of sameness was now pulling me back into a state of distress and regret. This state burrowed into a deep, invisible pit that led to my groans turning into nauseous pants and my hunger into a dizzying sickness. I felt like I was being choked and all of my insides were melting with a progression that creeped towards my throat. All of this culminated in me realizing one thing: if mother could outlive me even after I killed her, then I shall too. Though, a strange feeling resided within me that how I'll live will contrast how my mother will live. What she'll feel each day that goes by after her death; what she'll think; what she'll say. I don't really think my life will be comparable to how her's will be. Perhaps death was never a given aspect of life, and mother wasn't telling the truth when she taught us that. Maybe the end is not absolute. Kind of like how I lied whenever I hadn't run during fitness enrichment and didn't want to tell her out of fear the exploratory robot would hurt me for not doing as instructed. Maybe she was afraid to tell me the truth. What would the exploratory robot do to her? Is that why she terminated me as her son? Out of fear?

My eyes began to meander away from the bumpy edge of the creek and travel from point to point shot opposite of me in the dim, purpled night. I began to wonder if my mother was trapped, and if I could save her. Maybe the exploratory robot could be stopped; maybe I could stop it; maybe I could kill it. That would be the only person I would actually desire to kill. I believe the exploratory robot is a human. I mean, it doesn't look like the other human life forms or even mother, but I feel a strong reaction to it just like the presence of my mother or the thought of the little boy. It wasn't like when I stared at where the floor and the wall combined into a thin black strip or the creek surface; those were fixation points. The exploratory robot was something I watched as it moved and pursued objectives. I watched what it would do next like I watched for my mother's movements.

Strangely enough, I couldn't figure out why I felt no adversity towards killing the exploratory robot. Mother and the little boy I was terrified to kill, or at least to remember killing. The thought of killing the exploratory robot, however, bestowed no such reaction from me. I felt my insides grow inflamed, but not in the way I felt when thinking of my mother. My fingers began to grow stiff and curl into my palm, despite one of them being burnt and blistered. My body grew tense and my brow furrowed. I couldn't quite explain such a reaction. I don't know if I've ever felt that way. It wasn't distressing, to be fair; but, it felt the same way, in a sense. I think the only time I've ever felt this way is when thinking about killing the exploratory robot. I'm indifferent about killing the exploratory robot, while simultaneously feeling extremely connected to the idea of doing so.

I turned over onto my back, my eyes escaping the dark outline of the creek and staring up into the blue pillows of thick, moon-lit fog that filled the sky up above. My body was now warm, and holding my body in a tight, contorted half-circle was no longer comfortable. Watching the sky with a heartbeat that steadily rolled within me in a quiet rumble, I began to visualize the plan I would undertake to kill the exploratory robot and save my mother. When my eyes opened in the morning and the sun blanketed me in a muted, yellow light, I would be ready. The sun shining down as a distant, obscure ball of light would be the signifier tomorrow that my plan was about to begin.

Maybe I don't have to be terminated after all. Maybe my role as a son can be saved as well.

My eyes opened to the bright, almost colorless sky of the sun-lit morning, though not much sleep resided beneath them during the night. I was almost completely aware of the sun rising as it crept through the reddening insides of my eyelids and basked my body in a mild, wind-swept feeling of warmth.

I sat up from the muddy ground I laid upon, my abdominal muscles straining as I shot my hands forward and leaped onto my bottom, positioning myself upright. My back ached from the stiff, flat ground I had rested on for hours last night, contrasting the soft, pleasurable feeling I felt every morning I awakened in my bed. There was no exploratory robot to arrive in my room and approach my distressed, unnerved body, or a dark, gray room made of concrete to be drowned in the sunlight found piercing the area outside of my room. And, there was no sign of my mother to greet me with the same, bright demeanor she presented within every morning. I longed for that same routine that I experienced every day for so many years. It almost made me feel sick inside realizing I dreaded that routine recently. Now, it was forever gone, and I'm unsure if I'll be able to ever retain just a mere remnant of that in my daily routine going forward. But, with my plan, I'll be able to save my mother and kill the exploratory robot. I've seen inside the exploratory robot's body many times before; mother is confined to it by a long, metal arm that connects to its internal body made of metal plates and rubber wires of various colors.

I looked around for a little bit, finally concluding the watch of my peering eyes at the fine edge of a light-brown strata in the dirt and pulling my body up off of the muddy ground. I felt specks of dirt and loose sticks wander off of my body onto the ground surrounding my feet, collecting in an uneven boundary that just barely contrasted the ground's slightly darker color. As I stood up straight, I glanced over at the creek scattered with dead trees, shallow, muddied water, and a periphery broken up into a neverending trajectory of browned concrete shreds and twisting pipes. Stepping onto the path of dirtied asphalt without any consistent shape connecting its diverging bits, I glanced at my hand, and eventually my pointer finger. Brought to a rough, discolored prong of blistered flesh, I bent it back and forth, watching it bend towards my palm with a similar bent formation projecting onto my other fingers. Feeling the continued figment of heat that swarmed my pointer finger in a ticklish pain, I remembered the face - *my face* - in the creek water I stared at and touched with that now blistered finger. I then recalled my mother's face, and how they were virtually indistinguishable from each other. I'll be saving my mother with this hand; I'll be able to see her face again because of this hand, and the plan it'll partake in. I flexed my fingers before me, straightening them out and pointing them indirectly at the pile of concrete rubble sprawled out thirty feet ahead of me. I then gripped my fingers into the center of my palm, watching veins begin to slightly protrude through the back of my hand as an inflamed sense of warmth drove all throughout my body.

Casting my eyes ahead of me at the broken-apart path of asphalt that stretched twenty feet wide and ran for miles ahead, I released my grip, experiencing a tingling feeling fill the tiny indents in the flesh where my fingernails had dug into. I then proceeded to walk in the direction of the road lined by endless piles of destroyed buildings and jagged artifacts they left behind, stepping over the stratified pieces of dirt and rock lining the creek's path.

This was a path I traveled along for many years before. Yet, I felt different walking along it in the direction of the building I had previously resided in with mother and the other human life forms. Usually it was evening when I had, and the environment right now was cooler and sunnier. The sunlight penetrating the thick clouds of pollutants washing over the skies illuminated everything in the environment in a murky-golden hue, rather than a dimmer, grayer color. I was also stepping down this path intending something different to happen. Something that was extremely different from anything I had ever done willingly. Typically this was a path I traversed every evening after fitness enrichment activities, or, after disregarding the instructed activities while hiding along the creek's sloping hills. If I did the latter, I would head back to the building with the others when I assumed it was best to go get checked on, eat dinner, then go to bed. Now, I was heading back to essentially discontinue that sort of lifestyle for the others. I was going to kill the exploratory robot, and remove my mother from its control. I will kill it in the same way it terminated me. I will remove it from its role as the exploratory robot and terminate my mother from her role as everyone else's mother. I will destroy the very building the exploratory robot built for the very reason it controls each and everyone of us.

CRRRCH! CRRRCH! CRRRCH!

The sound of something moving relatively close to me filled my ears and eventually led to my body coming to a stop and my head becoming the only thing moving. I rotated it cautiously on my neck and peered with two enlarged eyes at the rubble around me, lining the path in bumpy edges of destroyed concrete that poured slightly over the discolored asphalt. I looked on both sides of me, feeling myself become aware of my environment with a distressing sort of immersion. Those same feelings of warmth and a quietly rumbling heart became hijacked by the distress that filled my body at the sudden sound I heard. I looked around, turning back and watching the sight of the creekbed with dead, neighboring trees along its side winding its way along its edges and swaying in the mild morning air. My eyes then slowly traveled along the edge of the rubble stumbling towards the edge of the creek, moving with my carefully revolving head. I then proceeded to watch the other side of the path with the same, breathless gaze, before sighing and looking ahead of me at the remainder of the path that dwindled down into a cloud of polluted haze. I had no idea what I had heard. I felt as though it came from the left of me in the pile of rubble, but I was unsure.

I took a step forward, and another, hearing the sound of loose pebbles and dirt slide under my heels. I stopped before I could move any farther, as a pair of indecipherable voices collected nearby in faint murmurs. My heart beat quicker as my body came to a jolted stop, turning my body in the same direction of the previous *crrrch!* noises. The heavy breaths I let out merged into a dreadful cacophony accompanied by the voices. I knew they were voices; they sounded just like my voice or the voices of the other human life forms, but deeper. Rougher, almost, and with no words spoken that I could understand. It was a quick slur of words I couldn't interpret, and had no knowledge of who was speaking.

I felt my body become awash in a heavily stimulated feeling, almost like I was running while standing stiffly in place watching the pile of rubble. I pushed my big toe against the edge of my shoe and dug the shoe's rounded tip into the patched asphalt, tempted to run but engrossed by the mysterious noises I heard from nearby.

My eyes moved over the disformed pile of building remains, looking for something I wasn't quite sure I was looking for. I peered closer, bending my neck forward and moving my head watchfully. The voices faded into light, stammered breaths, accompanied by the *crrrch!* noises I had already been hearing. My eyes squinted at the pile of concrete that shot towards the sky and diverged roughly five feet from the ground into little, dark openings. They then widened at the sight of two heads emerging from the space of darkness located beneath a displaced stretch of roof unwinding at its edges into jagged, sharp edges of wood. The heads moved in a space of darkness that stretched into a rough diamond-shape of overlapping chunks of concrete, coinciding with the *crrrch!* noises that littered the nearby environment. Soon enough, my shocked stares met with a couple of faintly colored eyes that stared right back at me.

I ran without hesitation, feeling my heart slide into my stomach in a pulsating rush as I darted in the direction of the building I had been migrating towards. My breaths escaped my heaving chest and exited through my mouth in a culmination of distress. Piles of rubble passed by me without much stimulation so as to pull me from the destination I awaited dreadfully. Nothing could stop me from running away from the creek, and the heads I saw within that pile of rubble. I had no idea who that was, or what that was. Were they people? How do I know they were people for sure? I just barely found out how my face looks, how would I know they were people without seeing their full faces?

Suddenly, I was running from something that distressed me in the now to something that had previously distressed me in the past. I ran from something ambiguous by nature to carry out a plan I was sure about. Though, with those mysterious pairs of eyes lingering in that pile of rubble, I was unsure how to feel about them trailing in the back of me as I ran from them, shrinking into small, unnoticeable specks of color and flesh. The building near the destroyed hospital grew larger and larger and became realized as a block of opened doors and bloodied insides, absent of any belonging human.

JACEY-ONE
MARCH 6, 2366

I looked through every room of the building, stepping up and down the partially exposed hallway and discovering the same traces of blood splashed unevenly over the rooms' floors. None of the human life forms were anywhere to be found; all that remained of them were the mere legacies they shared as the previous occupants of the bedrooms. As I neared my old bedroom doorway, placing my hand on its rough, concrete edge and peering inside, I noticed something: it was marked by scratches and indentations that exposed the brown, wooden insides of the previously closed planks. The hinges they rested upon seemed to be loose, as the doors all sagged closer to the floor than usual. I brought my hands into a light clutch and ran my connected fingertips against the door's exposed insides, feeling the splintery material run against my skin, leaving little cuts in it. To my own distress, I brought my eyes into the bedroom's insides, dragging my sights over the dim gray floor in a wide-eyed gaze. It met at the sight of the new baby's crib, which connected to me by a sporadically placed trail of fresh, red drops of blood running from its metallic edges. It was the same color that shone brightly beneath the dying body of that little boy, spilling into the exposed hallway and merging into several partially dried paths that ran up and down the hall towards the other doorways.

I could barely move, barely backing into the corridor filled with the dim, polluted light of the sun. My eyes remained on the intersecting paths of blood that all messily lined up right where my feet stood, one towards the interior of my room and one towards the other end of the hallway. I tried to breathe but could only let out quick pants of air, heaving my chest up but quickly retracting it as I felt my lungs constrain. It was happening again; someone was killed. Everyone, perhaps. The baby, included. *Was this my fault? Did I cause this? Would they come back?*

Fluid filled my eyes, rendering everything a blurred presentation in front of me, swaying in shiny, crystalized remnants of what actually stood there. As the fresh morning breeze of the local area brushed against my eyes and chilled the shield of fluid trickling onto my face, I had no desire to close them. Shock paralyzed my body and led my head to rotate in the direction of the blood seeping into the dry concrete as wide, crimson-colored strokes, my eyes held captive by that distressed gaze. My eyes moved along the concrete path that hovered in my vision as a red sea of haze, before moving back and forth between my feet and the edge of the concrete corridor. The corridor was bordered by broken-apart asphalt and dead plants that stretched for a couple-hundred feet towards the remains of the abandoned hospital just beyond the building. It lined the edge of my sights in a dimmed, brown hue, but melted into the blood-covered floors that ran beneath my feet.

Looking up and down the path in a continuous flurry of distress, I stopped at the doorway positioned right in the middle of the corridor, connected to the converging trails of blood by a significantly thinner path of small drops of blood. It was the room the exploratory robot rested in with mother every night, and also where the human lifeforms and I learned curriculum every day of the week. My eyes fell towards the edge of the blood-stained floor that rounded near the hard edge of the concrete path in an unevenly curved border, before looking back up at the doorway. It was open just like every other doorway in the hallway.

I began to step near the doorway, feeling my breaths return to the tight contortion my heaving chest projected heaved breaths from. The smooth, awkward feel of blood brushed beneath my shoes as I stepped towards the door, staining the sides of the light-colored material wrapped around my feet. My eyes remained fixated on the edge of the doorway signifying where the door would meet under normal circumstances. Though, inside of my head was a flurry of images flashing before me at the same time, leaving behind a mysterious trace of potential scenarios I could not entirely experience. Small chunks of material loosely atop the concrete rolled under my stepping shoes with a meek skid noise. As my body neared the doorway to the room, fronted by my nervously placed legs, I began to grow stiff in the wake of the door's arrival. I stopped just a foot from the opening of the room, sighing deeply as my eyes drifted into a distressed stare off to the side. My eyes then shifted to the inside of the curriculum room, the same walls of concrete rising from the floor and uniting the concrete floors with the concrete ceiling.

I had sat on the floor of this room countless times throughout my life. These memories were usually marked by me just passively receiving instruction from mother, and fixating on the indented strata formations within the smoothed-concrete floor. I would trail my finger over the curved, parallel design, feeling dirt and grime cling to my finger and leave a thick, gray film of dust on my finger. The exploratory robot was positioned at the front of the room, while mother presented herself on the rectangular screen bound to the outstretched arm of coiled metallic material.

Now, as I stood in the edge of the doorway, both of my feet positioned towards the sight I dreaded to behold,. I stared at the exploratory robot dressed in elusive, crimson-colored handprints that could just barely be seen. Those handprints lined the sides of the bulky gray box of compartments and entangled wires, bordering the exploratory robot in a coating of distorted handprints connected by the fading aura they exuded. Loose wires sprouted from the insides of the exploratory robot in diverging ends that all rose toward the ceiling, almost like the dead plants that littered the dry dirt all around the building I currently stood in. The door that closed over the exploratory robot's body was bent so far back that it hung loosely on its metallic hinges, with the sharp corners of the door leaning unevenly towards the floor. Thin, fleeting billows of sparks protruded from the insides. Ripped from its place inside of the exploratory robot was the long, coiled arm that connected the rectangular screen displaying mother to the exploratory robot's insides. The screen she was usually projected upon caved towards the floor, bowing towards the wall opposite of it and at an angle from where I stood in the doorway. It didn't move; mother didn't move, or greet me as I watched over her. The only thing that moved was the sparks released from the torn apart wires and the robot's exposed insides ripped into an unrecognizable patchwork of former metallic compartments.

I remained in place staring at the exploratory robot. Not a single inch of my body moved, except for the small, dry croaks that left my mouth serving as the only form of shock I could audibly express. My eyes began to collapse into a burning orb of fluid, hammering down my face and wetting the previously chapped remnants of my already tear-shed face. I released a lone sigh, breaking the breathless spare of shocked croaks as I began to speak, albeit without any structure.

"Mother?" I called, moving my head with a guideless bob.

That warm liquid continued to flood my face, corresponding with the scattered breaths I just barely managed to choke out. I waited for a response, only to receive a brooding wave of silence meagerly interrupted by my own whimpers and the slight, sizzling noise coming from the exploratory robot.

"Mother?" I called again, letting out another staggered release of breaths.

She remained unmoved, the rectangular screen still leaning motionlessly towards the

floor. I began to near the exploratory robot, removing myself from the point in the doorway I firmly mounted my unnerved body to. I placed one foot in front of me and then met it with the other, sliding cautiously across the floor with a stiff step. Images of that bloodied, dying little boy filled my head and juxtaposed ambiguously against the compartmentalized shred of metal parts that represented the exploratory robot. I could feel my body tightening with every step I took closer and closer to the exploratory robot, until I remained stuck a couple of feet from its blood-laden sides. My legs strained in place, as these feelings of unnerved distress paralyzed my entire body and made the physical manifestation of my will to move a painful experience. I shook in my place, unable to move but fully immersed in the desire to do so.

"Mother?" I called once more, before realizing there would be no movement produced by my mother. No greeting; no response; nothing.

Coming to that realization, I curved my lips with a slight grimace contorting the rest of my face. I tried to make an *oh* sound with my mouth but all that came out were hollowed breaths choked from my tightened chest. Standing there, feeling the morning breeze tickle my backside and the body hairs that stroked the inner fabric of my clothing, I realized something I could barely fathom: someone had killed my mother, along with the exploratory robot. Possibly all of the other human life forms if that's what the blood wrapping around the corners of their bedroom doors and into the corridor as dry, crimson brushes signified. *Who did this? Why?* I pondered to myself, finding my eyes locating the indented edges of the exploratory robot's backside and fixating on the misshapen corner of metal.

My skin grew hot and rife with a prickling feeling as I felt the room seemingly cave into my body and press me into a sweaty, humanized mold. I began to turn with an adrift sway accompanying my rotating feet. Staring at the path of drying blood that ran along the concrete corridors with the same curved flow like the nearby creek, I realized something: this was my fault. I killed them; all of them. If I hadn't failed mother as her son, surely everyone would still be alive; the exploratory robot wouldn't even have to be killed. Everything would still be normal. I mean, I believe normalcy is what I longed for. I was unsure if I'd ever be able to get it back.

My legs began to wobble in their shakily pinned places upon the floor, just before they buckled and I collapsed to the floor, slamming into the backside of the exploratory robot. It didn't move at all, only responding with the pain its metallic body manifested in my trembling side. I could hardly feel my legs as they sprawled across the floor in a lazy collection of bone and flesh, twisted numbly over each other in an awkward positioning. The hunger in my stomach turned into an almost insensible twist that just barely scratched at my insides, as I involuntarily feasted upon the pounding heartbeat that reinvigorated throughout my body. I stared ahead of me at the room's wall opposite of my leaning body, entrapping in my muddled periphery the exploratory robot's bulky right-side wheel and mother's sagging screen.

I don't even know what's the truth anymore. I've never thought about that, but it's true. I don't know at all what's true about the world I collect myself within, or the larger world I spill myself viciously into. I'm unsure about death; I'm unsure about life; I'm unsure about *me*.

Continuing to look ahead of me at the bottom edge of the wall opposite of my leaning body, I began to think about everything I had assumed up until this point. I assumed mother to be able to outlive her death; I assumed my relationship with mother was unique to only me; and, I assumed I'd die with her. I don't know why I assumed any of that. I guess I just did. I assumed all of those things and now truly began to realize them as false assumptions. I suspected this would be the outcome of my assumptions before, but managed to fool myself into believing otherwise. Now, realization pounded into my body and strangled my mind, leaving me thoughtless as I just barely managed to grasp my official reality.

Mother was gone. Unlike when I first assumed she was dead, she now was partially disconnected from the exploratory robot, and totally disabled. The wires and levers that connected them were compromised into a fizzle of sparks and diverging segments of metal insides that reached towards the ceiling. I now leaned just a couple of feet away from her against the exploratory robot, watching her dead presence through the thick patch of transparent fluid blanketing my eyes. I lost my mother;

she's dead. I don't know how to feel about that… Or I do… Or I don't… I don't know. The feelings that manifested within me. No other distressing moment could compare to the amount of distress I felt rain down on my body and leave me in a neverending descent that never actually materialized. I just sat there, processing what I saw through blurred eyes and feeling my body disintegrate into the floor of lines smoothed into the concrete floor of the room. Yet, when I thought about it, I was still there. My arm still pushed into the exploratory robot's indented backside, aching in a pain that ran along my clothed arm wrapped in a grimy fabric. My bottom side languishing on this floor I had sat on for so many years, yet never even dreamed of sitting on in this same context.

My eyes began to waver shut, casting the wall ahead of me and the thin black line at the bottom of it in a blurred stretch of obscurity. Nothing registered with me as anything anymore. It arose as once being something, but continuously fell into a visual pool of nothingness. I saw the large, black wheel that belonged to the exploratory robot become a swaying sea of blackness, merging with the sights neighboring it in mired hues of gray and white. I tried to hold them open for a little longer, though I was unsure why I strained to leave them open. I had no use looking any longer at the sight ahead of me. I was exhausted. Dying, perhaps.

I suppose the only thing that left me willing enough to hold my eyes open was the shadows ahead of me that grew larger and larger and moved within the still field of muddled colors. It was almost as though one of the blurred objects before me arose from the dismal fray before my wetted eyes and grew sentient. I don't know who or what it was, but I didn't seem to care. My eyelids opened only a few more times, lazily closed at intermittent moments. My eyes soon closed to the sights they had previously beheld, shunning the world I once found myself being violently forced into. Inside I was a pocket of dying blood and bone, and outside I was the muted symbol of my looming fate. Mental and physical exhaustion made their final slashes at my body, leaving me crumbling into my place with internal twists and pulls of hunger and distress. All that could be heard were those same distant murmurs once collecting at the jagged edges of that random pile of rubble, growing louder and louder near my dying body but amounting to nothing understandable. Not that I would have the ability to understand it, let alone the ability to outlive this fate I painfully encountered.

JACEY-ONE
MARCH 6, 2366

Voices circled above and around me in a cacophonic swirl of varying pitches and intonations, just barely registering with me as any voices I recognized. The voices shot through a plane of darkness that enveloped my surroundings and left no human trace of the collected voices. It was a group of voices; a group of people speaking to each other. Or, perhaps, just speaking individually at the same time in the same vicinity of each other. I don't know. I can't see anything. *Where was I? Was I dead?*

I could feel my body again. The feet that clung to the light-colored shoes I wore, once covered in blood and dirt stains; the legs and torso that filled out the jumpsuit stretching along my body; my head, seemingly resting on something, much like when I'd rest my head on my pillow in my old bedroom. *Was that where I was? Who's voices were it that surrounded me?*

My eyes pulled open a little bit, visually consuming a bright, piercing beam of white light that cut through the infinity of blackness found behind my closed eyelids. The dark outer ring of my periphery merged into a similarly brightened circle of light that melted into what I slowly began to perceive. I tightened my eyes and contorted my face into a tight cringe, flinching from the bright light that nearly blinded me much like the fluid that previously choked my vision.

A light, brown hue layered my eyelids, indicative of the polluted skies I assumed to descend upon me in a distant collection of colorless clouds and sunlight. The voices that hovered over my body were now right next to me, as if we were in the same room speaking over my sleeping body. However, based on the movements that tossed and rolled beneath my resting body, I could tell this wasn't a room I had ever been in before. Perhaps it was no room at all.

As I became more aware of my body, I felt the bumpy, lopsided movements beneath my resting body jolt me in a rough, side-to-side motion, forcing me against straps that ran horizontally across my body. I opened my eyes with a slow, gradual retraction, a quickening flash of blinks culminating in my eyes completely opening.

I'm alive. The same, polluted skies up above that filled the atmosphere with thick, bleak lumps of brown collected above my body in the daylit sky. The cool, springtime breeze that meekly nabbed at my sides. I'm alive, and not dead. Not that I'd know what it's like to be dead, or could even guess.

Though, lining my body was not only the same familiar groupings of building rubble that emerged as a field of ambiguous structures, but also a party of several unfamiliar bodies attached to entirely identical faces. My eyes widened at the sight of them moving with me, talking amongst themselves and hovering above my laying body. I couldn't understand any of what they were saying; nothing registered with me as a familiar word, and instead passed over me as senseless vocalizations.

Humans. I didn't know any of these people, yet they were people in the sense that the human life forms were. I marveled at their bodies wrapped in tattered clothes imprinted with guideless designs from splotches of dirt and grime. Their hair which clung to their heads in tangled locks of strands that knotted and twisted over each other, all of which were shaded various colors of brown within the group. All of their faces displayed hair on the lower portion of their face, hanging from it in either long, sprawling hairs that collected a few inches from their jaw in thin curls, or clung to it in lightly shaded stubble. I had never seen anyone like them before. They were so much different than the other human life forms. They were different from my mother, too. Yet, they were similar, too. They walked like the human life forms; their mouths moved like the human life forms did; words, albeit unidentifiable ones, left their mouths and interacted earnestly with the words produced by the others.

Blood was also something found on them. It clung to the skin of their hands and exposed arms as dark red patches dried into their flesh, wrapped tightly around their fingertips and trickling along the backs of their hands with only slight glistens permeating at certain points. As the sight of the blood filled my eyes, I felt my eyes roll back towards the sky and become filled with that drab, colorless plane that stretched for an inexplicable distance. My body quivered slightly in the tight hold of the straps that I felt grind into my body with a burning pinch, culminating in the detached realization I began to approach: they killed someone. Who? I wasn't sure. Would they kill me? I wasn't sure about that, either. Like how I killed that little boy.

I could see it again: the little boy's blood dressing my hands in a darkly shining spread of redness, as I peered over his dying body. However, I didn't feel the same amount of distress I was used to feeling everytime I recalled that memory. In fact, I wasn't even sure I was distressed by that image juxtaposed against the murky skies as a traceless hologram projecting that cramped, gray room and the dying remnants of that little boy. Those chapped, bloodied hands that swayed in place as they hung by the sides of those humans led to the recall of that memory, but not the same response to it.

As I stared into the polluted skies that clouds barely moved in a soft, tan current, engrossed in a thought yet basking in a colorless light, the voices of the humans choked into a light rumble. I could barely even register the sounds heard near my body as belonging to the humans, only confirming the low-voices as I caught sight of the slowly moving lips of three in front of me. Their eyes pulled toward my laying body in quick, dark jabs juxtaposed against a pool of discolored whites. My own eyes had now fallen from the tannish skies down onto the humans in my viewpoint, watching their tongues slap the insides of their mouths at the quick verbiage lashing from their mouths in quiet mumbles.

The feelings conjured within my body were distressing, but not in the same way it was once distressing to think about how I murdered that little boy. I felt my heart begin to progress into a gradually accelerating race, but not enough to constrain me into a frenzied mess. I was almost calm, but my body's nerves became itched with an adequate amount of excitation to render me slightly distressed.

One of them reached their hand up and moved it up and down with their fingers fanned timidly apart, exchanging another frantic glance with me before turning back to the person walking with them across my body. Their head, along with those of the others, bopped along in an uneven half-ring of side-to-side movements, corresponding with their heaving backs. As they moved along with my lying body transported between their bodies, their faces remained stuck on the trajectory before them as they turned and marched with the bumpy movements of whatever was transporting my body. They turned ever so slightly to speak to each other, never twisting back enough to lock eyes with me. Their voices crept out in quiet murmurs, similar to the ones I heard when I saw those pairs of eyes in the pile of rubble a few miles from the building I passed out in. Staring at their tangled strands of hair overlapping in thick, greasy locks, I watched their heads of hair slide against the upper edge of their dirt-stained clothes, fostering a dimmed presence.

I wondered if they were who stared at me in the pile of rubble, exchanging a series of unidentifiable vocalizations as I stared at them from nearby. I then wondered if it was them who killed the human life forms, the exploratory robot, and finally, my mother. And, if I was next.

Ihad no idea where the humans were leading me. They didn't interact with me much, only producing a quick, abrupt glance over my body before moving their eyes ahead of them.

The sun passed slowly over us, making an incremental slide over the morning sky only genuinely realized when looking away long enough then back again. Yet, the bright sunlight that poured in my eyes still remained there even when I looked away, leaving a bright blue orb latently floating before me whenever I looked ahead of me at the humans' backsides. The bright blue orb bounced against their backsides with a detached shuffle across their dirtied backs and messy hair. I waited for it to stop and melt into the patches of dusted skin, diluting its blue hue into a light, shadeless brown. However, it just continued to remain before my eyes, interacting with me in a quiet, expressionless stare until the humans took its place. My body continued to jolt within the tight hold of the straps stretching tightly across my body, pinching the skin beneath my clothes until a burning blister could be felt.

The steps the humans waddled into the ground began to pull to a slowed rap of footsteps, until they brought the thing I rested upon to a halt and their pants collectively replaced the sounds of their feet being placed into the ground. They lined my periphery with their backs heaving towards the sky and their heads leaning toward me with a sagging bow, probably a couple of feet away from my resting body. They then all stood back upright and moved inwards toward my body, panting towards each other across my body instead of the ground.

Similar unrecognizable voices began to fill the area from a distance, nearing closer to where we were located alongside trailing footsteps that grew into footsteps slapping against the ground and leaving the sound of dirt and rocks crumbling beneath their feet. It was a sound similar to when my feet slid over the recently bloodshed floor of the building I had lived in, covered with infrequent patches of reddened dirt and rock when I last saw it. Several other humans crowded around the border of dirtied flesh and clothing building up around me, crashing toward my sides with intrigued stares and hanging jaws. Their faces were all similar, with the only thing distinguishing between their watching faces being the varying heights of their hair, which formed thorny crowns of scraggly, outstretched strands against the tannish-brown skies behind them. The group continued to multiply, growing larger and larger until all I could see were those dirtied, hairy humans standing around me for as far as I could see, even within the hazy outskirts of my periphery.

I had never seen this many humans. At least, I assume they're humans. The humans I was used to seeing amounted to 5 humans, whether behind a screen or in front of it, but never this many. They only forged a circle around me and nearly replaced the polluted skies up above with a plane of wide-eyed looks and unidentifiable voices. They spoke amongst themselves; the voices I heard exchange wordless dialogue grew into a whirlwind of voices that could be heard across a large distance, contrary to the much smaller range of voices I heard earlier.

My heart began to pound in my chest, surfacing along my skin with patches of ticklish sweat that began to soak my clothes and ferment my neck. The reality I found myself in felt more real than ever before. I was now experiencing it. I was no longer with my mother, nor the other human life forms. I wasn't at the building I grew up in. I wasn't near the creek. I wasn't anywhere I had ever been before. That was clearer now more than ever. As I saw these humans near me, surrounding me for an indefinite amount of distance, I finally began to become distressed after remaining relatively calm.

The changes I watched rip through my environment reflected in my nerve wracked body. The blisters burning into my skin seared into my flesh with a fiery scorch, nearly wringing the feeling of blood creeping toward those tingling indents in my skin and the surrounding surface. I could feel the voices hammer at the edges of my head and pulsate the firm outline of my skulls, overwhelming me as they crashed onto me in a ravaging sea of echoing murmurs.

All of this culminated in the towering presence of one of the humans approaching my body from behind my head, draping my body in its long shadow. It almost looked as though they were hanging from the ground beneath everyone and drooping towards the pool of tannish clouds that once reigned over us.

I pulled my eyes towards the skies, locking my eyes with the deep, brown irises of a human that looked much different compared to the other humans surrounding my body. They stared down at me, their body flanked by a dust-covered blanket that covered their arms and every bit of their body below their neck. Specks of murky light reflected in permeated slivers throughout the front of the blanket visible to me. It had a rough look; not soft or comforting like the warm, sweat-stained blanket I wore whenever I fell asleep in my old bed. A hole was torn into the top of the blanket for their head to stick through, with little, sharp strips of the ripped material pinching the edges of their neck and leaving behind trails of miniscule scratches. Their face was different from the other humans that surrounded me on all sides, most noticeably the presence of a beard was completely absent from his face. All that was left behind were crimson-red blisters that lined the lower half of his face where the beard would have normally been. Additionally, his hair was flatter than the others and less tangled, with barely any strands sticking up from the curved mass of hair sticking from his head.

Sunlight grazed the edges of their head, summoning a luminous crown that poked outwards with sharp rays. They carried a large, metallic container, made out of a material that looked similar to that of the exploratory robot. I couldn't tell what was inside of it. My neck ached as I forced the back half of my head into the surface I rested upon, facing the mysterious person. I reverted my neck back into a straight position, moving my eyes back towards the sky and relegating the person draped in a dusty blanket to the upper edge of my periphery, suspending him into a colorless blur.

Strangely enough, the unidentifiable words produced by the crowd dwindled down into a near-breathless stretch of silence, leaving the sound of liquid splashing against the hard edge of something emerging from the voiceless crowd. The splashing was followed by the sound of something small touching the ground beneath me; almost like liquid dripping onto a surface. It reminded me of the sound of rain clapping against the ground and creating a unified sound of neverending drips. However, this was not rain landing upon the ground in a blanket of liquified blades; these were isolated drips, heard individually after the sound of softly splashing water.

Drip! Drip! Drip!

A random memory appeared in my head, leaving my eyes entranced by the blurry, twisted edges of the polluted clouds in the sky and my mind subdued in an unearthed thought. I hadn't really experienced that memory in a while. I was a little boy, and it was dinner time. My mother was greeting me that evening, as the exploratory robot carried a container of water in one of its coiled arms, gripped in its rubber claws. As it maneuvered around the tables within the room, stopping and adjusting its wheels around every corner and edge it came close to, water splashed on the edges of the container, crashing onto the concrete floor beneath us. *Drip! Drip! Drip!* Soon enough, as the exploratory robot reached my table, it placed a half-emptied container of water next to my plate of mushy lumps of edible food, with the liquid remnants of the container's contents trailing behind the robot. I thought of that when hearing that noise. *Was the human carrying water in the container?*

Prying into my body and scratching at my ears, the human's voice filled me with that same distressing feeling I experienced every time a loud noise ripped me out of trances I held with random fixation points in my environment. His voice summoned my attention and held it through the hammering rhythm of my heartbeat and the frantic, wide-eyed stare I shot at him with quick movement. Everyone's heads around my laying body bowed towards the ground, creating a non-verbal union of reactions that stretched for as far as I could see, and as far as that man's voice could call to. I knew it was a man because of the depth of it; it was like the male human life forms, and mine as well.

His voice continued to speak over my laying body, accompanied by light sprinkles of a liquid from where the man stood. The liquid could be felt on my face and body as it landed on my cheeks and soaked at arbitrary points along my clothes. It landed on me as a mere drop, grazing my skin as a soft figment of liquid, before filtering into a tickle, an itch, and finally, cutting into my skin as sporadic burns. It was an uncomfortable feeling I experienced, though I had no ability to ease that discomfort. With my arms locked firmly into the bed I laid upon beneath those tight straps, the burns remained piercing into my skin without any relief, continuing to spread with every sprinkle the man dashed onto me.

The feeling of the water spraying my body reminded me of rain blanketing the ground in a liquid artifact of the dark, gray clouds of a rainy, thunderous day. I'm not sure if this burning feeling I felt scratch into my skin was what was also felt by the muddy, wetted asphalt broken up along the ground in fields of brown and black surfaces. Yet, that's what I thought of as the man spritzed my laying body in the water held in the metal container clutched in his arm folded against his side. Landing on my body with the same *drip!* sound of rain as it hit against the ground outside my old bedroom, passed out onto my bedroom floor, and washing over my body a feeling of pain just like when I dashed my finger in the creek while viewing my reflection.

JACEY-ONE
MARCH 6, 2366

It wasn't long before I was removed from the straps belting me into the table I rested upon, leaving behind a rust stain that marked where the strap ran along both my upper chest and legs. As I stood up from the table, stretching my limbs by lifting my body onto my toes and everything above toward the sky, I noticed the table looked familiar. It was perched on four wheels and wrapped in a shiny, metallic border, rife with rust stains and cratering indentations that grotesquely decorated its exterior. The very top of the table contained a thin material that lined the insides of the table's surface, seeping inward at random points and even producing jaggedly torn holes that exposed the wet soil beneath it.

A hospital bed; that's what it was. My mother had taught us about it one time. It was projected on a screen separate to the screen she was displayed on. I had never seen one before. Its presence filled my eyes and held it, seemingly consuming my eyes as I held a wide-eyed glare with the dimly reflected mass before me. The light that gleamed off of its sides, poking through patches of rust and dust, left a blurred, discolored haze bouncing in my eyes. I was transfixed by the object, but thought nothing as my presence fell into its grasp.

I could hear a group of individuals collecting at my backside with their hurried voices, stroking my back with their deep grunts. One of their hands gripped my right arm and began to pull my body with the aggressive pull they produced, averting my eyes from the partially shiny hospital bed to the moist patches of browned soil beneath our feet. I nearly tripped as the person pulled me with them, subsequently rotating me around to face them. They spoke to me, much in the same way mother had spoken to me, but without any of the words I understood. I grit my teeth together lightly, producing an awkward grin at them as I stared at their lips moving up and down and letting out deeply panted sounds. They pulled at my arm, pointing at the distance behind them and beginning to tug me with them in little trips and shuffles. I began to walk with them, reluctant to deviate at all from what they were intending to tell me to do.

But, as I turned with the person and began to step with them, I almost stopped making any movement as my eyes landed upon a vast body of water, larger than any I had ever witnessed before. It was like the creek when it was full; yet, without an end in sight, and no edge to splash against that edge. Instead, it flooded the distance for an indefinite, muddy stretch, deconstructing into an ambiguous trace shielded behind a barricade of thick, polluted clouds. A curved border of beige, grain-like dirt lined the edge of the liquid body, encroached at its edges in a darker shade of dirt and a thin layer of the murky fluid.

The dirt I traveled upon with the other humans was darker and positioned on slightly higher ground than the grainy edges of the water. A curved stretch of bumpy, disconnected patches of asphalt wound throughout the area, almost like the one that I had traveled upon everyday after skipping fitness enrichment activities by the creekside. Except, rather than being lined with endless piles of building rubble, it was lined in dead trees that either sagged over the width of the path or collected lifelessly at the sides of it. The dead trees that crowded the path with scattered branches and broken trunks reminded me of the creek and how it looked during the day. Though, without the depth that crept deeper into the ground and sank to the bottom in a thin, jagged line of water or a bank-to-bank current. With my arm still being held firmly in the person's tight grip, I was led. It was a strange experience walking over the path of asphalt and loose twigs. It felt like I was walking over two things at once; the creek and the asphalt road leading up to that one building, merged into one surreal path.

Tables were placed all throughout the upper ground we traveled along, spaced apart roughly twenty feet and connected by only the wet dirt ground they all stood upon. Benches were connected to the structure of the tables, perched on two rusted-metallic poles on both sides of the mass. Many of the tables were broken in half, with a portion of its surfaces either sagging down in the middle or disintegrated entirely, languishing on the concrete slabs beneath the structures as a space of vanishing wood dust and chunks. Yet, no matter what the tables looked like, there was always a series of dirtied sheets pieced together to create a building-like structure. Yet, none of them had the sturdiness of the building I grew up in made of concrete and metal. They instead seemed to sway in the light breeze penetrating their stature, held tight to the ground and the trees by several rustic metal pins. Shadows caved into the sheets' dirtied surface before sinking back into the edges of it as it expanded outward.

The humans crowded at the structures amassed between trees and the countless tables, some stopping to stare at me as I was led into one of the sheet-made buildings while others continued onward. One of the humans remained gripping my arm tightly in their hand, while another accompanied us into the building, grasping the middle of the expansive wall of sheets that met in a thin, embroidered edge. They held the sheet back in their grip, pushing their bent wrist upward to provide space for the human and I to enter through. The human pulled me with them into the structure, which stretched for around fifty feet before meeting with another two sheets that overlapped against the light breeze flowing through the area. Our feet stepped against the soft, ruffled surface of a bed of more sheets meeting each corner of the building in messy, stretched edges. The sound of the sticks and dirt meeting our steadily placed feet could be heard beneath us with a muffled *crunch!* We stopped just a few feet away from the pillows, which sank into the floor with their little, dim shadows eclipsing the grime-spotted masses. Dirty pillows were placed neatly ahead of me on the opposite end of the floor of sheets, with a large one in the center and two smaller ones accompanying each side for a total of three pillows.

While stopped, my eyes moved over the room surrounding me. I believe it could be considered a room. I mean, that's what it felt like.

There seemed to be a floor that met with the four corners of four intersecting walls. The room reminded me of the rooms found in the building I grew up in. The sheets that stretched across the dirt ground and stood as the room's floors seemed to have the same strata designs decorating its soft, footprint-trodden surface. At random points in the sheet-floor, scrunches collected in groups of three or four half-ring lines, almost like when the sheets on my bed became wrinkled after sleeping on it all night.

I remember the exploratory robot cleaning my bedsheets once a week. It would take one of its long internal arms and grasp the sheet in its firm, rubber claws, tugging at it at each corner in a traceless rectangular motion until the sheet was dragging on the ground while hanging from its grip just slightly away from the bed. Then, it would wash the sheets in a compartment holding a spinning wheel of flat blades flooded with a thick, bubbly slur, and finally dried it off in a separate compartment.

My eyes were soon averted from the shadowy collection of a few half-rings pinched messily into the sheets beneath us, as the same man with the deep, loud voice stepped past us and hovered over the middle pillow with a strained bend. He then placed his tan, dirt-smudged hand on his knee and swung his lower back side onto the largest pillow of the three I saw, spreading the rough, plastic-like sheet covering him. His feet could be seen sticking out from beneath the edges of his wraparound sheet, stiffly following his legs as he shifted them and finally crossing them one over the other. His feet were wrapped in a scraggly brown material that came together as a pair of shoes. It was noticeably different to my shoes, which were light-colored and stained with blood and dirt.

A couple of other humans trailed behind the man as he sat down, presented with a similarly clean style relative to most of the other humans I was able to see. One of them held a large metallic container in their hand, with a meek trickling noise splashing lightly against its edges. The other held what resembled a leg - a human leg. A small human leg, the same size as a baby's leg. It looked clean, except for the light prints of dirt that decorated its pale flesh in a sparse patchwork of hands. Their backs were turned to us as they brought their bodies to their knees, preceding their steady descent with a gentle bow to the man at the front of the room. They swiped one of their hands over their upper body, beginning with their forehead, crossing over their chest, and bringing their pinched grip to their mouth.

The man at the front of the room pressed his hands against each other, heading his tightly placed hands with the tips of his dirt-encrusted fingernails. I watched from the side as the two other men engaged in the same activity, effectively suspending the three of them into a group of closed eyes and hushed murmurs. The human leg and the container of liquid was now placed atop the floor of the room between the bent knees of the three men.

As the men engaged in the unusual set of behaviors united by their similar posture and vocalizations, I grew fixated on the leg placed at the center of the human triangle. Blood glimmering near the top of the leg, merging with the torn, scratched ring of flesh summoning a freshly bruised crown at the calve's edge; a bone poking through the nerve and muscle that emerged from the leg's edge as veiny, crimson-red striates; and thin little hairs that poked from a smooth, dusty surface of dirt and blood handprints.

My eyes began to wander away from the leg and to a sharp, dim ray of light forming a thin line at the bottom of the room's walls, expanding and contracting with the springtime breeze that brushed lightly through the area. As my eyes did so, I could see the blood-covered hands of the humans that transported me on the little hospital bed; and, the fresh bloodstains that formed a series of overlapping crimson paths in that building's partially exposed hallway.

I realized a connection between those three separate events, one bound by the blood that decorated those distinct surfaces as part of what I suspected the humans to have done. They killed the other human life forms. They were the ones who hid in that pile of rubble near the creek; they were the cause of those trails of blood staining the concrete floors in several crimson strokes. They had killed the human life forms, and eventually took me with them, albeit alive. Why they left me alive and took me with them, I couldn't quite figure out. Fixating on that thin strip of narrow, grayed light and watching a discolored haze emerge from that fixation point, I came to the realization that this wasn't a good situation to be in. Whatever that means.

The distress I normally felt when anticipating the exploratory robot's arrival was the same as how I felt watching those three men engage in a quiet, closed-eye conversation, and feeling that man's grip remain on my left bicep. I had that strange feeling whenever its wheels would zoom slowly towards my bedroom door and enter through it with its big compartmentalized body attached to them. Now, watching the severed baby leg rest on the sheet floor between the three men's legs, I felt my heartbeat seemingly sink into my stomach while protruding through the narrow tunnel of my throat. The lumped-sensation expanded in my throat until I could barely push out any breath from my constrained chest. A twist pierced through the rummage of starved, acidic waves that groaned from inside my stomach, scratching at my heart with a burning pressure. I took a breath - or, rather, several scattered breaths pressed out shallowly - before feeling a thick rush of my insides traverse up my throat and onto the sheet floor beneath me. I then sagged to my knees with my arm still in the human's grip, watching the room sway faster than my eyes could perceive. Its walls passed up and down and side to side without any sensible organization, filled in its oscillating cor-ners with the dim presence of the three men turning frantically to me. I watched through blurred vision as the metal container shook partially in one of the men's hands, leaving thick, darkly colored liquids splattering at its edges and trickling down its sleek side.

My heavy breaths patted the bile-stained sheets in shaken strokes that left behind mushy ripples just beneath my face turned towards the approaching men. My eyes remained on them but could barely conjure any stable image of the three men crouching near my side. Their dimly clothed bodies swayed into intensified obscurity, until their blurred presence all sank beneath a sea of darkness, and their frantic voices became quieted by my unmoved ears.

MARCH 6, 2366

I began to awaken atop a surface different from the one I passed out upon. This one was softer and almost comparable to the bed I awoke on every morning every day for years. My eyes opened with a detached sort of flutter pulling my eyelids back and forth into my head like the claw of the exploratory robot reaching for my fingertip, expanding and contracting. Except, there was none of the *reee!* sounds that could be heard as my eyelids opened. Instead, my breaths leaving my mouth and filling my head with an atmospheric sound of deep rumbles and pounds could be heard. As I opened my eyes, looking up through the blur obscuring my vision, feeling the sickening heat unnerving my body, I realized I was around the same men once again, crouched over my body and dowsing my lazily agape mouth in a thick liquid. It had a lukewarm feel, and left a mild trace on my lower face.

I don't think it was water that I passively let enter my mouth and slide down my face. If it was, it was unlike any water I had ever drank before. The taste was salty and somewhat bitter. As I began to process it filling my mouth and clogging at my throat, I began to cough, sending thick jets of the liquid through a stammered choke. It oozed along my jawline and collected on the plush bed I laid upon, collecting awkwardly along my neck. As the liquid left my mouth and emptied onto my face and neck, I gasped, feeling a cold flush of fresh air vacate my mouth and chill the thick film outlining my mouth's interior.

The men sat crouched around me with their wide eyes and nervously hanging lips collecting on my wet face. The man I had first encountered earlier today while spraying my body in the water sat farthest from me, with his right hand placed opposite of his ribs over my two legs. The other men sat closer to my face, with their deep brown irises pooling at the edge of their eyelids and casting a glaring look at me.

Watching the men and beginning to realize the unnerving feeling of the thick, bitter liquid coating the edge of my face, I began to lift my hand, sliding it weakly by one of the men's tensely bent knees. His eyes fell to my slowly lifting hand, along with those of the other two. My eyes remained locked with theirs, locking my hand nearing my face in the blurred regions of my periphery. The silence that was found in the room felt strangely different to realize; the room had been relatively silent for a few minutes now, yet suddenly could be felt pressing down onto me. I could hear my heart beating lightly in my chest, beginning to pick up agonizing speed as I neared my hand to my lower face.

I touched my pointer finger to my face, feeling the thick, slimy film caress the tip of my finger and sink beneath my nail. I looked between the nervously watching faces and the wrist of my hand, pulling my wetted finger from my face and aligning it with the half-ring of men crouched over the edges of my body. It blocked the dimmed rays of light blanketing the insides of the room from the overlapping sheets representing the front of the room, pointed weakly upright just a few inches to the side of one of the men's dirtied cloaks made of rough, almost metallic sheet. Staining my finger was a dark, crimson color, sending a hollowed ripple of various shades of that blood-red color imprinting my fingerprint. *Blood.* That's what was on my face. That's what they were forcing into my mouth. My head moved over the several encounters with blood I had experienced today alone - the blood lining the partially exposed floors of the building I grew up in; the blood covering the hands of the humans transporting my body; and the blood seeping onto the sheet-floor from the amputated baby leg. *Was this the human life forms' blood they had given me?*

I frantically moved my eyes from my bloodied finger to the overlooking heads of the men, feeling my breaths paint the air in stiff, stammered figments of air. I felt the strong urge to vomit again, but could only conjure the dizzying feelings that were summoned whenever I began to throw up. There was probably nothing left in my stomach but the sickening buzz that meandered through my stomach and sluggishly exited my lips in pained groans.

The men began to grow frantic once again, with the one farthest from my face pushing himself away from my laying body and crawling out of my vision. The other two's heads turned with his body shuffling quickly towards where the pillows had been placed, with all of them speaking anxiously amongst themselves. My eyes shifted abruptly to the right sides of each socket, trying to see what the man was searching for without moving my body at all. I was unsure what the other men would do if I were to move at all.

My eyes quickly cut back to the man crouched over the lower end of my laying body once again, fumbling with the baby leg in his hands. He then pinched it by its foot, twisting it over in the small grip of his pointer finger and thumb pressing against the balls of the foot and the soft top of it. I watched him reach over my body, holding the man sitting next to him by his right shoulder and beginning to hover the baby leg over my quivering lip.

The smell of clean skin mediated by the overarching aroma of dirt and grime filled my nose, along with the cold feel of the amputated baby leg nestling chillingly against my lower face. The men spoke frantically at me, facing me from where they sat stretched over my laying body. My hands flexed at my side as the rest of my body awkwardly stretched beneath the three men, along with my head that turned side to side with my grimaced lips shunning the leg with a disgusted cringe. I barely opened my eyes, squinting them at the ceiling away from the men. They began to yell, with the man who had spritzed the burning liquid over my body beginning to shove the baby leg against my teeth.

I groaned, but not from the hunger that cut into my body in pained stabs and deep rumbles. I groaned from the flesh that was wetted by the saliva lining my teeth, initiating a moist connection I dreaded having to partake in. A muffled grunt pressed from my chest out of my strained-shut lips. I wanted to breathe, but doing so would allow the man to insert the baby leg into my mouth.

The two men closer to my head began to shift just beside my ears, pulling my hair beneath the placement of their knees. This pain was worsened by my insistent desire to rotate my head side to side so as to avoid the insertion of the baby leg into my mouth. They began to place their hands on my face, quickly muttering under their breath nonsensical gibberish as they began to grip my jaw and yank at it. I clenched my teeth tightly into a pained grin, feeling my cheeks pulled upward and my jaw dragging towards my moist neck in the men's grips. I could feel the skin on my face burn beneath their pinched fingers tightly tugging at my face.

The man crouching near my hips roughly thrust his right knee over my body, clashing with my penis tucked beneath my jumpsuit and pushing it with his leg wrapping over my side. It remained tucked under the man's knee pressed stiffly against my left testicle. I screamed, and then felt my jaws pressed open with the dirtied thumbs of the men pushing down and up on both rows of teeth in my mouth. I panted, feeling the saliva pooling at the back of my mouth gargling as I nearly choked on the pained groans I let out.

I felt the soft, warm flesh of the baby leg being pressed in between my teeth, littering the insides of my mouth in a dry layer of dust that progressed into a sickening taste. The man pressed harder and harder, until the skin on the leg became pierced by my two front teeth and led to a trail of blood trailing the roof of my mouth and staining that warm pool of saliva in its metallic taste.

The same words were screamed at me repeatedly, though I had no idea what they were saying at me; I just could tell they were the same words based merely on how they sounded and the pain I felt trying to ignore them beneath these three men. As they berated me with their bodies overlapping uncomfortably over mine, I felt distress worse than

I had ever felt. It felt worse than when the exploratory robot hurt me, zapping me until I was painfully numb or locking me away in my room until I was mercilessly hungered upon the cold surface of my bedroom floor. For my whole life, that's what distressed me the most. Now, watching those three men gather around my body, clawing frantically at my face, I think my experiences with the exploratory robot were second to this experience based on the level of distress I felt.

Watching their mouths stretch and push their cheeks into strained contortions, showering my blood-covered face in the saliva carried in their mouths and landing on my face with their loud interjections. Feeling their hands grip at my face and burn my skin harder than any zap ever projected onto my body from the exploratory robot. All of that made this the most distressing experience I had ever gone through in my life.

All of this led to one of the men gripping both my jaw and the middle of my scalp in his thick hands and pressing the two ends in each other's direction. The man perched over my hips ripped the baby leg back, leaving a thin layer of the pale flesh in between my teeth. The backs of my teeth remained awkwardly parallel to each other, leading to the undesirable bite my front teeth penetrated through the flesh with between bloodied teeth. I could feel the veins tangling along my gums tickle the moist flesh, languishing in my jaw as the men held my jaws together.

Their screams faded into words produced in focused pants, just barely descending from their tongues onto my passively sensitive ears. I relaxed my clenched teeth in their tense grip, allowing the chunk of bloodied flesh to slide along my teeth and nestle in the cranny stiffly situated by my molars. I tucked my back-teeth softly into the flesh, hesitant to bite into the skin and muscle forced into my mouth. I knew I had no other choice. I wasn't getting out of here. I wasn't surviving, and I had nothing to survive for. My mother was dead, and I had no idea where the building was that I grew up in. I had no reason to try and circumvent the force of the men.

So, through that thick layer of liquid relegating the men to figures in an obscure haze, I stared at the dimly lit ceiling up above, beginning to press my top layer of teeth into the bottom one. The piece of the baby leg was tough, bitter, and stroked my gums unpleasantly. I continued to chew at the flesh until it melted into a bitter sludge of blood, veins, and muscle. Several droplets of the liquid lingering in my eyes trailed down my cheek as I took my last bite, and swallowed it, panting as the tender mush sank down my throat and left a disgusting taste languishing in my mouth. The men began to pull away from my body, releasing my head from their grip and beginning to stand and allow the rough, shiny sheets they wore to flow in the light breeze brushing through the room. Then, the man with his legs placed over each side of my body unfurled my penis from beneath the firm placement of his folded knee, standing.

JACEY-ONE

MARCH 6, 2366

After the interaction with the three men, I was led to another room made of sheet walls strung together by nails hammered into dead trees scattered throughout the area beside the body of water. I was helped up by the three men, who forced me off of the three pillows I had been laying on with my arms gripped tightly in their hands. The short glance I managed to pull with the three pillows loosely placed together in a straight line revealed a smeared patch of blood shaped in the region my neck had been laying on. They were the same pillows the man had been sitting on or beside, placed a few feet away from where they had been positioned. The man stayed behind and organized the area within the room.

At first, my eyes flinched into a stinging blindness, leaving me unable to open my eyelids beyond a mere squint. I lazily dragged my feet along the ground, skidding over dirt and rock and occasionally stepping on something with a slight *crunch!* As I opened my eyes, expanding them until light touched my irises without a shocking burn, I realized I was being brought into a room.

The room was around forty feet from the room I had previously been in, concealed behind several overlapping sheets that produced an entrance faced with several light-brown stains. The stains lined the sheets in unevenly shaped patches of tannish hues, almost like the clouds that filled the sky with a polluted, sunlit glow. I believe the room's entry was facing towards the body of water rather than away from it, unlike the room I was first brought into. As I stepped into the room with my legs idly placed one after the other at the edge of the room's sheet-floor, my eyes landed upon a person standing ten feet away from the men gripping my arms and me. They had long hair like everyone else I saw, but it landed past their shoulders in tangled, dirt-speckled locks of hair, much different to the neat, almost-straightened head of hair crowning the men in the room I first appeared in. Their face nestled a beard that wrapped around their jaw and lower cheeks in a downward stretch of thin, curled hairs. They also wore clothes similar to the rest of the individuals that had circled around the hospital bed I had been laying upon earlier. Their upper body was wrapped in a tattered garment of clothing that ended by their hips, and rustled gently over the lower half of their attire in dirty gray streams of fabric.

In their hands were similarly colored fabric, folded over each other until they sat as inch-high and foot-wide stacks of the gray-colored material. The two men unfurled their tight grips from my numb biceps and left me standing there positioned with a subtle sway in my posture, beginning to speak with the person. One man stood slightly aback from the person with his outstretched hands producing a meek fan-formation over my bicep.

The person had a soft voice, one that strangely enough reminded me of my mother's voice. I didn't understand what they said, just like I didn't know what the two men said as they spoke quickly amongst each other. Their voices captivated me, leading me to avert my eyes from the stack of clothes in their hands and to the lips ejecting every unintelligible syllable brushing the edge of their mouths. My eyes twitched slightly, almost falling to a blink as a thin line of liquid protruded along the edge of lashes bordering my bottom eyelid. The person - the woman, perhaps - reminded me of my mother. She didn't look exactly like my mother. In fact, she looked much different. It was just her voice, higher pitched than any of the other ones I had heard today and in recent memory, sounded like my mother's. My heart raced slightly in my chest, leading to my breaths leaving my mouth in an uneven beat, pounding stiffly against her voice.

After a moment of my eyes fixating on the edges of her lips stretching into countless rings of dirty-pink flesh crossed with the tangled strands of facial hair overlapping, the men left the room. I barely realized their departure as a jet of air stroked my back and the sound of sticks and rocks cracking and skidding in the dirt nearby filled my ears. I turned my head back to face the lightly rolling borders of the sheets behind me, pushing in a flood of light that entered and left with every push and pull perpetrated by the local breeze. I looked back up at the woman who was now speaking to me, gesturing to the collar of the garment cloaking her upper body. My eyes were now wide and filled the corners of my wind-swept eyelids, locking with her moving lips.

I didn't form any response to the words she spoke to me, instead swaying slightly in my place with my eyes fixated in an entranced marvel on the smoothly widening lips she ejected senseless words out of. Strangely enough, I could see my mother's face plastered onto the woman's face positioned towards me, shielded behind a mask of dirtied hair and grime, removed from the screen she was projected upon and standing before me. I just couldn't understand a single thing she was saying.

The woman stepped towards me, smiling softly after speaking to me without any movement reciprocated from me. She reached her hand up to the zipper hanging stiffly at the edge of my jumpsuit's collar, placing her hand on my side and taking a step back to peer along the length of my body. The small hairs layering the edge of skin forming around my waist tickled with her sudden touch, corresponding with the warm tickle that brushed along my backside in the delicate draft caressing my body near the door to the room. My eyes moved with her averted gaze moving up and down my body, jabbing through the gentle bed of warm breaths scattered from my agape lips.

She gripped my collar, dragging the zipper further and further away from my neck and her fingers pinched against it until it met my waist in her other hand's grip. She then placed her hands lightly by my neck and pinched the unzipped corners of my collar, pulling them towards my shoulders and stretching them down my back. She leaned in as she did so, pulling it down my back about halfway before turning to my sleeves, pinching them in the dirt-lined fingertips and nails of her hands and pulling them downward towards her side. My arms surrendered to her grip as she pulled the sleeves off of them, with the only movement produced being the warm heartbeat that sped lightly in my wrist.

She placed herself on the floor with her knees grazing against the tips of my dirtied, bloodied shoes and planting into the sheet-covered ground scattered with occasional bumps from pebbles and twigs. She dragged the sleeves down until the insides were exposed outwards and the cusps clung to my wrists and flung my hands back an itch when releasing them. She then removed the jumpsuit from the lower portion of my legs, along with my shoes, tossing them both to the side in an unevenly piled lump of dirt-stained fabric and shoes. My eyes landed on the pile of fabric cut through by one of the shoes tipped towards the corner of the room to the left of me. The inside of the clothing contained soft, minute thorns that bristled in the air and sported nearly invisible shadows in the dim afternoon sunlight.

I turned my head down to my bump-covered skin, connecting the slight patches of hair and tannish skin clinging to my forearms and the pale, hairless coverage of my bicep. The woman stood from where she had been kneeling, pointing to my underwear and allowing her pointed finger to fall back to her side in a loosely held grip.

My hands moved almost automatically to the waistband of my underwear, flinching with the rest of my arms subdued under the itch of my naked arms trembling in the room's sharp breeze. I looked at her for a moment before bringing my eyes down to the crotch of my underwear, tucking my thumbs behind the garment's soft belt of elastic and pressing my four fingers into the underwear. I bent my knuckles forward and dragged the underwear down my legs, arching my back with the bend of my arms until I was naked before the woman. Standing back up straight and allowing the draft billowing into the room to hug my backside, I faced the woman with my penis and testicles pointing outwards.

The last time I was naked was when I still lived in that building with my mother and the other human life forms. I undressed in front of the exploratory robot and felt my mother's bright, gleaming eyes fixate on my naked body, as she instructed me to practice intercourse with a beige-colored object similar to my waist. After zapping me until I was numbed and pained into the floor with my body languishing on that cold stratified concrete, I was terminated by my mother. I watched the screen she was projected upon fade into a rectangle of dimly-illuminated blackness and retract back into the exploratory robot's compartment. I thought she was dead, and that I killed her, then began to wonder if she could be saved from the exploratory robot. Now, I believe she's been saved. She escaped from the exploratory robot's screen. My mother was now here standing before me, preparing to dress me. The humans saved her; they killed the other human life forms but saved mother and I. That's why I'm still alive.

"Mo - mother." I gasped with a breathless stammer, casting her body behind a shield of liquified blur as she bowed by my feet. She was beginning to place a garment of clothing near my feet as the name came out.

I could feel the air press firmly against the insides of my cheeks and leave my lips in warm pants, with the name still circling throughout my head and tickling the shape my lips had been paralyzed into. It was hard to process what had just left my mouth. But, I said it. I said my mother's name.

She stopped what she was doing, bending her head back after bopping it lightly while working to pull the garment of clothing over my naked legs. She began to pull her body up, straightening her torso to face parallel to the pale surface of mine. Her eyes squinted and her lips twisted into a tight pull, pushing her left cheek up and revealing a disproportionate share of her yellowed teeth. She said something I didn't understand, but could perceive as a question. I wasn't sure why or how, but I could tell she asked a question.

Her eyes moved between my widened eyes and my breathlessly agape lips, shifting up and down quickly. She then moved her eyes away from my body and bent on her left side, filling her face in the golden sunlight that poked through the dirtied sheet doors of the building. She took one last look at me before stepping away from her position on the floor a few inches away from me, calling the same word repeatedly as she pushed through the sheet doors out of the room. I turned awkwardly around to face the meekly shifting sheets pushed and pulled by the local drafts of wind pushing through the area and the fresh amount of force the woman perpetrated against it.

I was now waiting for my mother to return to the room. I stood there naked with the several garments of clothing both used and unused by me collecting at my feet in a border of unattended piles of fabric. Though, where I was and what I was doing didn't preoccupy me. Rather, everything that surrounded me and affected my presence entered my senses passively, overridden by my active obsession with the woman I now believed to be my mother. I could feel the wind tearing beneath my skin and uprooting the hairs that nestled in my body's flesh. This realization was a feeling I could feel spread in my chest like water touching a dry-throat and flooding a dehydrated body. I truly assumed that earlier today my mother was killed. Now, I could be with her again, and this time it felt more real than it ever had. I could tell mother looked somewhat different than when she was last projected on that screen. Although her face wasn't remarkably different compared to everyone else's faces, she did have a beard on her face, and her skin seemed to be dirtier. I wondered what happened so quickly for her face to change in appearance.

Mother came back with another human - a man, I believe - and pushed through the sheet doors of the room, brushing my backside with both the entering breeze from outside and the abrupt passing of their approaching bodies. They orbited around my body in a half-ring, lining up next to each other with the fresh words their voices spoke hanging off their tongues in loose, hefty pants. Their eyes stared widely into mine, falling far short of ever closing into a single blink. The woman spaced her fingers apart in a detached fan-formation, opening her lips to form soundless vocalizations and repeatedly pressing her hand to and from her face. The man's face followed closely with her hands, moving back and forth steadily as his eyes remained on my lips. My lips hung open, revealing my two rows of teeth spaced apart by a barrier of saliva layering the hard edges meeting between them.

Does she want me to speak? I wondered as she continued to direct her hand from her mouth towards me, producing shapes with her mouth but producing no words.

"Uh - um, mothe-" I stopped, casting my eyes on the body of the man standing next to the woman. I couldn't speak any longer, pausing my voice and diminishing it into a string of breaths unlike anything I had ever produced before.

It was like how I felt whenever I pressed that warm, sweat-stained blanket into my lower mouth and filled my nostrils with the comforting scent relishing the soft fabric. Yet, catching sight of his body and fixating on it, it was also like viewing the towering presence of the exploratory robot drowning me in its boxed shadow, forcing me into a state of despair I had to relent to as it grasped for me and hurt me. I was distressed, while simultaneously comforted. I liked how I felt.

I don't know what led my eyes to become so preoccupied with the man's body. I drew my eyes all across his shape in frantic glares, fixating on the soft, almost blended edges of his body. The edge where his clothes wrapped tightly around his legs and flowered towards his neck along his torso, producing a shape almost identical to the letter v, or where a soft bump protruded from the intersecting point where his crotch joined the two edges of his browned, dirtied pants.

As I stared at the man's body positioned before me and reigning over the meek presence of my naked body, I felt the strangest sensation I had ever felt in my life. My penis began to fill with something almost like a fluid, rushing towards the tip of my penis like the water in the creek streaming toward a hazed point in the distance. I clenched my hands into a flexed grip, protracting my knuckles against my skin. I nearly brought myself to the tips of my toes, feeling my big toe digging into the sheet floor and pressing into the sharp, jagged edge of a hidden stone. All of this happened almost automatically as I forgot where I stood and who I stood in front of, feeling my penis grow into a hard, long block of tannish skin and protruding veins. It bounced lightly as an extension of flesh from my crotch area, tickling in the draft flowing through the room.

Looking down at my penis and shooting dense breaths down at the strange formation, I felt my heart hammer in my chest and appear in the hat of flesh enclosing my head. My vision blurred; not from a fluid, but rather from a genuine haze that locked my vision behind and filtered into my brain in a warm, buzzing feeling.

"Wa - wa-" I panted, beginning to stammer breathlessly as sweat covered my chest and wetted my hair. "Water. Water."

I looked up at my mother and the mysterious man, finding them rotating their heads between my face and my penis before locking eyes with mine. But, as I panted those words to them with several pauses breathed heavily into my verbiage, gesturing frantically at my parched mouth, I felt a thick, hot liquid seep from the tip of my penis. My legs began to shake uncontrollably, erratically displacing the tense flex I had strained my legs into. I watched everything turn into black around me and my body buckle beneath my trembling weight, forcing me to the ground. I laid there, encircled by the voices of the two individuals yelling around me.

WE ARE SOME-
BODY'S DILEMMA
TRAPPED IN THE
MIND OF A TOY.

ARE WE SOME-BODY'S DILEMMA TRAPPED IN THE MIND OF A TOY?

MARCH 6, 2366

By the time I opened my eyes and cast my surroundings in a thick shell of haze, I was already in another room, placed atop a bed similar in feel to the hospital bed I was transported on into the lakeside area. My breaths were the only thing I could hear loud enough to understand as occurring around me, depressing the voices of the people nearby into muffled gibberish. Clothes pressed gently into my body. They didn't feel the same as the clothes I had worn before, and for everyday for the past year or so. It wrapped around my body in a loose grasp, concealing me in a bag of dirtied fabric.

I could feel liquid enter my mouth and drip down my chin, either tracing my neck in thin streams or falling onto my covered chest. The water tickled my throat as it sank down that dried tunnel of flesh, leaving behind an itchy film in it. I coughed a bit, closing my eyelids before rolling my eyes and exposing them to the room I laid in. My eyes landed upon the man and the woman I had passed out in front of, standing at the foot of my bed with a nervous stare stretching their faces into wide eyes and stiffly agape lips. Hanging just below their presence a few feet away from me was a man dressed in that same shiny, almost plastic sheet, with his arm bent into a border wrapped along the lower portion of the two's legs. His shaved face contrasted the hairy faces of the man and woman standing in the background of his straightened mast of hair wrapping around his head. He brought a metal container to my lips, filled with a pool of liquid that hugged my bottom lips and flooded beneath my top lips, filling my mouth in a hot, ticklish feel. Yet, the liquid was refreshing. It didn't have the same taste as the water my mother used to supply us when she lived behind that screen. Though, it washed down the dry, pasty feel of my throat beneath a sheet of fresh water.

The man giving me the water turned to the other two with the container still bent over my chest and brought to my lips, speaking with a slightly pitched voice as a subtle smile lit up his face in a reddish glow. He looked back down at me, removing the container from my lips and leaving behind a liquid artifact caressing my chin and hurtling towards my chest in small, occasional drips. My eyes followed his hands leading his concealed arms to a bedside table from beneath his sheet draped entirely over his body, placing the container on the table. It was a small, metal table, overrun with stains of rust producing irregular shapes and designs. He stood back upright from the table he had crouched momentarily over, turning to me again and bending over my resting body. He closed his eyes, hovering his hands over my body with his thumb tucked into his palm as he produced a swiping motion over my upper body. I watched as he brought his hands together like how he did in the first room I had been in with him, producing a clap suspended in a placed slant angled towards the ceiling. Muttering beneath his breath an even faster string of words, the man and woman at the foot of the bed bowed their heads with him and gripped their hands tightly, tightening their eyes towards my legs sprawled towards them.

As their heads bowed towards me and their hands remained pressed tightly against each other, I examined the clothes strung around my body in loose jumbles of dirtied fabric. My clothes were gray, but permeated by extensive patches of dirt and grime that created a stretch of browned blotches crawling towards my feet. My feet were concealed by shoes that exposed the edges of my feet with a beige-toned line of toes poking over my body. Straps spaced an inch or so apart ran horizontally across my feet, fostering a patterned line of exposed flesh and brown leather obstructed by melted material and winding pieces of connected fuzz.

I felt different. I had never dressed like this in my entire life. Ever since I could remember I wore a beige-colored jumpsuit and shoes. They clung snugly to my body; the articles of clothing I wore pressed loosely into mine, leaving behind pockets of space that blanketed my skin in chilled air. This wasn't how I have ever dressed; this wasn't how the other human life forms back at the building I grew up in dressed either. Now, however, I dressed like everyone else in this local area. I don't know why, but they dressed me in their same type of clothing.

I looked up from the overlapping knuckles of my mother and the man's interlocked fingers, looking frantically around me at the room I was in. I wondered where my clothes were as I tried to see if they were anywhere nearby. I couldn't see any of my clothes lumped in a pile on the floor, or flattened neatly into a warm, soft stack like when the exploratory robot would wash and dry my clothes. I don't know why, but not being able to see my clothes distressed me, like when I would hear a loud noise randomly while fixating on something in my environment.

All I saw around me were the same walls and floors of sheets melded around either the sticks and rocks flooding the ground or the trees they pressed against. There was not much else in the room except for the table beside my bed, carrying the container of water, and the bed I laid upon just a foot away from it.

Feeling the countless sprigs of fuzz twist and turn within my clothes' insides and bristle against my windswept skin, I realized so much in my life had changed so abruptly. The place I had lived in for so long was now abandoned, and had no place in my life anymore. Now, I was in a different physical environment surrounded by more human life forms than I had ever encountered in my first eighteen years of living. They all looked different from the human life forms I had grown up with. Even mother looked different from when she had been projected upon that screen extended from the exploratory robot's insides. I don't know how to feel about all of these extreme changes. Strangely, I didn't feel any distress experiencing all of these sudden changes in my life. The frequency these changes all occurred at rendered any experience of pulsating, panting distress flattened into a mere numbing buzz.

My eyes moved over the sporadically folded edges of clothing wrapped over my body, trying to cling to a thought that could barely be pictured. I tried to realize what was now my life - a life based in a physical environment I had never laid my eyes upon before this morning, surrounded by people I had never met before then either. Yet, I felt that buzzing feeling in my head heighten into a pain that strained my head and crossed my eyes over each other and blurred my vision. I didn't know how to process my new reality. Rather, I just existed at the center of it and passively allowed everything to emerge carelessly from the periphery, acting onto my body and senses without restraint.

Their heads would soon retract from the bow they tilted their heads into, swiping the pinched grips of their hands over the upper half of their bodies in the same swiping motion. The time I remained in the room with the three of them was short; soon after, I would be led out of the room to a massive table where countless individuals congregated around with jagged-edged plastic slabs in their hands. It seemed to be the same vast amount of people that had previously gathered around the hospital bed I had been transported on. Now, they were only differentiated by the hundreds of sharp glares shooting from the tons of plate-like objects in their hands and rendering an illusive glow hanging throughout the crowd. I would be led by the man in the dirtily shining garment cloaking his body in a dirtied haze, who sat me down behind the table and in front of the vast group of people stretching along the shoreline of the lake.

The chair was unlike anything I sat upon in the building I had grown up in. It had a long sliver of metal that shot towards the sky in a thin, inch-wide stab, coated in a dark gray paint roughened by numerous white scratches. The center of the chair's square seat sank into a softer gray depression of the same metal material, with the tannish sunlight illuminating the layered colors of the seat. Sitting down in it, it was unlike the seat I normally sat in when I ate in the building I used to live in, which featured no backing and was just a bench bordering the edge of a table positioned a foot or so higher than it. I took a moment to process it, feeling a strong urge to just bend my back towards the cold metal back and allow it to penetrate through my browned clothes and chill my skin. I remained sitting up with the three men standing just around me, occasionally relenting and allowing my back to graze the cool metal back of my chair.

Several trays lined the middle portion of the table in rustic metal slabs erecting a fortress of meat built in lazily assembled lumps. The pieces of meat twisted and turned over each other in blackened, crisped segments of flesh, exposing the grayed bones inside them that poked from cut edges. Alongside those large metal trays roughly two feet long, were smaller glass and plastic slabs lined in jagged edges that entered the round borders of them in a large severed chunk and ended as a thin crack. They were covered in the same green and orange mush I was used to eating every night for dinner, glistening in the dim sunlight in soft, almost bubbly hills of puree.

Looking up, I realized everyone was beginning to seat themselves in the same metal chairs lining the table for a long distance. The table stretched towards the lake roughly a hundred feet to my left side, and stretched for an even greater distance in the other direction. They sat down together in almost perfect unison, huddling along the table's crowded edges with a murky horizon arising from their knotted heads of hair. The man beside me remained standing, quietly bowing his head towards the table covered in countless trays and plates. The voices that filled the area in nonsensical chatter fell into a silence that stretched across the table and only became obstructed by the occasional peep coming into earshot. Within seconds, there was not a single sound heard along the entire table. Everyone, including myself, sat down in their chairs with their two feet planted in the dirt ground providing a dusty bed for the tables to position upon. Looking to my right side away from the lake, engaging in a visual traverse bogged down by countless heads and identical faces, I noticed a large nest of concrete rubble stretching towards the sky with a rough, jagged presence, positioned a couple of miles ahead of the table's end. A long valley of dirt, rocks, and smaller portions of building rubble separated the two points.

It was the remains of the hospital, clouded in haze and illuminated by the border of sunlight touching its irregularly shaped edges. My eyes falling to the curved edge of the cooked piece of meat lying meekly a few inches away from me, I realized something: I had never been on this side of the hospital's remains. Now, sitting at this table among a group of humans I had never before seen, I was on the opposite side of the building I grew up in. I knew it was the destroyed hospital building because of its shape and how it clung to the dimly-lit haze polluting the distance. It was almost like I was seeing it from the creek I had always hidden by, but instead saw it opposite of the creek near this much larger body of water.

I believe the man standing next to me had been speaking to the people around the table with a loud belting of senseless vocalizations. His hands were brought next to his shoulder and bent with his palms parallel to the sky. I hadn't paid any attention, instead finding my eyes enveloping the crisped edges of the meat before me that crinkled into blackened edges and pooled into valleys of browned skin. Hills and valleys of various cooked flesh covered the meat. I had never seen anything like it served on a plate before at a meal. I knew it was something to eat based on how it was presented on a plate-like object, surrounded by countless other individuals with plates laying before their hands gripping twig-like objects in their hands.

Strangely enough, despite never seeing anything like this meat in my life, I experienced a hunger for it that I had previously felt whenever it was about to be breakfast time. I was usually laying down in my bed with my blanket pressed into my nose and filling it with the pleasing aroma of the soft blanket bristling against my nostrils, rather than sitting at a table surrounded by other humans like I was doing right now.

Everyone spoke one short vocalization in unison, before shifting in their chairs with a widespread patchwork of *ernt!* noises erupting through the area, reaching into the various plates of meat. The meat shifted with the grip and pull of their hands, rolling into varying places on the plates until a greasy metal surface was revealed. They all planted their elbows on the table's edges and bent their hands towards their face with the meat in their greasy hands, tearing thick, red chunks of flesh from the meat.

I brought my eyes down to a piece of meat positioned in the middle of the metal tray parallel to my sitting body, caving towards the edge of where it had been amputated and rounding it out in a veiny red front. I blinked, feeling the urge to grip the meat and put it to my lips like the rest of everyone prickled at my bent fingertips restrained into a loose curl. Averting my eyes abruptly to the man I had felt my penis harden to, I eyed his sitting body over the piece of meat separating our bodies. I felt my breaths leave my mouth in isolation, juxtaposed stiffly against my entranced eyes and suspended heartbeat. Any blink I felt inclined to produce was fastened to the circumference of my sockets and edged in a windswept burn, as the sight of the man consuming the meat in his two, brawny hands filled my eyes. I could feel my penis begin to harden once again in my clothing and push past the baggy folds of the inside of my clothing.

His eyes met with mine as he took another bite from the meat, widening as he raised his eyebrows steadily. Taking a strip of meat in a slow bite, he held the piece of meat slightly beneath the point of his chin, flashing a soft grin at me with his lips rimmed in a greasy ring of black-dust and shine. I felt my penis press against my leg and harden against a fold rolling over the far-edge of my right pant leg, implanting a firm cranny of flesh and fabric. I looked away, gulping as I passively looked at the soft, bristled edges of the severed pieces of meat.

Beginning to feel the hunger I had been experiencing for a couple of days tighten in my stomach and pulsate in my throat as a wobbly lump, I eyed the pieces of meat before me, realizing I could eat some too. I felt the saliva in my mouth pool towards my lips and liquify the chapped edges of it as a groan shook my stomach in a rumble and riveted my body in a deep bellow. I licked my lips, reaching my hand up to the meat before bringing my outstretched hands to a stop.

The man beside me, who had spritzed me in water earlier today and pressed the baby leg into my mouth, grabbed a piece of the meat, exposing the discolored presence of a cooked foot. A human foot, just like mine and any of the other human life forms, whom I always assumed had feet just like me. The bones in the feet clung tightly to the blackened, specked flesh wrapping them in a firm mold. It stretched all of the way to where the knee would be in a stream of stratified colors like the lines populating the concrete floors of the building I grew up in. Instead of a knee, there was the dimmed, gray mass of the exposed knee joint poking outward.

Noticing the mush that the humans each plopped wetly onto their plates one-by-one, identical to the food I was used to eating all of my life, I realized for sure that this was all of the human life forms folded onto this table in disjointed limbs and muscle cooked to a dull crisp. The hunger in my stomach wavered and shook off into a slight pain in my chest, but didn't fade away or sag into a sickness. I actually wanted to eat these pieces of human meat, and didn't mind it at all. It felt strange, and almost distressing to come to such a conclusion. Despite the distressing feeling, looking around me at the man who had spritzed me in water and left me in burns, as well as the man who had grinned at me, I began to reach my hands forward and grab hold of that spare leg.

A shell of dust pushed against my fingers as I hesitantly gripped the leg, leaving behind a slippery film of grease on my fingertips. I fixated my eyes on the diverse strata of cooked flesh blocking everything else out of my sight, recalling the human life forms this leg likely belonged to. I took a deep breath, feeling that inhale pound into my stomach and almost cause me to vomit what little I had left of my insides onto the rusted table before me. Then, I placed the meat to my mouth, bringing my teeth to the flesh and pressing them beneath it. The hairs on my legs struck upright as I took a bite, feeling the grease from the cooked skin coat my tongue and the veiny meat fill my mouth. I chewed the meat between my teeth, grinding it awkwardly into a moist sludge. I swallowed it, feeling it grate against my dried, itchy throat and land precisely in the empty pit of my stomach, visualizing a ripple effect transiting across the acidic pools of that pained chamber.

As I put the meat to my lips again and took another bite, this time quicker and more comfortably, I thought of when I dashed my finger into the creek's surface at the sight of my reflection. Pressing just beneath the water's surface and leaving behind a rippled trace, and removing it with a burnt, blistered ring decorating it in a discolored red. Except, swallowing the chunk of mashed meat and feeling it drop into my stomach like a utensil onto the cold, concrete floor of the building I grew up in, I felt satisfied. In fact, it was the most tasteful thing I had ever eaten.

The warmth of the meat in my hands and its chunks in my mouth filled me with a comforting feeling I only have ever felt when nestled into my bed and awaiting my mother's arrival. I rotated the meat in my grip, with my bites scraping meat off of the leg quicker and quicker. I ate away at the meat until moist strands of the meat barely hung off of the bare bone of the leg. I ran my tongue against the firm bone and bit the little strands off of it, feeling the moist touch of the bone wetted in my saliva paint my cheeks and nose in a cool, crisp feeling.

The span of time between the first bite I took and the aggressive slide of my teeth against the bare bone was quick; practically no time went by as I spun that leg of meat viciously between my two rows of teeth. Rapidly, I transformed it into nothing more than a dim, gray piece of bone with exposed pieces of fatty flesh permeating at random points. I placed the bone down onto the table and exhaled deeply, feeling the warmth in my chest tinge my breath in a tasteful flavor. I felt satisfied with what I just ate, strangely enough. That was the most satisfied I had ever felt in my life, I believe.

Now, sitting here with my back leaning into the stiff metal chair and falling into my legs lazily sprawled beneath the table, I could feel sleep creeping into my body and taming the shocked pull they had into my sockets. While I was distressed over the pale, almost undead baby leg that had been forced into my jaws, I experienced no such feeling recalling the big, meaty human leg I had just eaten. This feeling would remain throughout the rest of the day and into the growing hours of the night, falling onto the lakeside area in a purplish haze as I was tucked in the same room as the man who my penis had grown hard in front of and fainted in front of.

JACEY-ONE
MARCH 6, 2366

It was strange falling asleep in this room made of sheets and a floor covered in two lone mattresses. Even more so than falling asleep in the soft, stratified layers of mud bordering that creek. Seeing the sky collecting far above my head in purple clouds and eventually moon-lit haze was more comforting than seeing the sheet-made ceiling of this room push up and down in the drafts of wind swarming through the area. It was strange. The bed I laid upon was comfortable enough, despite the springs in it poking through the thin material of the mattress and itching against my back. I suppose I felt more comfortable feeling isolated from everyone I knew and languishing on the dirt ground. Even the light blanket that grasped towards my chin with little fingers of loose, winding threads couldn't comfort me. I'm not quite sure what this discomfort was based off of. However, it felt similar to how I felt when first encountering that man in the room where I was undressed.

He slept next to me atop a mattress separated from mine by about a foot of space. The dimmed presence of the man with his head bent back into the mattress hung in the periphery of my eyes, along with the slow thump of his chest heaving. His chest created a hill in the shirt he wore to sleep, spread to his biceps which were much larger than mine. The arm closer to me was folded behind his head, filling his shirt in the firm, round muscle of his bicep and pointing towards the ceiling in the tight edge of his bent elbow. I tried not to look too long at the man, only occasionally tucking my head nervously into the bed to glance at his resting body. Still, I couldn't help but shoot countless glances at his body, pivoting my eyes from the blurred periphery I held them in and fixating them with my turning head.

After roughly an hour of frequently looking at the man, and feeling drool bury the edge of my mouth's interior and wet my lips, I turned my head towards the ceiling. Laying my eyes on the dim pool of light grays and whites swaying in the windswept sheet-ceiling, I fixated on the darkly tannish stains that cut through the soft, drab space of gradation. It wound through the ceiling as it pushed and pulled in the wind, lightening in color as it caved towards my body and darkening as a shadow filled the belly of the wide sheet pulling toward the sky.

I tried to close my eyes to the room I found myself in, finding it strangely difficult to hold my eyes shut, even as the weight of rest dragged down on my body in a wave of drowsiness. Perhaps willingly deciding to neglect my physical environment and surrender to sleep was a difficult decision to make. At least when I passed out I had no input in that decision; where I woke up, covered in thick streams of blood or itchy ones of water, was not my fault, and I had no choice otherwise. At least, I don't think I did. I don't know. Choosing to stay awake felt like the right choice to make. Every time my eyelashes meshed together in a soft kiss, suspending my vision behind a tired blur, I ripped them back open, finding myself awakening with my heart racing and my breaths quickening. I would always find myself drifting back into the climax of that intoxicating cycle, feeling the pleasing presence of sleep wash over my body before being forced back beneath the tight hold of my shakily awakened body.

There seemed to be something missing everytime I began to fall asleep. Something I typically experienced in the closing moments of my day of wake as I rested upon my bed. Just trying to figure out what it was that was missing was enough to keep me awake. I could almost feel the word build at my tongue and hop off of its slippery precipice in a breathless gasp. I could see it there building in the haze of my tired eyes, almost as though those same tannish stains above me represented a trace of that missing thing. It was like I could touch it, even though I couldn't quite recognize what it was that I was missing as I began to fall asleep.

It was a little boy that languished in that stain; in that pool; that pool of dark, red blood, irregularly shaped like the tan-brown stains stamping the sheet ceiling. He sank into that pool of blood and into my blurred vision, becoming realized as the thing I missed from the routine I pursued prior to my sleep as I progressed into that period of rest. That little boy covered in blood on the concrete floor of his bedroom, blanketed in a strata design of minor, gray indents, and the distress that I felt when viewing that distant memory. That's what I was missing.

That memory almost faded behind the dark pull of my unconscious, when I was awakened all of a sudden with a large mass crouched over my body and breathing heavily on me. My eyes ripped open, folding beneath the creases of bone lining my sockets and focusing on an insignificant jumble of facial features. I couldn't tell who it was that stared into my eyes, steadily holding their face over mine and breathing onto my chapped lips. My heart raced in my chest, pounding within the warm mesh that tensely brought my body together beneath the person's.

My penis began to harden in my pants, tightening against what seemed to be the leg of the person crouched over my body. I could feel my heart beating in it, pounding repeatedly like water dripping onto cold, hard pavement. *Drip! Drip! Drip!* My body became inflamed, but not in distress; rather, it was an intense warmth that radiated throughout my body like the sun washing over my presence on a hot summer day. I almost automatically brought my hand to the person clinging to my laying body, feeling their tense, muscular leg, beginning at their knee and bringing it to the round shape of their buttocks. I could just barely bring myself to breath, finding pleasure in the dizziness that paralyzed my mind and suspended me beneath a sky of static haze.

The withered flesh of my two lips became wetted in the moist kiss of the person's lips pressed against mine, sealing our two faces locked into each other's. Their nose dug into my cheek, swiping against the upper edge of my cheek filling the space bordering my lower eyelid. It didn't bother me feeling their nose jab into my face and grind against the bone of my upper cheek bone. Strangely enough, I barely even noticed it, even as I simultaneously felt the roughness of bone against bone, only barely buffered by the layers of flesh separating our faces.

The person leaned back and sat upright with his two legs bent over each side of me, revealing the heaving back of the man who had fallen asleep beside me. He stared at me, his dark brown eyes bouncing steadily with his head moving with the rest of his heaving body. Gripping the hastily embroidered edge of his shirt, he flashed two veiny hands redded behind a shell of sweat. He pulled his shirt up his body and over his shoulder, folding his arms with the shirt clinging tightly to his elbows and large biceps, concealing his head with it. Finally, as he removed the shirt from his torso, he revealed the muscular shape of his hairy flesh, corresponding with a wave of pleasurable sensations washing over my body, leading to my head bending back into the mattress and my toes flexing.

Tossing his shirt to the side of the bed, I watched his back flex with his arms tucked into his sides and his hands gripping the hemmed band of elastic, kneeling on one leg and beginning to stretch his shorts and underwear over his legs. Finally, he pried the two garments of clothing off with his feet picking at it into the inside edges of his heel until he was naked. Revealed, in the middle of a patch of curly, dark brown hairs that collected at his crotch like the beards hanging at the bottom of everyone's faces, was a penis - a notably large one, long and hard. The thick, bright red tip of his hard penis grazed against my sweatily clothed body with almost a foot of space separating us, probing at me like the arms of the exploratory robot. It looked a lot like mine. I assumed all penises looked like mine and his, but I couldn't be too sure.

He then removed my clothes from my body, pinning my arms to the thinly veiled surface of coils in the mattress and gripping my legs as he exposed my naked body. I was sweaty and shakily planted at the mercy of his towering presence. As he gripped the shaft of his hard penis, with his head of moist, wavy locks positioned towards my head with a dim hang, I flashed a loose smile at him, just before feeling the insides of my body melt into the massive lump I felt inserted into it. I believe it was his penis he was inserting.

I let out a gasp that almost jumped into a scream lept from my strained lips, leading the man to grip my mouth and line his firmly held palm in the moisture of my heavy breaths. The tangy flavor of dirt and the food from earlier today lingered on his hands, filling my nose in a strange aroma and my mouth with a flavor frothing into a salivated paste. My heart was racing faster than it ever had in my life, and I could barely breathe. However, I wasn't distressed. The feeling of what I assumed to be his penis pressing against the inside of my body was the most satisfying feeling I had ever felt in my life. I never wanted it to end. Despite the pain I felt as it pulled against hairs in my butthole and lined it in a tunnel of gashes and fresh blood, I enjoyed it. The fluid that had been common whenever I was in pain or panicking was now filling my eyes, corresponding with a light laugh pressing from my lips and barely registering as a muffled breath leaving my nostrils.

A rough, ticklish feeling could be felt in my body, like the threads of my childhood blanket stroking my face but erupting through my body and paralyzing my stomach. My stomach was warm and the end of my butthole broke down into a hot, pricklish mass. I felt his penis press against the end of my butthole, harder and harder until the hairs inside of that tunnel of flesh wrapped around the circumference of his penis and grinded between the two surfaces interacting. Fluid lined the edge of my penis, coating the tense tip with each push of the man into my body, as sweat collected at random edges of his face and dropped onto mine like rain onto the ground.

Eern. Eern. Eern. I could hear him grunt atop of me. His grunts corresponded with a cycle of events that was suspended beneath the numbing blur fostered through the pain and pleasure of this ordeal. My moans caught at his hand and left my body only as a muffled breath, understating the inflammation fracturing my body into stimulated bits.

The event culminated in the dissolution of my insides, sinking from my stomach towards my butthole. It collapsed like the hospital building falling towards the ground in concrete bits and melting to it beneath a sea of acidic rain. My insides filled my butthole and flooded towards the edge of it, trailing along my buttocks and bordering the edge of my bent back in a thinned, grainy sludge.

I think I'm finally dying. I've assumed this to be the case many times in recent days, and now felt it to be definitely true. As my insides poured towards my butthole and surrounded me in a repulsive stench, seeping beneath my back and tarnishing this mattress in a brown paste, I realized this was my death. I was finally accepting death. The feeling of the air leaving my chest as that massive lump became quickly removed from my body, spritzing my body in specks of the warm liquid, I accepted this as the final moment of my life.

Staring up at the sheet ceiling now crossed into an acidic sea of flashing reds, greens, and blues, seemingly falling to me but never landing, I realized I was now alone in this room. The man had left. I was now alone, laying in a sea of my insides that reeked of a foul aroma. That was all I realized. All I could see was that sky of electric haze, and juxtaposed beneath that, the memory of that little boy languishing in that pool of blood, just before I was reprimanded by the exploratory robot for killing him.

Somehow, I smiled recollecting that memory, feeling satisfaction comfort my entire body, rather than distress paralyze it. I drifted off into sleep, warmed by the insides of my body layering my backside in a thick slush, and content with the death I assumed to be what I experienced.

Strangely enough, it all felt similar to when I pooped in the bathroom while living in the building I grew up in.

JACEY-ONE

MARCH 7, 2366

I woke up fermented in the dried mush of feces clinging to my backside and solidifying a cold, icky buffer of paste between my body and the bed. I felt cold and disgusting, blown into my bed with the fresh draft of the spring morning planting me firmly into the poop-stained mattress I laid upon. Shivering in the cold led to me pushing the feces farther and farther up my back, sealing my back in the foul, brown paste. I had never experienced anything like this before. Whenever I pooped it was in one of the bathrooms found within the building I grew up in. Now, after the ordeal that occurred last night with the man, I was covered in it, too distressed at the thought of getting up to clean myself in a place I've never been, yet too distressed to stay here covered in feces.

The man had come back some time after I slept, falling asleep on the same mattress beside me. Any chance I got to partially roll on my side summoned the presence of his clothed body, with his hair clinging to his head in moist waves of dark brown locks. I don't know where he went after what happened last night between us. He removed his penis from my body and flung some of the poop onto it, which now dried into my stomach in brown specks of mush.

Looking up from where I lay, I stared at the thin strip of white light bristling in the light sway of the sheet. My eyes enveloped the strip of light moving towards and away from the edge of my mattress, either hiding the dry, pebble-ridden surface of the ground or exposing it. Regardless, a bright blue figment of light bounced along the breezily fluid border of the room, shifting in my eyes as a neon strip of light.

I don't know why, but something about this morning seemed to unnerve me. Watching the bottom of the door to the room made me feel as though there was something I was supposed to expect to happen, yet I couldn't figure out what that happened to be. It distressed me trying to figure it out, staring at that strip of light I had never before seen and finding no clue appear in the vicinity of my head. Waiting for it to appear led to my heart beginning to race in my chest and my breaths leave my lips in heavy pants. My back lined with sweat began to merge wetly with the shell of feces coating my back.

I could hear feet shifting in the rocky dirt outside of the room I shared with the man, kicking pebbles and sticks in broad steps that grew louder and louder. *Skkrt! Shhh! Skrrt! Shhh!* The sounds grew louder and louder, until the skidding noise concluded and the shadows of four feet filled the edge of the sheet and stretched over the rest of the sheet in the towering shadow of two individuals. Watching the beige tips of a dirty set of fingers grip the edge of the sheet and begin to flood the room in the bright light from outside, I closed my eyes almost automatically. The hairs bunching along my legs in soft curls stood upright, as my body felt the absence of a soft, warm blanket covering my body. I tried to act like I was asleep, feeling the cool morning air lash my body in chilled licks and the dim, polluted sun penetrate my eyelids in a dull, golden hue.

It wasn't long before the two individuals entering the room began to frantically shout at each other, scurrying along the sheet-floors and bumping the edges of my mattress. I opened my eyes slightly, realizing the presence of the man who had forced the baby leg into my mouth and my mother, who were now beginning to grip my arms firmly in their hands. They lifted me up and sighed heavily, a tinge of disgust hanging on their constrained voices and their contorted faces. I looked between them with a stiff string of breaths hanging out of my agape lips, watching them exchange their voices frantically with each other as they turned to the man who had been sleeping next to me. They gestured towards him then to me, and he shrugged his arms with his bent hands brought close to them. The two groaned while holding me in their hands, beginning to pull me with them.

They pulled me through the sheets overlapping in the front of the room, shuffling me into the brightly lit area surrounding the room in a prominent path of dirt and rock, as well as more buildings made of sheet. The two turned to the right with me in their grips, leading me past sheets pushing and pulling in the cool morning breeze and encasing the tucked outlines of countless individuals, all of which poked their heads out, watching me pass by. Their faces all looked practically identical, popping out of the sheets like stars flashing through icy clouds filling the darkly polluted night skies. They stared at me, with some of them pulling out from behind the sheets and standing at the foot of the buildings they had resided in, watching my mother and the man lead me farther and farther up along the path.

Eventually, we rounded a corner that revealed the massive body of water wrapping around the landscape of dead trees interconnected by pinned sheets, bordered by a brown, grainy shoreline encroached by soft waves. They led me to it, our feet skidding over rocks and twigs with the occasional pebble skipping a few steps ahead of us with a small *clitter-clatter*. I felt my body grow colder as I neared the body of water with them, feeling the breeze of the morning intensified by the water it bounced off of in chilled billows. I shivered in the grips of my mother and the man, shakily placing my feet one after the other as the three of us neared the shoreline of the lake.

My feet soon grazed upon the soft, cool surface of the dirt, sinking half-an-inch into the dirt and kicking multiple thick specks behind me in my tracks. The dirt surrounding the lake was damp and thick, differing from the thin, almost dusty blanket of dirt covering the stiff terrain of dirt and rock most of the encampment was positioned upon. It grew damper and muddier the closer we got to the water, until mud created a thick, black ring bordering the edges of my toenails and collected along my feet in wet, grainy trails.

I gasped as the two brought me into the soft, icy shore of water, sinking my trembling feet beneath the surface. My arms hung tensely in their grips, just barely managing to exert a rough jolt as we stepped further into the water. The cold water rose up our sides, all of the way until our hips floated atop the edge of the water, relegating our legs beneath the soft, rippled surface. The water was dark and murky, and showed no more than the curled edges of my pubic hairs as a muddy current partially rubbed against it, exposing it in the light morning sun.

The man released me from his grip, standing away in the water and allowing the same, almost plastic-like sheet he wore to float in the water. He brought his hands together and closed his eyes, beginning to murmur to himself. My mother held me tightly in her grip and led me towards his front side, stopping our feet in a soft, muddy point in the dirt littered in little rocks and softened twigs. Then, turning to me and placing one of her hands behind my back and the other to my chest, brushing her breasts against my body, she laid me back into the water, bringing the chilled liquid to my neck.

I brought my whimpered pants to a soft, pitched whine, nearly feeling that same liquid fill my eyes out of panic. My body began to burn all over as she sank me beneath the water, wetting my hair and prying off the feces folding over my back. My face eventually became spritzed in the same water, inflamed with multiple minute droplets inflicted by the man who now spritzed me with one of his gripped hands. It was practically the same as what happened yesterday atop the hospital bed around all of the people, hammered by the frantic murmurs of the man and the repeated motion of his clenched, wet hand flicked towards me.

I felt tempted to bring my head to the side and pull my eyes away from the thick, gray clouds reigning overhead in drab strokes. Yet, I feared what the acidic water would do to my eyes if I were to tuck my right eye beneath the rippled surface and view the man with my other one, feeling as the water itched at my outer eyelid. So, I just hung there in the grasp of my mother's hands, finding my hands bend awkwardly against her forearms and straining against her soft, beige flesh. The tips of my fingers grasped at the slightly hairy surface of her skin, trying to cling to something as she began to tilt me from side to side in the water, swaying me gently.

The hairs on my head were now sopping wet and floated calmly in the current my head sank into. Although I felt cold entering the water, the inflammation burning into my skin hidden beneath the muddy surface of water almost heated it into a satisfying blanket of warmth.

Staring at my mother and feeling the man continue to spritz me in the water, prying into my skin in meandering burns, I felt calm. A smile tucked the corners of her lips into the folded flesh of her cheeks, tightening her eyes into a bright squint. The face grew warm, though not near as inflamed as the rest of my body hidden behind the murky current circling beneath the soft ripples of the water's surface. I think I was smiling; I could feel my cheeks stretching into a tight contortion and the wind beginning to chill the salivated case glimmering along my teeth. My heartbeat in my chest in a slow rumble, almost like the warm water in the building I grew up in pumping into my childhood bathtub in gradual streams. We continued to smile at each other for a few more moments, as the moist clumps of feces originally occupying my back floated to the water's surface, fostering a grimy halo around my wetted head.

She then lifted me out of the water, casting my body's naked torso in a red glow and a burnt feel. My mother grabbed me by one of my biceps and twisted my body in the opposite direction of her, gripping her hands along my back until it was facing her. I now stared into the cloudy horizon filling the far-end of the water in gray blobs and a mystic trace of the still body of water. I shivered as I stared at the polluted horizon, unnerved by the imagined yet hardly realized distance of water tucked beneath that murky curtain brought over the edge of the water. I couldn't look away, barely even noticing my mother begin to brush the lower edge of my back, removing particles of feces from my skin.

It was only when she began to slide her hand between the cheeks of my buttocks and cleansed the stiffened layers of feces sealing the hole together that I pulled my attention away from the thick clouds, gasping.

The insides of my butthole became seared in the acidic liquid, prying into rough cuts and sinking a burning feel deeper beneath them. Her hand reached deeper, until the feces was effectively removed and filled the chilled spring air in a foul, muddy stench. The dirt and grime caking the upper beds of her fingernails in a deep brown line stung the insides of my butthole, almost ripping open the bruises circling it in a tunnel of burns and gashes.

I was eventually fully cleaned with the acidic water I stood stiffly in, turning around with my feet buried beneath soft specks of the moist mud swarming its surface. As I did so, the mud I kicked up from the water's floor spiraled to the surface, disrupting the mild float of several particles of feces collecting between mine and my mother's bodies. My body was now covered in burns, poked at all over by the cold breeze of the body of water harshly encircling me.

The soft border of haze dissipated from my eyes as I stared breathlessly into my mother's, with the man now holding my mother's hands in his and murmuring once again. Their eyes were closed, and their hands wet, connected by the slimy trails of thinned feces lining their hands in brown liquids and small clumps. My mother's hands were clamped together between the man's hands gripping hers from bottom to top.

As I stood there silently without interfering in the quiet interaction initiated between the two, I caught sight of the encampment standing behind them, hidden behind a wall of the same polluted clouds lining the horizon of the water. The sheets strung between dead trees could just barely be seen, registering as gray blocks loosened by the beams of light pouring through them. The trees, however, could still be seen, surmounting against the reign of the polluted rays of light and stretching its countless tiny branches towards the sky. Beginning as a large, massive trunk, and stretching into meandering branches that faded behind the dim haze. I thought of all that stood in the concealed distance stretching behind it, including the decimated remains of that old hospital building and the creek I had stayed around during fitness enrichment activities. I felt the cold brush of air chill my wet locks of hair, electrifying the droplets hanging from the thick clumps and falling onto my back. Then, I remembered the body of water behind me, fading into nothing more than a still surface blanketed beneath clouds.

Turning away from the faded sight of the encampment and the mum interaction of my mother and the man, I stared into the clouds at the far edge of the water, remembering the polluted horizon hazily wrinkling the rocky edge of that creek's terrain. My eyes widened and fell into the endless trek of water hidden behind the clouds, intensified by the speculations I held for what laid beyond that edge.

Maybe it connected back to the creek? I thought to myself, stunned by the strangely hollow sight hazily erected from the water's edge. *Maybe the clouds at the edge merged into the clouds found at the far-end of the creek?* I watched it for a moment, feeling as though my heart was sinking into my stomach and burying the oxygen in my lungs with it. I was perplexed by the edge of the water, and felt strange realizing the potential connectedness between two different facets of my physical world that didn't seem to connect at all. The far edge of this body of water seemed to sit miles away from the far edge of the creek, yet was connected nevertheless by the barricade of clouds rapping down on the water in hazed slaps.

This connection sat with me but hardly registered, instead collecting in my mind amidst confusion as I was led back to the encampment with my mother and the man, the three of us emerging from the polluted fog and relegating the water behind that same illusive shield.

JACEY-ONE
MARCH 7, 2366

After being led through the rows of overlaid sheets strung across dead trees, I was taken back to the room I had been sleeping in with my mother entering with me alone. The mattress I slept on had now been removed, and there was now only the other man's bed. A couple of individuals kneeled on the floor where the mattress was originally found, scrubbing at the sheet floor with a soaked rag clumped into their hands and rubbed aggressively against the floor. Several wet stains seeped into the ground, lamenting the soft terrain in dark brown patches sporadically placed near the two individuals. Just next to them was a strange bottle that had a jagged cap at its top, revealing the sharp edges of a broken hinge on its pale-blue edge. They glanced at us, speaking words to my mother. I didn't listen, instead focusing on the act they partook in as the marks of wetness lined the traceless remains of my mattress. The disgusting aroma of feces hung in the air beneath the minor trace of a floral scent. It was almost more distasteful believing the trace of facade hanging in the room's confusing scent.

After speaking to the two people who kneeled on the ground beneath her, my mother pointed to my clothing laying on the ground in dirtily lumped piles, then gesturing to my body. I stared at her for a moment, my body seering in pain with every mere flinch I initiated. Reluctantly, I kneeled down alongside the two individuals, quickly scooping up the clothes in my strained hands as I felt the burning sensation wrapping my body inflame across the flexed bend of my back. I sighed, standing back up with the clothes in my hand and feeling my skin retract against my bone and muscle, sizzling against my skeleton.

By the time I had dressed myself again with the same clothes, my mother was smiling at me, shifting her eyes steadily up and down my body. She didn't say anything, instead producing a small grin leaning more so into one side of her face. I smiled back, feeling that same warm feeling heat the insides of my chest and boil softly into my stomach. Her eyes then stared at my lips, averted from my beaming gaze as she began to bring her hands over my sides, planting them softly on my hips and caressing them over my backside in a gentle wrap. My mother's face was now a couple of inches from mine, angled parallel to mine as I rotated my head awkwardly to stare down into her eyes. Her breaths touched my face, filling my nose with a fowl aroma and brushing my face in soft strokes. She began to near my face, puckering her lips in a firm, chapped bunch and planting her lips on mine, to which I did nothing in response. She pulled her lips over mine, lining them in the saliva painting the inner flaps of her lips as she folded hers over mine. It was a strange experience, one that reminded me of my experience with the man last night but without the same feelings expressed. I don't know why, but feeling my mother close to my body with her lips fixed on mine felt unnerving, and almost distressing. I don't think I like it.

Once she pulled away from my mouth I looked into her eyes, feeling my brow furrow slightly and sweat chill the creases of my cheeks. She produced a small smile, her eyes gleaming at me in a slow gaze transfixed on my lips.

As she brought her hands away from my backside and began to step away, the man who had slept next to me the night before approached us, riding a crashing wave of crunched skids and kicked up rocks and dirt. I felt my breaths stop and barely move out of my mouth in stiff pants, occurring as I felt my penis harden in my pants.

He smiled between us, then turned his head as he spoke with my mother. I watched him closely, focusing on his dark brown eyes planted on my mother in a gleaming gaze. I just barely looked at my mother, finding the feelings I felt with the man's presence overrun by the strangeness I felt remembering that kiss from my mother.

The exchange between them soon concluded, ending with the man reaching over my mother and placing his hand on my left shoulder and beginning to walk with me brushed with his firm grip. I walked with him, looking back at my mother only briefly who watched us depart the area, smiling through the tannish light that burdened her face into a furrowed squint. Glancing up at him as we walked, he didn't say anything, instead leading me in silence throughout the encampment with his eyes loosely focused on the ground before us.

We arrived at another one of the buildings propped up by several sheets overlapping between a few trees. The man pulled one of the sheets back with his free hand, his other still placed over my left shoulder blade. Entering the room, I almost stopped in the pull of his arm hanging against my back, feeling his grip tighten over my back as I viewed the tons of bookstacks lining the edge of the room in a discolored array of pages and leather covers. Glancing back at me, he paused, before I stiffly resumed my steps in the man's grip, stepping into the middle of the room covered only in two pillows and remaining empty until meeting the border of the room lined in various stacks of books.

I followed him into the center of the room, treading slowly across the floor with my eyes moving rapidly over the stacks of books erratically rising from the sheet floor in unevenly stacked columns. The man sat down on the pillow, similar to the one the man had sat upon in the room I was first introduced into. Watching the space inserted into the path of books near the entrance of the room, I brought my eyes to the man beaming up at me from where he sat on the floor. I glanced down at the empty pillow positioned roughly half a foot away from his, connected to him only by his angled foot concealed by the browned, tattered leather of his shoes. I steadily sat myself down on the pillow, shakily brushing my feet against his and feeling the air in my chest warm and the skin on my face stiffen with a mask of prickles. My stiff penis pressed against the fabric of the lower garment I wore, grating against it as I sat there and stared at the man's smile.

I had no idea what we were doing, or what was going to happen. I hadn't been in a room with so many books before, only ever seeing the occasional one the exploratory robot would guide us through once it printed five copies for us. My eyes fixated on the sun-lit surfaces of the books meeting with the tannish stains of the sheets, buffered by the man's body and continuing on the other side of it. I remembered those books we would read, where the exploratory robot used its gripping arms to place the books in our hands as we one by one approached the robot with mother guiding us through the text. The dark leather backs were filled with pages that turned at the brush of your fingertips and sliced at your skin as lines of text slid beneath your bent grip. The words entered your head and conjured various images, while still remaining printed on the book's pages. It was strange.

"Hi, Jacey-one."

The sound of those words filling my ears didn't phase me at first, instead entering and relinquishing a frenzy of memories of mother greeting me. I stared at the darker edges of the tannish stains intersecting at the tattered edge of clothing encasing the man's biceps, thinking over the words I heard. The voice was deep, and sounded nothing like my mother's voice. Rather, it sounded like the voice of the man who sat with his legs crossed parallel to me, watching me closely.

Averting my gaze from the tannish stain pushing and pulling in the steadily adrift spring draft, I stared at him, positioned in the center of an even larger stain stretching around his sides. The sunlight beat down on the sheets and produced a golden hue eclipsing his dirty body, illuminating the brown stains unwinding on the sheet behind him like the wings of a bird preparing for flight.

His mouth hung open like he had just said something, held rigidly agape as his eyes moved over me. I briefly looked away, beginning to form my mouth into an o-shape as if to say something, finding nothing but the stifled intent to speak, burdening the edge of my mouth in unintelligible noises and panted breaths. Returning my gaze to him, I managed to barely let out an aloof "Uh-", repeating the short term for several moments. The moment words connected into sentences inside of my head, they were lost at the abrupt shift of my face into a contorted grimace, furrowing my brow and remembering all of the unrecognizable words spoken by the man to others. *How does he know how to speak my language? How does he know my name?*

"I can speak your language." He continued, placing his hand to his chest and tapping it against it. "I can talk to you. I lived with you before."

The words landed in me like the massive hospital building collapsing to the ground, falling into my ears and registering as a string of words suspended in isolation. I was panting now, moving my eyes rapidly between the man's arm and the stained sheet walls, struggling to process what I was hearing now. Looking back up at the man juxtaposed against that long stain, I recalled the memory of that little boy laying in that pile of blood on that bedroom floor, seemingly dying and eventually dead. Dead because I killed him, which I was reprimanded for by the exploratory robot. Now, widening my eyes and feeling my face grow hot with a prickly feeling, I realized the man before me was in fact that little boy. The little boy survived death, and now sat before me, alive and all grown up. It was a surreal experience basking in his presence, and realizing his life beyond that one distant memory. The feelings of distress that normally accompanied my recall of that memory became blurred into a frenzy of conflicting feelings. I felt my heart racing, like I would if I was alone and distressed in my bedroom growing up. I also felt warm and comforted, like when I thought of my mother while smelling the blanket I wrapped myself in at night. I felt all of these feelings envelope my body in a polarizing crash of symptoms, leaving me only certain that the man before me was the boy I killed, and the person that survived it.

"You-" I paused, leaning on my arm now and looking away before looking back up at him. "You're the boy. Are you? Are you the boy? Oh-"

"Yes. I am." His hand was now placed on mine, summoning my averted gaze to the veiny surface of his gripped hand. "I know what you're thinking. You probably thought I died, a very long time ago. You probably thought the robot killed me. Well, it didn't. Rather, I was given up, and eventually taken in by this group."

I ran my eyes frantically over the fuzzy, stripped edges of a tattered hole torn into his shirt near his shoulder, trying to process everything I had just heard. I sighed, feeling my head suddenly begin to pain and the skin around it grow heated. Caressing my temples, I closed my eyes briefly, before returning my gaze to him away from his eyes, too nervous to stare directly at him.

"What - I don't understand. You're - you're that boy? The exploratory robot killed you? I didn't kill you? But, I thought I did. I thought I killed you."

"We were both so young and it happened so quickly. The robot had knocked me over hard enough to where I struck my head on the floor, which was made of a really hard material, and so I bled. It stitched the cut closed, but for some reason the robot then picked me up by its arms and left me outside. I wandered for a bit before being taken in by this group. That's my only memory of that place."

"So I must've not killed my mother then." I remarked quietly, almost saying it to myself in a hushed voice as I remained entranced with the soft edge of the room's floor.

"Wait, what do you mean? Of course you didn't. She was just as much a part of the robot. The only way you could have killed her was by destroying the robot itself since she was related to it, like what we did. We destroyed the robot."

"You killed my mother?" I said sternly, almost disrupting the last breath made by the man. I felt my heart racing and my head suddenly lift up, almost automatically pulling myself to the floor as I scooted abruptly.

"I mean-" He paused, looking at a point in the sheet walls overhead before continuing. "I suppose we did kill her. I don't think it's like me killing you, or myself, or someone else like us. I'm not sure. I've scavenged some books that might help me know."

The man leaned back atop his pillow, pulling his legs closer to his chest as he twisted to the side and began to run his fingers along the spines of multiple books, the bend of his head angled in the direction of his pointer finger. Continuing to stare away from the man, I felt my hands grip tighter into a fist, redding my knuckles and planting into the flesh of my palm the sharp edges of my dirty fingernails. I was beginning to shake, starting out as a light tapping of my feet in the tattered brown leather shoes I wore and worsening into a tremble that shook my whole body in place. That same fluid began to fill my eyes and collect in crystalized bits at the edges of my eyelashes, dripping down my face and electrifying the hellish surface of my face. My shaken breaths morphed into scattered gasps, starting out in my tightened chest and choked out.

As the man twisted back to face me and quickly leaned toward me with his hand placed against my trembling cheek, I stared at the torn edges of his shirt's collar. It hung with the bend of his body and revealed his hairy torso concealed beneath the shadow of his shirt. He spoke to me softly, viewing me with widened eyes and brushing his voice warmly against my face in tender breaths. I could see my mother's face on that screen she had been projected on for so many years. Her voice I could hear chirped from that screen and register warmly within my body, only to be corrupted by the fact that she spoke in the same voice with the same exact words to everyone else she encountered. I could see my mother pressed against my lips with her head of messily placed strands of hair winding towards my head and brushing against my eyes. Most of all, I could see what my mother was finally. She wasn't real. She never was,

"SHE'S NOT MY MOTHER! SHE'S NOT MY MOTHER! NONE OF THEM ARE!"

All-of-a-sudden, my tightly gripped knuckles were brought to my head, almost pounded against my skull. I knew only of their rough placement against my head because of the pain that penetrated through my skull and rounded my forehead into the pained clench I held my face in. I bit down both of my jaws, biting into nothing but the ring of saliva laminating the two rows of teeth. Feeling the man's hand holding the side of my head in his relaxed grip, I threw my body back to the ground, tearing my fists from my head and placating them viciously at my sides. I stared at the ceiling moving in the soft draft of air brushing it into little rolls moving across the tannish stains of the sheet. The ceiling was blurred and obstructed into dozens of sparkling lights, casting the dirtied sheet behind a liquified shell. My legs were now bent awkwardly to the side, pushing into the man's bent knees and twisting past his side. I was now laying with my back angled to the floor, twisting at my hips and planting my shoulders achingly into the floor.

Panting, I watched that man begin to rise from the blurrily crystalized bounds of my periphery, conjuring the only slightly clearer version of his presence hovering over my body and juxtaposed against one of the tannish stains stretching unevenly across the ceiling. He stared at me, saying nothing before beginning to speak again to me.

"Are you okay?" He asked me, now hovering over me with his body perched on his left arm fisted into the floor by my side.

I stared at him for a moment, continuing to pant before providing a breathless "No" as a response. Shifting in his seat awkwardly hanging off the soft edge of the pillow he had sat on, he pulled his arm into his shirt, gripping the edge of the sleeve and leaning over my body, pulling himself to his knees. He wiped my eyes, elbowing me slightly in the stomach as he did so in the shirt that clung almost too tightly to his body.

"Jacey-one-" He began, leaning back to sit up and poking his arm back through the sleeve. "Of course you don't have a mother. I don't even have one. Any actual mother we had probably died a very, very long time ago, before you and I were even born."

"What do you mean?" I replied, furrowing my brow and watching him closely.

He sighed, itching the bridge of his nose loosely connecting his eyebrows in thick, meandering hairs before gripping his hand over his hairy jawline, speaking slowly.

"I - I'm not sure I can explain this in a way you might understand. Well-" Pausing, the man sighed again, before continuing. "Based on some work I've done, I've found that some time ago - I think around three hundred years ago - humans, like you and I, all died, and left behind these robots, much like the robot that raised you and kind of me. They were designed to raise humans using the fertilized eggs of mothers and fathers from that time period. Those mothers and fathers are dead now, but their fertilized eggs - the babies they were going to produce, are alive now. All of the robots have raised them throughout the world."

"Wha-" I began to ask, my voice trailing off as I grew lost in my struggle to understand what I was being told. "What? I don't understand what you're saying. I don't get it."

I tried to make sense of what the man was saying, squinting my eyes and angling my eyebrows in a firm slant, only feeling my head growing hot and the same man before me remaining all I could see. I struggled to picture what the man was telling me, only seeing the same images of my mother projected on that screen connected to the exploratory robot. *Fathers?* I thought to myself. *Fertilized eggs? My real mother's dead?*

"I don't think you'd be able to understand it. It was hard for me to grasp it."

"So I don't have a mother?"

"You did, long ago. So did I, but they're both dead now."

"Well how do you know? How do you know they can't be brought back to life? Can't they escape death?"

"What?" He replied, taken aback as he tensely produced a single laugh. "Of course they can't escape death. Nobody can. There comes a point when everyone dies, and your mother died. So did mine, and you and I will one day die. There's no way to escape that fact."

My eyes moved away slightly, fixating on the jagged edges of a tannish stain seeped into the sheet walls. I remembered what I used to think about death, with it being something that you could escape. I thought that's what happened to me when the robot terminated me but I was still alive.

"So, you can't escape death." I began, "Which means I didn't escape death… whiiich means I never died. But that robot-"

"It didn't die, because it was not alive." He interjected, his eyes remaining on the averted drift of my gaze.

"Oh, okay. Okay." I said, looking away with my slanted brow bone bending over my right eye and tightening it into a squint.

I tried to think over what the man had been telling me, finding the new information entering into my mind and leaving my body in focused breaths and a burn that slowly heated the sides of my pained scalp. All I could view was the man sitting before me and staring down at me, with loose traces of unrelated memories and scenarios permeating through the ambiguous breaches of my deep entrancement. Drool filled the edge of my lips and poured over the chapped edges of it in a long, thick droplet, trailing my chin in a warm stream and tickling the windswept edges of my hairy legs in a chilled jab. I couldn't think of anything regarding what he was saying.

So, I looked back up at the man, wiping my mouth on my arm and swallowing the drool, drying my bent wrist on the rough layers of fuzz wrapping around my side. He watched me cautiously, bending his head forward slightly and pursing his lips as if to say something. Nothing came out but a weak grunt produced as a strained hum.

"Well, I think that's all I can really tell you right now. I'm really not sure if you'd be able to understand anything else I'd tell you."

I nodded slowly, following the slow movements of his eyes grazing over the sheet-floor as he stroked his chin. My blank stare and thoughtless mind only validated the claims of his response.

"Maybe I can show you something to help you understand better. Maybe later today in the building rubble near the camp."

I glanced mindlessly between the edges of his body, recognizing the words he was speaking and finally understanding what he was trying to say. I thought of the piles of rubble that stretched across the miles of dirt and asphalt covering the dead earth, starting at the dirt ground in loose fragments of concrete and metal and rising from the ground as a boundless configuration of nothing. Squinting my eyes and moving my head side to side as if a heavy breeze carried it lightly in its windswept pushes and pulls, I thought of the times I would head back to the building I grew up in after skipping the fitness enrichment activity. How I would ponder about the insides of those building remains, the jagged, fragmented layers of those environments that faded into the polluted horizon into erratically pronged edges and lured me to its mysterious insides. I thought of that, and my passive desire to hide within that rubble, despite me never pursuing the piled remains.

I looked into the man's peering eyes, beginning to nod my head slowly and panting heavily, morphing my staggered breaths into a breathless "Yes please."

"Okay," he replied shortly, tucking his lips into his mouth and grinning awkwardly at me.

Our time in the room was spent in not much conversation, instead stifled with the tense exchange of our breaths as I looked around the room. Pivoting my body with the border of books stacked along the softly ruffled insides of the sheet walls, I examined the words found on the books' surfaces. Some text placed near discolored images or found juxtaposed entirely against a solid, faded color. Some engraved into a leatherbound book shredded sporadically at its firm edges, while others printed into the shiny, wrinkled surfaces of the books, sunlight traveling bumpily across it like the dried cracks found in the dirt bed of that once-waterless creek. My eyes stopped on one, featuring light, blue letters that flowed over the rough lumps found in the thin, wrinkled cover. The text read, "HISTORICAL OVERVIEW OF CATHOLICISM," read awkwardly in my brain and hanging on my tongue without much accuracy in my aloof pronunciation.

As I looked away from the book, the faded blue text bopped around in my vision, propagating the tattered edges of the man's shirt in the hazed bounce of the words. I had no idea what the words meant, and what meaning arose from the words connected in big font on the cover of that book. It only remained a dimmed yellow haze in my vision, providing a blurred signal of what might be a book read by the man sitting before me. I had no idea what it was about, and could only speculate within the pained bounds of my aching head and burnt skull.

Later, we departed the tent, leaving in the same fashion of pulled sheets, steadily ducking our heads. The man and I walked across the same dirt path littered with sparse rocks and twigs, shuffling in the dirt past the same watchful eyes and timid bodies we remained subjected to in our traverse through the encampment. I looked back at them as rocks skidded randomly across the dirt path, sliding additional rocks along the path in a patterned glide of stone.

"Why are they staring at me?" I asked the man, almost without thought.

I watched some of them on my right side as we stepped down the dirt path, turning towards him walking with me on my left side and watching his head turn in the direction of the onlookers.

"We've never saved someone we were supposed to eat. Usually, when we go out and hunt, we eat every human we target. You, however, won't ever be eaten. We saved you, and want to make you a part of our culture. So, everyone is staring at you because they're curious about you. We've never seen anything like this before."

We continued walking and began to turn a corner marked by the discontinuing of the line of trees connecting the countless overlapping sheets hanging in the collection of dead trees. I heard everything he said, but processed it with a furrowed brow and agape lip, staring away from the humans beginning to emerge from their tents on the side of the man at the sounds of our voices. I couldn't quite process what he was saying, only understanding that I wasn't eaten like other humans were. In an extended effort to process his words I silently repeated his words in my mind. The man made it sound as though the group typically hunts humans. What other humans were there besides the human life forms I grew up with?

I looked around blankly, continuing to walk forward slowly with the man stepping at my side. Looking up at the rows of sheets strung from tree to tree and caving inward and out in the soft breeze that also stroked my skin, I realized something. The humans I met here were the first I had ever met besides the human life forms I grew up with. Noticing the shadows of humans planted shakily into those windswept walls and the unintelligible murmurs cloaked behind them, I realized that these were humans just like the human life forms I had grown up with. Perhaps, just like me.

Realizing this was more than just being aware of it; I could feel it in my body that there were more humans than I was ever previously aware of. It felt like the sensation of water filling your gut and pleasantly caressing the nerves of your body, stretching to every heated nook of your dehydrated stature. My entire life I assumed the other human life forms and I were the only humans alive on this planet; that's what mother had always told us. Now, looking around and realizing the loud, rough voice of a man approaching the man and I, I realized that wasn't true. Strangely, realizing this fact didn't even feel real enough to be realized.

We stopped, turning to the other man approaching us alongside others, forming a group of five. They all carried something in their hands, whether it be rusted tools like hammers and saws, or heavy bundles of ropes or nets carried in their arms folded over their chest and just barely managing to contain the bulk of loose, tangled edges hanging over their forearms.

The man spoke in a different language as he turned to the group, who stared at him and only barely allowed their eyes to slip from their tamed gaze surrendered to the man's beaming, muscular presence. I stared up at him, watching his jaw move up and down and his tongue flick in his mouth as he spoke incomprehensible words to the men. They nodded at him, the strands of hair curling from their head and glistening in the dull, polluted sunlight moving latently with their head.

They spoke for a few moments, with individual men chiming in with random, grunted vocalizations and fostering a cacophony of raspy grunts arising from their uneven heights. I could barely distinguish between any of them, finding my eyes drifting among the men and discovering the same shallow vocals attached to each rugged man's body.

The man then turned around and started walking again, gesturing for me to follow as he curved his arm over the soft spring draft and gently breathed "Come on." I started walking with him, glancing shortly at the men behind me who crowded behind us in a jaggedly trotting group before returning my gaze to the dry, dirt path before us. They didn't glance at me, instead staring ahead of them at the back of the man's head covered in tangled locks of hair and a net of sun-bathed particles of dust, holding the materials in their hands.

It was my first time migrating near the place I had grown up in in days. The sight of the polluted skies melting into the ground in browned haze was familiar to me, broken up by the same sights of dead trees and chunkily barbed edges of destroyed buildings littering the distance. I noticed the slight indents found in the blanket of loose dust floating along the dried surface of dirt, rock, and disconnected islands of asphalt found beneath our feet, along with countless patterned footsteps imprinted into the ground. I managed to figure out the origins of the tracks, connecting it to the hospital bed I was strapped into and transported upon by several of the humans, the wheels leaving behind uneven tracks only obstructed by minute rocks and twigs.

Stopping in my tracks, I rotated my head with the path of bumpily curved lines and placed steps etched into the ground's dirt, twisting through the group of men behind me and trailing off into the horizon behind a cloud of yellow fog. The men bumped into me, glancing down at me before crowding around me and relegating me to the back of the migrating group, molding their traverse around my still body. Noticing the tracks from when I had been transported atop that hospital bed, I felt strange watching the tracks drift into the clouded haze indicating the location of the massive body of water, only represented by the little branches winding towards the skies in twisted jabs. I could feel the burns left behind the blistering grip of the straps that went over the sides of my body, tingling in the cool breeze and distracting me from the acidic burn that washed over the rest of my body.

It was strange being at this standstill between those two points in the distance; the decimated remains of building after building bumpily blanketing the area surrounding the creek, and the sheet-made encampment lining the massive body of water. I don't know what this feeling is, becoming subdued in its isolated feeling as I panted softly and watched the small troves of dirt bordering on those engraved footprints in the ground. The grains of dirt lined the footprints in soft hills and bristled slightly in the flowing air, picking off individual specks of dirt that floated to the surrounding ground broken up into a sea of loose asphalt and dirt. I saw two ends of my life represented by these two opposing sides of land, inferring the past and future relegated to these two parallel horizons of haze and polluted sunlight. I was awestruck by this feeling and the sights that sank into the blurred corners of my periphery, only emerging in my head as diluted memories of them.

"Hey, Jacey-one," I heard the man suddenly call out, prying me out of the entrancement I held with the footprint sinking into the ground.

I opened my mouth to say something but could only bring myself to issue a mere "Oh" with my blankly agape lips. The men behind him stopped for us, watching the man and I closely.

"We're almost there. I was hoping to show you the insides of the rubble of this old building. I believe it was a hospital at one point."

I stared blankly at him with my eyes widened and stomaching his sudden presence, averting my gaze from him and looking past his arm wrapped in tattered brown fabric at the vast pile of concrete and metal erected from the distance. I stared breathlessly at the sight illusively fermented in the sun beaming through the polluted clouds and meeting its jagged edges. Almost automatically I began to step with the man as he pivoted in the direction of the men facing us with their tools messily lumped in their arms and hanging over the hairy flesh of their limbs. The man gave a short nod, giving a silent command to the group of men who now turned and began to lead us to the pile of rubble.

I almost slid my feet lazily against the ground in a grainy shuffle against the dirt- and rock-ground, lost in the sight of broken apart concrete that reached up to the sky and almost crowned itself in the haze reigning above. The minute hills of dirt and rock emerging from the borders of the men's footprints ruptured with the nonchalant slide of my feet concealed by the loose, leathery brown material of my shoes.

As we got closer I surprisingly felt colder, as the polluted morning sun became swallowed by the towering presence of concrete emerging before me. We stopped at the foot of the sight, where a sea of cracked asphalt and dead plants dried into the Earth and laid a sprinkled path of broken glass for us to walk upon in cautious crunches.

I carefully placed one foot down on the field of broken glass and jaggedly dissected sections of asphalt, moving my eyes over the massive structure of rubble and watching the rest of the group gather at the edge of my periphery. The area wreaked a wet fragrance, like the rain water that soaked the muddy banks of Earth along that creek and produced a salty smell. I had never stepped so close to this destroyed building, recalling the massive cloud of concrete dust that had swarmed the area beyond its scattered edges and locked me in my room, relegating all contact with the outside world to my ears and the billows of air trouncing over the area.

Looking closely at the building's side facing all of us, I could make out the edges of some walls not completely destroyed, instead slanted towards the skies and breaking off at its outer edges into loose, bent metal rods and sharp glass. There seemed to be windows not completely broken and fallen into thousands of miniscule glass shards, instead planted into the walls that remained standing and revealing the grayed, rusted insides of the decimated remains.

"Jacey-one, come on." The man called, bringing my eyes to his body now angled towards me ten feet away.

I glanced back at the building's remains, walking with the man and meeting the group of men who began to place their items on the ground and gesture at each other amidst unintelligible discussion. The man standing next to me quickly inserted himself into their conversation, blending his deep voice into the frantic cacophony of grunted words. One of the men began to hand the man standing next to me a bundle of rope, holding it in his hands and allowing the loose, ratted ends of the tannish cord to dangle near his exposed knees. The man nodded at him as he grabbed the rope from the other man just opposite of him in between the several other men carrying tools, proceeding to quickly drop himself to one of his knees with the other bent near his left bicep. Another one of the men placed the pile of net on the ground between one of the men's feet and the kneeling man's hands quickly handling the rope bundled beneath his bent leg whilst caressing his folded knee planted into the dusty ground. He gripped the weblike network of thick, black threads intersecting every few inches for roughly ten feet of space, beginning to tie the rope into the edge of the net, over and under the intersecting threads. By the time he twisted the rope back over to his gripping left hand where the beginning of the line of rope was found, he tied the rope together, twisting it multiple times over it until it formed multiple overlapping loops, and eventually, a tightly bound knot.

Speaking to the men who gathered at the edge of the laid-out net, he stood up from the ground with his collar gripping his neck and the bust of his tattered shirt clinging to the firm outline of his muscular chest, folding over the edges and leaving a pocket of space revealing his hairy torso. Heaving, he placed one foot forward and the other back, flexing his thick legs as the men all stood atop the net, pulling the rope back as hard as he could and allowing his biceps to flex into a veiny, hardened shell of flesh. The rope was tightly bound to the net, as evidenced by the lack of puncture sustained to the strained rope and tilted net.

I could feel my penis hardening beneath my clothing, poking against the rough insides of the fabric like a pointer finger curiously scraping at the surface of a hardened stain on a table. My irises plopped to the bottom of my eyelids and inhaled the sight of his heaving body, watching him through strained eyes as he tossed the firm rope to the ground, speaking to the other men. As he finished speaking to them, he turned to me, quickly brushing his veiny fingers bent around his lightly pinched pointer finger and pulling his shirt down.

"You ready?" He asked, panting and flashing the firm outline of the staggered push and pull of his chest.

I almost didn't respond at first, instead allowing drool to collect at my lips and soak my chin in a salty film. My response became the soft sound of drool falling off of my chin and crashing into the dry ground, dripping quietly. *Drip! Drip!* Eventually, feeling everyone's eyes fall onto my still body, I mindlessly nodded at the man, who watched me carefully.

The men draped the net over the erratically placed steps unofficial to the rubble beginning at the ground in uneven slants, bunching the rope on the ground between their moving feet. I followed closely behind the man, who hid most of the placed net behind the muscular shape of his back's upward stretch. He spoke to the others in quick slurs, grabbing the patchwork border of the net and beginning to lean against the rough frontside of a large slab of dusty concrete, dug into it with random cuts and scrapes. I stepped closer to him, watching the men nervously as they grunted and spoke unintelligibly to each other. The man began to lift his body up onto the slab, pivoting on his bottom and folding his legs to his chest, standing up as he gripped another concrete slab slanted in a different direction nearby. Sighing, he turned to me, pausing for a moment before holding his hand out to me.

The thick, dark hairs on his arm brushed in different angles, sprouting from his arm in thick, bristled clumps. It produced a rough spiral design around his arm in a hairy cast, almost like the minor, metallic indents found wrapping around the exploratory robot's arm in a thread-like spin. I watched his outstretched hand hanging stiffly from his arm, looking back up at his beaming eyes before grabbing hold of his hand. He gripped the right side of my back with my shoulder blade tucked firmly into his grip, pressing my held hand into the muscular slope of his chest and pulling me against his body, positioning me next to him. I slipped slightly back along the slant of the large block of concrete I stood upon, before steadying myself in the man's slightly loosened grip.

"Alright Jacey-one, we're going to climb up these rough blocks of rubble, and hopefully we'll find a room still intact from the original hospital. I see some windows still remaining up high."

He gripped the net in his hand, nodding to the men collecting a few feet away from us, a few of them gripping the messily bunched rope in their hands and studying themselves with their feet placed apart. Turning to me, he smiled briefly, before pivoting atop the chunk of concrete and sliding his feet with a soft crunch sounding with the turn of his body. He examined the bumpy stretch of the building rising towards the sky and hiding beneath the beams of sunlight in a cold, dark shadow, cloaking us in the same dim shade. Then, he started to climb up the steps provided by the erratically overlaid concrete slabs found in the rubble, positioning himself on the slab standing a few feet from our own feet. Turning on his knees and pushing himself into a stand with his hands, he reached out his hand for me to grab. Looking around awkwardly, I placed my hand into his and grabbed it tightly.

"Just climb up onto the slab I'm standing on - that's it. And we'll be doing this for the rest of the way."

I kneeled onto the cold, rough surface of the slab, feeling it wither against my hairy calves and twist the softly curled strands along its scraped edges. Standing up with both of my hands either placed within or over the man's grip, I stood next to him on the slab, hearing the crunch of loose pieces of concrete slide beneath the tattered underside of my shoes. I peered over the massive pile of rubble erected above the ground and surrendered dimly beneath the polluted skies, before traveling up another slab with the man, and another. The process would be repeated for every slab we encountered, moving over it with scraped legs and gripped hands painted in the pale, white dust blanketing the slabs. Our bumpy ascent up the pile of building rubble was occasionally broken up by the irregular placement of each subsequent slab, or large segments of metal pipes winding from inside the rubble towards our bodies. We moved around them, being careful not to slip against the intermittent slopes of concrete dust and small chunks we moved in cautious shuffles along the way. At one point, the tip of my foot brushed against a larger chunk of concrete, sending it down the turbulent slope of concrete sinking a hundred feet beneath our stiffly planted feet.

Looking down behind me, I watched it bump along the chunks of concrete placed over each other in jaggedly cut pieces, skipping over several at a time and trailing along the length of the stretched rope connecting to the man's held net. *Crick! Crack!* The distance almost swayed beneath the bend of my head and watch of my widened eyes, shrinking to the small, shadowy profiles of the men standing at the base of the rubble. I felt almost pulled by the unnerving tide of the pooling haze obscuring the Earth far beneath my feet, to which the man grabbed hold of me and consoled me.

He gripped my right forearm tightly in the awkward placement of his grip, wrapping his other arm around my back and tucking my face roughly over his shoulder. I looked timidly with wide eyes over him, relegating the visible portion of his muscular back to a patch of blur as I watched over the folds of concrete rubble we stood near. Pulling me away, he gripped my shoulder firmly, bending his head down a little in a half-bow and pushing his eyebrows upwards and wrinkling the skin covering his forehead.

"You alright?" He asked, only barely receiving a soundless nod as I stared behind him in shock.

We were nearly at the top of the pile of rubble, standing at the crumbled borders of a large opening found in the rubble. It crunched at our shuffling feet in soft churns, and stretched beyond us into an almost perfectly intact room found beneath the stacks of rubble. A pane of glass bent over a slab of concrete and rusted paint that broke off inside of the room into shredded layers. Several other pieces of concrete pressed into the glass, folding the pane neatly over its pressing corners along a web of lopsided diamond shaped cuts waiting to crumble into countless shards. My reflection could be seen in it, but only through my blurred vision. For, just beyond the room before us and fading beneath a sea of dull haze was the creek, stabbing through the Earth in a thick, murky line. A sea of concrete rippled in rough, jagged waves towards the creek's bank, carrying a tide of rolling folds of concrete, metallic rods, and various broken windows that shined and glistened in the polluted sunlight laying bare the dirtied Earth.

The man held my right forearm in his grip, allowing me to steady myself on the concrete slab just a foot above our feet aching in the loosening threads of our tattered leather shoes. I peered deeper into the room, noticing the outline of a paint-chipped door twenty feet away from the room's entry and blocked at its midpoint by a tannish metal shaft that sank beneath the room's ruptured floorboards, lined by a crumbled current of concrete and stripped wood.

"I have to check if the floor is sturdy enough to hold our weight." He stated, brushing against my right bicep with his fingers brought into a swift fan.

"Stay right there, and hold on to this net to keep yourself sturdy."

He placed the net in my hands, looping its weblike border around my fingers as I just barely latched my hands onto it, staring in awe at the insides of the room. The man kneeled over the edge of the opening, bending his right knee upward and burying the other in a patch of pale-gray concrete dust surrounding the opening. The loose pebbles and troves of dust crunched beneath his shifting feet, blanketing the tattered backside of his lower garments of clothing in a stamp of white that formed a plump shape around his muscular buttocks. He stretched his left bicep over the patch of concrete dust and placed the rough fold of the concrete slab beneath it in his massive grip, painting the strands of hair wrapping around his arm in silver specks. Steadily positioning himself, he kicked down on the floor beneath him, slamming his feet down onto it with several loud *thumps!* and allowing a thin white cloud to arise from the depths of the room. He loosened his grip on the edge of the concrete opening, pushing himself slightly deeper into the room and tapping his foot onto the floor closer to the door.

The man then returned his gaze back towards me, smiling shortly before reaching to me with his hands beginning to take the net away from me in the pull of his grip. I released it, and watched as he allowed the net to sink by his feet with the rope following its gripped path. He turned to me, reaching both of his hands out to me with only the portion of his body visible being exposed at his chest near the hill of concrete dust. His face beamed up at me, hovering beneath my bowed head and nestled just above the border of ruins tainting his body and clothes in white dust.

I kneeled before him, surrendering to his grip as I shuffled with my folded legs in the concrete dust and felt it dirtily embrace me in a cold touch. He wrapped his arms around my back and pulled me with him, shoving my face in his as he nearly tripped back into the room behind him. My legs fell against the bend of his, then pushing off of his with the jab of my knees and standing up before him. Standing up as he released me, I brushed the concrete dust with my hand that circled in the air and assaulted my eyes in a wave of hazed, dimly lit blur, just before it settled and left behind speckled traces.

Looking around, I was able to adjust to the dim presence of the room unseen when cloaked by the reigning sun and its polluted rays, discovering that the room stretched even deeper than I initially imagined. Looking past the man as he began to flatten his net over a patch of space beneath his folded knees, I peered into the rest of the room, finding an additional fifty feet or so of space covered in fallen metal shafts dissecting the scattered floor, glass beds that broke in half beneath them, and tons of intersecting sections of concrete. There was surprisingly a lot of space hanging over our heads, with the ceiling collecting over our heads roughly four feet above us in sagging segments of metal pipes and wires seeping out of the torn ceiling. Some pieces of the ceiling were closer to our heads, whether they be rusted metal pipes bent over the jagged folds of sagging plywood or glass tubes that collected in rectangular crates and remained loosely connected above by tangled, discolored wires.

I began to step around the man, who now stood up and began to rotate his head with the perimeter of the room, sighing. The floor crunched under my feet, kicking up minute pieces of glass and dust that slid beneath the step of my feet. The man's eyes followed my body, his two dark eyes pouring through his hairy face and eventually fading into the blur of my periphery, surrendering to my backside. The slow crunch of thin clumps of concrete and sparing glass shards turned into a cacophony of steps against the floor as the man began to step with me into the room, beginning to examine the wires hanging from the ceiling in tangled clumps of white and gray cords. I looked around the room as I stepped deeper into the room away from the opening, soon bringing my eyes to a small glass bed that clashed with a large metal shaft laid diagonally from the ceiling. The only light found in the room tapered off into dull rays that barely touched the ends of the room beyond the entryway, illuminating the door opposite of the hole left by the dissecting segments of concrete.

I don't know what entranced me about the bed, with the end of its dirtied mattress lifting past the glass edges of the bed and crushed beneath the metal shaft lifting the whole bed upward. Something about it looked familiar to me, like it was a bed I had seen before. I stopped by its side, slowly placing the tainted fronts of my legs at its side until it brushed coldly at my legs and tingled the hairs along it. A slight rattling noise could be heard from near the bed, as I noticed a dirty-white blanket grouped into a soft clump of shadowy folds. A soft shuffle rolled beneath the blanket, stopping the moment the rest of the bed stopped moving with the brush of my legs.

I could hear the man in the background begin to collect items in his hands and place them somewhere behind me, moving them in his grip with light *clitter's* and *clatter's* following the passing of his hands. The noises just barely registered with me beyond mere recognition, the automatic shift of my head towards the sound sidestepped by my preoccupation with the blanket. I knew there was something that looked familiar about this bed, something that made me recognize it as something I had seen before. I looked at the cracks that cut into the sharp, jagged edges of the glass border meeting with the fallen metal shaft. The dirtied mattress that lifted towards the disfigured ceiling and sank beneath the pressure of the metal shaft, leaving behind an elevated trail of brown stains and a film of dust. The blanket was soft and turned over and over again into untouched ruffles caked in a dusty shell. It looked so familiar, and felt so familiar as I unconsciously reached my trembling hand out to it, feeling a warm feeling caress the nervous ping of my heart and the gentle rumble of my breathing chest.

The feel of my hand sinking into that soft lump of fabric, coating my fingertips in a thick layer of dust and brushing against two firm holes. The feel of both of my hands pouncing onto the pile of blanket and burying it in my grip, ripping it from its dirtied place at the end of the pressed-down mattress and shoving it against my nose. It was all culminating in the foul stench of the blanket paralyzing my nose in a dry, tangy scent and caking the skin of my face in a mask of dust. Just beneath my twitched eyes lay what seemed to be a collection of human bones, grouped together beneath the original place of the blanket and scattered with light rattles.

My mother had taught us about human bones once. They all connected to each other to form our skeletal system, clinging to our flesh and hardening our skin in thick, firm coatings. The bones were small, roughly the same size as the baby that I had been replaced with, and who's leg the man in the large, shiny cloak had fed me. I stared at the bones collecting dully in a rustic-brown pile, holes and grooves caving all along its rough surface. The skull had a large backside, curving around it and brushing against a cage of bones stacked along each other. The cage represented a single row, with the rest of it broken off and brought to a brittled crush beneath the metal shaft.

I felt the blanket slip from my grip as my hands dangled at my sides, planting the dusty pile of soft lumps against the tattered rounds of my leather shoes. I stared breathlessly at the skull, isolating every other pale gray or white object surrounding it and hearing only my breaths paralyze the air in the room. I stared into the holes found beneath the miniature brow bone of the skull, staring at the sea of black flooding the hollowed out insides of the skull behind it and feeling the skin around my eye sockets tickle. I blinked with a sputtered twitch of my right eye, beginning to reach my hand out to the skull and feeling the dusty air filling the room tickling the upright hairs found along my arm. I furrowed my brow and pulled it back into a relaxed state, pushing and pulling it back and forth as those same droplets began to blur my eyelids and clump at my eyelashes in sparkling flashes. Sticking the tip of my pointer finger into the baby skull's skeletal eye socket and rubbing it on its rigid edge, I coated my finger in the thick, pasty brown dust found along the brim. I ran my finger all along the circumference of the eye socket, feeling the droplets of fluid fill my eyes and flood my face in a chapped, heated feel. My finger began to tremble within the socket, bending the farthest knuckle up and down, right against the bottom half of the socket. I continue to furiously release the fluid from my eyes, blockading the skull behind a wall of liquified blur.

It continued to twitch within the empty eye socket, pinching back against the bottom edge of the lid towards my finger. Eventually, the tremble of my hand produced a hole in the eye socket along the browned rim of the eyelid, tearing a slight chip into it with a plastic *crack!* sounding with the fold of my pressing finger. I pulled my finger back and brushed it against the sharp points marking the split in the skull's eyelid, pressing it harder against the edge of my fingertip until a blister formed on the outer crease beneath my dirtied fingernail. Holding the crooked bend of my fingertip, I flashed my wrist towards the ceiling, my forearm painted in the white concrete dust and my pointer fingertip trailed in the brown dust left from the skull. The tip of my finger was redded, with blood grasping at the surface of the skin and warming the scratched inside of the knuckle.

The chipped skull sat before me in browned, disfigured blur and burrowed below my pointer finger, as I realized that it was in fact a baby skull before me. Much like the baby I had been replaced with, and ultimately fed.

"You know, I believe you were born here. Some time before it collapsed, obviously. I must've been born here, too. It's a sort of informal guess on my part, but if this was a hospital, it must've had enough shelter at the time for the exploratory robot. Can't imagine how it'd get up this high, though, given its structure."

I paused, shifting my eyes against the right sides of my sockets and turning slowly to the man, who had collected several baby skeletal remains and carried them in a browned, erratically shaped pile in his arms. He stopped by the net, folding his legs into a kneel and carefully placing each bone over the weblike network of thick threads.

"What do you mean?"

"It'd probably be difficult for you to understand. I just think this is where you were born, and raised as a baby, at least."

"Raised as - as a baby?" I asked, my body positioned at the awkward standstill of an uncommitted pivot shared between the space of damaged beds and the man.

"You were raised as a baby here. You were a baby at one point. Everyone is. In fact, my partner is pregnant right now. She'll be giving birth any day now."

I stared blankly at the man who crouched below me, fastening the hold of his shirt's sleeves against the firmed flex of his outstretched arms moving over the piled skeletal remains as he quietly assembled them into a neat group. *Partner? She's pregnant? What does this mean?*

My head grew wrapped in a hot feel, seemingly producing a heated glow that hovered close to my head. I felt a drool pool from my lips and line my chin in a warm streak, dropping onto the floor a few inches from the frontside of my tattered shoes and the edge of the net. He ceased to move his hands over the bones he sorted, staring ahead of him before glancing up at my blank stare and loosely hung jawline, standing up quickly.

"Oh, don't worry." He began slowly, placing his left hand against my neck and gripping the stiff tilt of my head in it. "She doesn't have to know about us. About what you and I do. Why we do it. Or where"

His voice was shallow and caressed my face in deep trickles of air, hanging in my ears and floating latently in my head. He began to pry his fingers between the torn elastic band tightened against my waistline, stretching against his pointer finger and following with the rest of his right hand, grazing against my hardened penis and squeezing it gently in the grip of his hand. I gasped, feeling my eyes roll back towards my forehead and hiding them behind the slow close of my eyelids. I forgot everything he said, and everything we had been doing in this room. My attention was now focused on the grasp of his warm hand that wrapped around my penis and the shield of ticklish pings that ambiguously separated them. I could feel my heart racing in my chest and speeding up my throat in sputtered trickles.

The soft, gentle brush of cool afternoon air caressed my buttocks and caused the minute strata of hair lining my legs in curled stretches to stand upright, as the man pulled my tattered shorts down my legs, dropping them at my feet in a lumped pile of fabric. He gripped the base of my penis in one hand, roughly wrapping his hand around the crimson shade of its flesh and placing his puckered lips over the exposed tip. The wetness of his saliva electrified the ticklish prickles digging into the flesh of my penis, lining the rest of it up until his loosened grip at its base as he shoved the entire penis in his mouth, stroking the moist back of his mouth and stretching his uvula with its devour.

I gasped, beginning to shudder in place like it was a cold environment exposed to the hostile jabs of a windswept winter night. My feet shuffled erratically in place like I was preparing to march forward along a familiar trek steeped with the smoothness of my step and etched with the confidence felt. I shuffled back without much control in where I moved myself, feeling my penis begin to slowly pump a thick substance into the man's mouth as he choked a little, slashing his tongue throughout the walls of his mouth in thick licks. Shuffling against the side of the partially destroyed baby bed, I felt my heart lurch into my throat as the bed shifted away from the scattered slide of my body, and fell over into dozens of minute glass shards. The man pulled with me and barely moved, just as the large metal shaft once jabbed into the bed slid into the side of his head with a loud *thud!* He bit into my penis slightly, before relaxing the grip of his jaw against my penis and eventually sliding all of the way off of my pelvic area and falling to the ground, accompanied by the traverse of the large metal shaft crashing into his head once more. The shaft now fell to the floor with another final *thud!*, crashing into another bed and breaking it into countless additional shards of glass, the sound of scattered bones rattling beneath it.

My penis was now softer than it had been and hung lightly at the bed of pubes it stretched from, dripping with a thick, discolored-white substance that sank along the tannish, chipped side of the shaft and falling onto the man's resting face. I stared down at him, panting as my heart began to slow to a soft buzz in my chest. He didn't move, his face now planted into the dusty floor in a motionless slant as the rest of his body folded over the strain of his bent knees. The thick white substance had collected in a glossy pool near the lazily hanging lips of the man. A gentle trickle of drool hung at the corner of the man's mouth, landing in a thick, muddy slur as it mixed with the concrete dust on the floor, colliding with the grayed edges of the substance that dripped from my penis onto the floor.

My eyes looked over him blankly for a moment, registering nothing about the sudden descent of his body to the floor. My legs shook timidly in place, preceding the tense jerk that brought my knees roughly to the floor, feeling the grains of concrete dust grate against my exposed knees. I began to crouch closer to the man, lowering my face as I bent my back towards the ground, staring at his face. I could feel the breaths in my chest ceasing at my lips in muffled pants, held stiffly behind my redded cheeks as I listened carefully while watching the lifeless tilt of his half-hidden face. I could hear nothing. No matter how hard I tried to hold my breath, or focus my hearing on the man, I couldn't hear anything coming from his body. The only sound I could hear was the billows of air flowing through the area outside of the hospital remains, whistling with a muffled pitch and kicking up grains of concrete and rocks in the fluid catch of its breeze, trickling in light skids like water dripping from a faulty pipe.

I looked back over the rest of his body, quickly glossing over the loose threads and bits of meandering fuzz that sprouted from his torn articles of clothing. His body didn't move in its place, only remaining stiffly upon the ground beyond the crook of my twitching nose. I pushed against his body with my hand remaining slightly above his shoulder slanted parallel with the twisting metal shafts above, watching it move back into place without any response. I was holding my breath as I kneeled there hunched over the man's body, watching him with wide eyes that pressed against the skull of my head attaching my sight to distressing conclusions.

I felt that same fluid begin to fill my eyes that had done so many times before. I felt it line my eyelids and mark my cheeks in chapped trails, dripping off of my cheeks onto the dusty ground below and fostering an erratically combined mixture of muddied white and brown substances. I pushed against his shoulder again, then again and again, shaking him with the push of my frantic grip. I sniffled, beginning to pant in choked breaths as I saw that same little boy languish into that pool of blood on my bedroom floor, fading into a dark crimson shadow and falling into the back of my head as a damned memory.

Kneeling here with my buttocks partially exposed and my knee wetted by the mixture of substances decorating the floor, I began to realize who this person was. Despite being told just over an hour ago who this man was, I barely came to the realization this was the human life form I had grown up with. The one I played with, exchanging childish giggles with our legs crossed over a floor of stratified concrete and our hands moving roughly with female dolls personified with the swing of our tiny grips and chirps of our pitched voices. The one I ate with throughout the day, consuming plates of discolored, pureed mush and scooped dismally with little metal spoons. The one I killed, or thought I did at least.

Now, feeling the moist artifact of his mouth cling to my softened penis and reverberate throughout it in hollowed prickles, I realized this was my fault. He was now dead. He didn't breathe anymore. He didn't move. He was dead, and I killed him. I didn't kill him as a kid, I killed him now. He died while his mouth was caressing my penis. I killed him with my penis. It's all my fault.

JACEY-ONE
MARCH 7, 2366

Enough time had gone by to where the sun now poured into the room at my angle and illuminated half of the scattered metallic remains I sat within, slicing me down the middle into a half-lit, half-shadowy naked figure. I had become too exhausted to keep crouching over the man's lifeless form. Choosing instead to sit, I leaned cautiously against the tilted, rustic metal wheel of the overturned bed. My leg muscles remained tensely flexed, bracing for the unlikely but feared moment when the man might abruptly come back to life.

It never happened, leaving an aching pain in my uselessly strained legs as I watched his motionless body become further illuminated in the waning afternoon sun. The hollowness of this room isolated at the top of this configuration of stacked rubble became intensified with the sweeping billows of wind that swept through the area, picking up speed and carrying larger scatters of dust and pebbles in its heavy pass.

I had no idea what to do, instead swiping my eyes frantically over the man's dead body and the metal shaft that pressed against his skull, partaking in a one-sided transaction of exchanged visuals. My heart raced in my chest and bristled shakily against the heaving pumps of my breathless lungs. I could feel it sink into my stomach again and again as I came to the realization of what had occurred earlier, leaning my head back and panting at the ceiling, bringing the back of my head into an awkward bow with the rest of the room. A lump grew in my throat and tensed with every heavy breath I made, attempting to clear it but only feeling it solidify in the walls of my throat.

My eyes drifted toward the opening in the fractured concrete wall, lazily watching it through the heated wrap of my dizzied head. I could feel vomit twisting in my gut and piling into my shakened throat, choking me with the wettish slur that filled it. I could hear footsteps skid against the scattered rocks and blanketed concrete dust that covered the rubble, cutting into the roughened drafts of wind that slowly dusted off the hospital rubble. Louder and louder they got, tracking up the hill of rubble on an upward trajectory of patterned crunches. I could hear deep voices jumble erratically together in a cacophony of unintelligible conversation, spoken alongside the loudening steps.

The net that carried the skeletal remains of the baby slid toward the opening in the wall slightly, shifting once more before being yanked against the cracked remains of the still-upright wall, tossing the loose remains against the motionless feet of the man. They scattered around his feet with a light rattle, dancing to an emotionless beat of *clink's* and *clunk's*. Deep, raspy grunts could be heard as the shadow of a man cut into the beaming rays of sunlight pouring into the room, several loose pebbles and a large cloud of dust sliding into the room with the rough insertion of the man's feet as he sat atop the wall. The cloud that crept into the room in chunky waves of dust obscured the man beyond a mere sun-lit silhouette, blurred behind that mystic shield as he waved the dust away with his hand.

I shook my head, feeling my frantic heartbeat leap into my throat and shake the walls of bile burning it, watching the man jump into the room from the ledge provided by the wall and decorate me in the dark fall of his shadow. He turned back towards the opening, speaking frantically to a couple of other men that crouched along the wall's edge, beams of light creeping past his rotating head and jabbing me in the eye with bright stabs. I flinched, pushing myself back against the fallen over bed and shifting it beneath the timid push of my strained back. The man turned his head in my direction, speaking at me and stepping towards me. The scattered skeletal remains of the baby crunched beneath his feet, other pieces tossed carelessly to the side with the rough kick of his steps. It wasn't long before his feet ran into the slanted placement of the man's feet tied over each other in an awkward contortion of limbs, bringing his eyes down to the man's dead body. He began to lean over the man in his tattered brown clothes, gripping the rusted edges of the metal shaft and lifting it past his head bent back away from it, peering closer to the man with the shaft still in his grip. The man glanced up at me, before looking back down at the man before me with a look of shock on his face. He then noticed the chapped layer of that thick white substance glistening at the soft tip of my penis, leaning his head over the man's body and staring closer to the man's face. The same chapped substance dried to the edges of his lips, lining them in a thin, discolored-white ring erratically lining the pinkish flesh.

The man stared at me with wide eyes, glancing back down at the man and reaching his hand to his mouth, rubbing his firmly pinched fingers against his lips and bringing it to his nose. He watched me closely, brushing his gripped hand side to side beneath his inhaling nostrils and continuing to lean over the man. Then, allowing his hand to fall to his side and shifting his other that had remained planted against the dusty ground, he crouched over the man and eyed me with a brooding glare, beginning to stand with a pounce frozen into the barely moving dangle of his arms and folded legs.

He grabbed hold of me by the arm, pulling his body back into a reclined stand and tearing me from the floor, stretching my arm in his dirty grip. He dragged me over the man's body, pulling his head upward with the slide of my foot as he tossed me against the wall opposite of where I lay. I panted within his grip, unsure of what he was doing at first as I frantically looked around at the slanted room just before a cloud of concrete dust arose with the slam of my body. He grunted, staring down at me with his brow bone furrowed and his cheeks reddened into a blistering blush, puffing his chest as he slowly approached me and eventually kicked me in the stomach. My head was now painfully pressed against the barricaded door still intact within the room, cringing as I felt pain paralyze my stomach and send the vomit thickening my throat in a thick paste onto the floor between us. I groaned, curling in the shadow of the two men crowding the opening in the rubble.

I grimaced at the floor, beginning to cave my pained stomach towards the floor when the man took a step back, leaning towards me in a bend and swinging his fist against my penis, bruising the chapped rod of flesh dangling from my pelvis and transforming my deep groans into a soft squeal. The pain could be felt all throughout my body, erupting at my pelvis and burning throughout my tensed muscles. I felt sick, desiring to vomit even more of the bile that muddied the dust on the floor in a pool of bloodied chunks and dirtied my hair as it trailed down my cheeks. The man stood back, heaving his chest and wiping his nose roughly before reaching down and scooping me into the grip of his hands, propping me up against the wall with a viscous shake, slamming my head back into the wall as I stood up with it brought to a pained bow.

He growled in my face, droplets of saliva painting it in chilled licks as he spoke to me in unintelligible banter. I could hardly bother to care about the pain of his firm grip stretching the flesh of my bicep as he pressed his grip towards the wall away from him, his dirtied nails siering into my skin. The pain starting at my bruised penis sank into my body and caused my stomach to ache, leaving the dizzied rumbling of my heartbeat echoing throughout that paralyzed chamber. I didn't look into the man's eyes. Instead I winced them in the direction of the door blocked by the fallen metal shaft leaning over its front, bringing my head to a lazy bow and leaning my tilted forehead in line with his eyes. His snarled voice entered my ears in unintelligible words and slurred sounds, caressing the side of my face in hot breaths and punched sounds.

The man turned to the two crouched in the entryway to the room, shifting and beginning to enter the room as he loosened his grip on my left arm and began to tighten his on the other, pivoting me towards the two men and forcing the dusty crack of the door into a hidden surrender with my tensed back. The crack in the doorway, cushioned by a thick layer of dust and just barely exposing a thin, dark line where the door met the floor, faded into the blur of my memory as I was now painfully turned to the men, who began to grab me near the edge and lift me onto it. The man behind me forced the lower garment of my clothing over my exposed buttocks as the men dangled me over the ledge in the room, awkwardly pushing the shaft of my penis against my stomach as he gripped the elastic helm over it.

The men then proceeded to step down the pile of rubble with me in their grip, carefully placing the tattered undersides of their shoes on each unofficial step that followed, manifesting in either large hills of dust and pebbles or firm slopes of concrete. One of them waved towards the men frantically, who began to quickly shuffle at the base of the hospital rubble and trade erratic shouts with the men who carried me. There was a moment of silence as the men stood in place at opposite ends of the rubble and stared at each other, eventually moving along the hill in careful steps marked by smooth crunches and trickling pebbles.

It wasn't long before the distant ground that swayed dizzily in a tannish haze became realized as the ground beneath my feet, quickly passing beneath my tattered shoes with patterned crunches as the men rushed me to the encampment. We would eventually arrive, the three of us watched over in frantic glares emerging from the passing tents, and soon enough, met with the concerned faces of the men who had crouched over my body and forced the baby leg into my mouth.

JACEY-ONE
MARCH 7, 2366

The man dressed in the dusty sheet of plastic stared with wide eyes at the men holding me in their sided grips, currently found on the floor with his knees planted into the soft, rippled sheets laid over the bare Earth. Someone sat kneeled opposite of him in torn brown clothing, decorated erratically with loose threads and holes exposing various patches of hairy flesh. They were turned to us, shifting their bodies knelt into the stained pillows beneath their folded legs and revealing a severed human leg cut into with various gnawed-indents, including an attached foot. A metal container stood to the left of the gnawed leg, chapped with thick remnants of dried, brown paste lining it in pseudo-drips.

He stared momentarily at the men gripping my arms, bringing the lazily pointed grip of his hand in front of him and hushing them quietly, returning to the woman kneeled before him and quietly murmuring repeated vocalizations to her. She shifted her gaze back to the man, cupping her hands in her lap and bowing her head in the direction of the man's concealed lap. I watched her quietly, feeling the gripped bind of flesh and dirtied nail numb along my arm as I grew transfixed with the somber sight planted before me into the floor along stained pillows and ruffled sheets.

The man in the plastic-like sheet stopped speaking, silently gripping the severed leg in his hands with one end staining his right hand in dried blood. The leg looked like it had just barely been attached to a living person, the balls of the feet painted in a soft, pink color and stretching along the softly hairy leg in a beige tone. It contrasted the browned layers of skin that crinkled atop the tender enfold of meat bound to the leg's bone I had eaten along, grease providing a grainy shimmer along the cooked flesh. This leg looked almost like it had barely been killed, the artifact of walk arising from its lively appearance.

He swiped his pointed finger over the woman's body, beginning at her forehead and crossing over her chest. Then, he brought the gripped leg to her mouth, just as she softly breathed a short vocalization and lightly placed her hands beneath the leg's fold broken up by various bite-marks indenting the flesh. She bit down into the flesh of the leg, shaking her head slightly from side to side and pulling her head back, the leg shifting in the two of theirs grip. She then tilted her head back, a slight *rip!* noise coinciding with the rough recline of her head as a piece of the leg's raw meat entered her mouth, followed by choppy, liquified smacks as she chewed on the meat. We stood there for a few minutes watching her chew on the tough piece of meat, soon followed by a loud gulp and a scatter of breathless pants as the chewed meat fell down her throat.

The man then placed the leg gently onto the space of softly ruffled sheet placed between their bent knees, then turning his head to the paste-stained container set next to the gnawed-at leg. He gripped the metal container in his hands, bringing it in front of him and allowing the woman to place the dirtied rim of the container to her lips, slowly tilting the container towards her nose until she grunted a tender gulp. A thick, dark liquid dripped from its rim as the man lifted it away from the woman's grip, placing the container on the ground again.

The woman then bowed to the man with her hands cupped a few inches from her chest, sitting back up and twisting her body around on the pillow, just barely brushing its soft, browned corner on the edge of the metal container sitting near its edge. Standing up, she paused just before she could move any farther, the corners of her thinly relaxed lips bending upward into her cheeks and producing a smirk. It was the woman I assumed to be my mother, her presence familiar to me from when she had kissed me earlier today. She walked towards the men and I, the two of them shifting as she stopped before them, smiling at me with a pivot breaking her walk as she kissed her hand, bringing her grouped fingers to my lips.

I could taste the bitter scent of raw human flesh linger on my lips as she dragged her grouped fingers down my lips, hanging my lip at a gentle gape as the saliva lining its edge wetted her fingers. It filled my nose in a foul stench, leaving behind a grossly sensed trace of her presence after she removed her mouth from my face, walking past the men with a smile grinning softly at me. As her hand brushed down my chin in a chapped trail of flesh, I felt a patch of short, prickly hairs pull with her fingers, bristling on my chin with a quiet *rip!* sound. Notably, the patch on my chin was rougher and more prickly than my chin had ever been before.

The men then turned me to the man in the dusty, plastic sheet who now approached us, dragging me by my feet initially as I mulled over what just happened and planted myself there in a paralyzed glare with the tranquil brush of the turning sheet walls behind the man. They spoke frantically to the man, gesturing to me in abrupt waves of their hands. The man stared at me, tilting his head to the side and leaning on his left foot. Biting down on his lip, he looked up at the ceiling with his hands brought in front of him in an angsty cup, tightening the spread of the plastic sheet as his arms folded over its side. The outline of his penis could be seen near his cupped hands, which became hidden behind the mild flow of his worn-sheet cushioning his body in air as he removed his hands from his frontside.

He gestured at the pillow positioned at a slight angle with the container of thick, dark substance, the men promptly beginning to shuffle me towards the stained pillow and hover me over it. I glanced up at the man who was now beginning to lower himself to the pillow, flashing a thin smile at me as he gestured to the pillow lying beneath my aching buttocks. I looked away nervously, feeling my stomach turn as I held my shaky gaze with a flowing stain melting over the soft folds of the windswept walls. I sat in front of him, the two men's gripped hands easing on my descending biceps until their hand was now placed on my shoulder, stepping back carefully.

The man bowed his head with his eyes remaining on the men, descending to the tattered sides of their shoes ripped loosely over random toes and exposing dirtied, long nails. In the blurred borders of my periphery the men bowed, swiping their hands over their upper body and turning to leave the room, sending a brush of cold air tickling my back and filling my ears with the gentle sound of wind washing over the area in chilly billows.

The bright edge of the two sheets stretching at the edge of the room remained in my periphery in a grainy ray of white fuzz, only surrendered to the stretch of my bent back as the man sitting before me gripped my hand, fixing my attention on him. He stared at me with a small smile pushing his smoothed, hairless cheeks into a gently wrinkled curl, blending into the mindlessly expanding pull of his lips and slap of his tongue as he spoke unintelligibly to me. He gripped my hands roughly in his, pushing his bent legs brought into a firm cross with mine and bowing his head towards me. He murmured frantically with his eyes sealed in the direction of my crotch, his hands beginning to shake with mine still fastened beneath his grip, my fingernails tucked beneath his wrist. I looked nervously at him, feeling my heart begin to rush into an erratically trickled beat as he started to rock back and forth, tears streaming down his face in sparkling, reddish hues as he muttered frantically to himself. I shifted with the volatile turn of his body as he shook his head, his lips stiffening and turning his spat mutters into heaved pants. He turned his strained face to the ceiling, facing his breathless frown to the ceiling and pulling my arms above his head with it. My eyes were now focused on the smooth, curved protrusion of his chin, lined in the droplets of fluid falling from his eyes.

He then ripped his head down and faced me with furiously widened eyes, the browns in his eyes sinking into an almond-shape pool of reddened, inflamed white as he glared at me breathlessly. He shoved his body onto mine, yanking the grip of his hands onto my biceps and tearing at my shirt's sleeves as he kissed me violently. I held my lips tightly together in a thin pucker, feeling my heart sink in a shaky descent as the air in my chest evaded any shocked gasp locked behind my sealed lips. His lips were lined in a pasty, tangy flavor, causing my stomach to turn awkwardly with nauseated pings as he continued to kiss me, wrapping his chapped lips around mine. His kisses were broken apart by grunted pants that tickled the hairs on my neck in a warm itch, the pricklish feeling spreading around my back.

He began to push his body even more onto mine, until my body was brought back into an angle with the floor beneath our bodies. I lowered my body with a slight trip breaking up the fall of my back, just as the man ceased to move over my body as the sheet he wore tugged at his collar bone. He hovered over me with his right hand planted by my left bicep with his fingers stretched into a strained fan on the sheet floor, tugging the sheet from under his bent knee. He exposed the hairy profile of his dimly lit stomach and legs, caked in a matted jungle of curled brown hairs that contrasted the smooth, hairless look of his face. He gripped the torn elastic hem of his underpants, tugging at it with his free hand and exposing his hard penis, plopping the shaft and the closely dangling testicles over the firmly strained band.

I breathed nervously, watching as he stretched his arms over the sides of my head and lifted the stiffly flowing plastic sheet over my head, quickly washing over me in a sea of black dots and countless gray cracks intersecting across the sheet. The stained ceiling pushing and pulling above my face in soft flows of fabric became hidden behind the fall of his sheet, the rest of the room relegated to a thin white line separating the edge of the sheet and the floor.

The man was now crouched over me with his face hovering over mine and grunting hot pants of breath and drops of saliva onto my face, tugging at my tattered brown shorts and shifting them shakily down my legs until my upper legs and pelvic area was exposed. My penis was soft and capped in a dimly shined transparent film, hanging limply from the bed of curled brown pubic hairs grouped between my legs. The man pulled the shorts down the rest of my legs, scooting over the remainder of my body until the plastic sheet was tugged below my neck and he hovered above my feet in a half-kneel crouch, his penis brushing against my calf as he removed my shorts from my feet. He grabbed the cup of thick, crimson substance in his hand, beginning to crawl over me in a tensely pounced traverse with his left hand guiding him across my body with a scattered shift, spritzing the length of my body in the liquid.

As the plastic sheet pulled over my head again and blanketed me in a sky of diamond-cut scrapes of plastic, he bent his head towards his hard penis, tossing the thick, crimson substance onto his penis and throwing the container to the side. He gripped the base of the penis and ran his hand along it with a slow, moist stroke, spritzing my pelvic area in its dark droplets. Then, spreading my tensed legs apart, he wrapped his arms around my knees and propped my legs in a contorted bend over his shoulder, forcing my bare buttocks onto his hairy legs. He then inserted his penis into my butthole, the thick, dark substance bounding his penis in a darkish glow tickling the hairs tangling around its edges. I felt the air in my chest leave in a unilateral gasp, an agape artifact of the huge breath left in my hanging lips. The man pushed and pulled back and forth with his penis inserted into my buttocks, slamming awkwardly against me with his grunting body leaned over the lower half of my torso. The hairs loosened inside my butthole and torn into bloodied gnashes tickled awkwardly at the slide of his moist penis, inflaming the burned walls of my butthole in one large, blistering itch.

Permeations of the dull sunlight basking the room in a brownish, stained afternoon hue could be seen ever so often every time the man pulled back with his penis inserted into my butthole, the sheet he pitched over us sliding up and down my forehead and illuminating my lips and the rest of my torso covered in the spritzed substance. We sat there for a few more moments with the man hunched over me in a grunted fold, my penis remaining barely hardened and brushed awkwardly up against his thumping frontside. Eventually, the end of my butthole tickled with the soft pumping of fluid against it, a gross, nauseating feeling trembling the rest of my body in chills and hair-raising itches.

JACEY-ONE
MARCH 7, 2366

Iwas led to the lake by the men who had led me to the man in the plastic sheet's tent, stripping me of my dusty, tattered clothes and dragging my naked body into the lake. My feet sank into a burning bind of blister and hotness as they stepped with me into the water, one of the men holding my arms behind my back and the other leaning over towards the browned, polluted ripples of water and cupping his hands. He then faced me and flicked his cupped hands upward, tossing a splash of the burning water onto my pelvic area. It seared against my skin and wetted my pubic hairs in a matted glow, tickling the roots of the hair and sinking into the tender indents left in the skin of my penis from the man's mouth biting into it. I bit my mouth quietly but opened it quickly to let out a hissed pant, fluid building in my eyes and staining the rest of the lake in a polluted blur.

The man stepped over to me, glaring at me with a grinned snarl straining his face as he began to fondle with my penis, tickling it with a spattered grip of his erratically bending fingers. I looked at him through the blur fostered in my eyes from the fluid, my heart racing in my chest and creeping up my throat in an electrified rumble. I gasped as I felt blood rush up the shaft of the penis and fill the man's fumbled grasp in hardened flesh, reaching a crown of pinkish flesh colored in several bruises.

He continued to stare at me with his lips curled into a breathless sneer, fondling with my penis for a little bit longer before wrapping his entire hand around it with a moist, burning grasp and yanking it violently towards him, causing an excruciating pain to start at the base of my penis and erupt through the rest of my pelvis. I sank into the man's grip bounding my biceps tightly behind my back, feeling his nails dig into the flesh of my arm as I gasped with fluid filling my eyes, my legs bending. The countless veins in my penis became inflamed with a fiery burn that tickled the walls of it in a painful itch. My penis became softer, leaving behind a painful trace of the man's nonchalant yank as he let it hang in his hand, soon removing it and eventually leading me and the man holding me out of the lake's shallow shore.

After being dressed again in my clothes, I was led to a massive group of people crowding outside of the rows of tents erected amongst the encampment, facing the other direction as we approached them. The man who had had sex with me just an hour ago stood at the center of the group, perched on top of a hospital bed with the dirtied undersides of his tattered shoes leaving a trail of grainy streaks of brown following his flowing plastic robe. I believe it was the hospital bed I had been transported upon by the humans, with the stained, torn sheets of its mattress crushed beneath the dirty positioning of his feet. He gestured his hands in circular waves that slowly bucked against the chilled breeze that flowed through the evening-stained area, pivoting in slight turns as he spoke to the audience with unintelligible hollers. His shadow moved against the edge of the crowd in a long stretch of black arched narrowly against the golden bed of rays that caressed the Earth in a warm hue.

The men led me through the group of people, pushing past them and charting a path bordered by shifting steps crunching against the grainy dirt and watchful glares coupled with a distant array of scattered murmurs. We reached the front of the group, the man in the large plastic sheet glancing at us with his arms still hovering at his sides, shifting atop the hospital bed. He stood next to the two other men who had helped force the baby leg into my mouth, who stood with their plastic sheets flowing gently in the moving evening air as they remained in front of the bed. Stopping in front of the large group of people that filled the vast space of dirt bristled with patches of twigs and pebbles, the men turned me to face them, watching a sea of bowed heads and occasionally glancing eyes mold around my timid, pained body.

I looked at them with wide eyes, noticing the dead trees erected in the distance and filling the polluted evening skies with sprawling twigs and overlapping sheets hanging from them. Their beards clinging to their faces in various shades of patched, brown strands filled the distance in a patterned sequence of tannish foreheads and varied beards, overlaying the space before me in a patchwork of indistinguishable faces. The strange pattern almost reminded me of the half-circles of pasted-over concrete scattered across the floors of the building I grew up in, or the ripples of water bouncing off of the penetration of my pointer finger or my feet against the creek's surface or the nearby lake. It all stretched into the distance in a rounded scatter, almost swaying before me with a numbing haze as I became engrossed in the patterned space of beards and their connected faces.

The man's voice could be heard from behind me, a brush of air sounding as the two men holding me before the group of people turned with me to face the three men surrounding the bed. The man standing atop the bed held his arms out with a frozen grip outstretched over the two men's gripping hands, grasping his forearm in their hands and assisting him to the ground. He stepped off of the bed's edge, the tattered edges of his billowing plastic sheet turning in soft folds of moving fabric as he stepped onto the ground from the bed with a blunted fall.

He stepped away from the bed and past the two men and I. The three of them blurred into the halted periphery of my rotated head as the slide of stepped crunches stopped behind us. I was led to the bed, the men gripping me by either the sweaty crevice matted in curled hairs between my arms and sides or the calves of my legs, my clothes folding against the edges of the bed and tightening against my legs as they laid me down. They laid the same several straps previously pinching into my flesh in blistering pulls, fastening the sharply tattered edges over my chest, waist, and legs, clipping them with a muddled buckle clipping nearby. They wheeled the bed around and faced me with my feet pointing to the massive audience swarming the area in a sea of bowed heads and shunned beards, my head directed away from the encampment. The sky blurred above me in a tannish spiral, settling in my eyes as a fading haze of polluted sun-lit clouds as the two men stopped turning the bed in the dirt; the swerve of grained dirt and rock sliding beneath the bed's rusted wheels coming to a crunched conclusion.

They stepped away, leaving my eyes subjugated to the sand-colored skies streamed in monotonous lines of haze further buried into the deep swath of polluted clouds. I looked to the side of me, breathing slightly heavy as the strands of hair caked in a dried sheath of vomit pulled between the turn of my head and the mattress beneath my body. The lake sank beneath the polluted haze of the horizon and erected a dark, blurrily rippled pool of shadowy water, occupying my eyes in its chilled depths. I turned my head back to face the skies above, feeling my throat harden into a tight, pasted bind at the sight of two plump, round pillows of flesh filling my eyes. Two small hands wrapped around the rounded edges of the beige-colored flesh, seemingly extending from the skies up above and caressing the tubes of flesh that hung from the universe barricaded by a manmade shield of pollutants. Two dark spots clung to the ends of the sloped tubes, marked by erratic rings of speckles of grain and filled with a dark brown color, illusive traces of the grainy substance lining the flesh in a faded strata design. The paste was almost like the mud by the creek, or the mud that surrounded the lake in a ring of sandy soil forming a beach that melted into the gentle shore of ripples. I could make out the shapes of two, large nipples beneath the brownish paste, moving around above my face like two frantic eyeballs.

One of the men who had carried me from the pile of rubble into the encampment fumbled with my penis as the tubes of flesh marked in mud and specks of grain continued to dance over me, with two gently gripped hands caressing the fluid slant of their movements. My penis was soft in his grip, a slight pain still felt in its tensed shape as the remnants of our interaction in the lake tainted my pelvis in a paralyzing sore. He shook his head nearby, speaking a few unintelligible vocalizations as his head of knotted strands shelled in sheaths of dust and twig bopped around in a dirtied blob hidden in my periphery.

The tubes of flesh bent closer to the edge of my head, as a woman's face emerged from behind the tilted descent of the flesh and plastered the burnt, tannish clouds in an eased aura, hiding behind my head and revealing the beaming smile of the woman I believed to be my mother. My lips tickled in the soft breeze that flowed through the area in heavy billows, brushing lightly against the bits of hair forming a haphazard shape of tiny curls around my mouth. I could feel her kiss on my mouth, and how strange it felt experiencing it. Her hand brought into a relaxed pinch as she brushed my lips. The mud that covered her breasts in a dirtied shell, painting her nipples in grainy shadows and tracing the edges of her breasts in fading prints of pulled fingertips. She continued to smile at me, her head upside down from where I laid.

The man off to the side then waved near the lower half of my body, temporarily pulling my eyes to the blurred gesture he made in slow swipes as the woman I believed to be my mother left my side, her smiling face trailing into my periphery and holding my gaze with a fading memory. A couple of crunched footsteps stamped against the shredded twigs and dried soil painting the earth in a bland field, followed by several grunts. I lifted my eyes to the top of my eye sockets and tried to look behind me, feeling a brooding pain fill the borders of my sockets and the shadow of my brow hover over my eyes. I couldn't see what was occurring behind me, only finding hazed shadows moving nearby in the gloomy evening sun latching onto the surrounding horizon broken into meandering rubble and a goldish hue.

The hairy, muscular chest of the man I had had sex with suddenly reigned above my face and dangled various curls of dark brown hair above me. I felt my lips shape into a gasped O and the air in my chest break into a broken choke. My heartbeat trickled in my chest in a scattered beat of distressed pings. I felt sweat ferment my cheeks in a moist paste, cooling in the evening breeze dancing through the area in lush drafts. The man's hand still hanging near my lower body held his gripped palm against my penis, feeling the aching shape harden in his gripped hand.

I could see the firmly gripped wrap of someone's hands cling to the space of flesh caved beneath his chest in hairy abdominal muscles, wrinkled folds of flesh pulling with the push of the person's hands. They held up his body in front of them, assuming that it was a human gripping their strained hands around him from behind his body, isolating their face behind his back and suspending his dangling body beneath the tannish skies. Whatever held the man's body over my head began to shift the wrap of their hands around his torso until it was only one of their arms holding up his body. They reached their other hand towards his penis, grabbing it and fumbling it closer to my face as the thick coat of hair wrapped around their arm in curled fuzz pulled against the man's hairy side.

I felt my penis grow harder in the man at my side's grip, until it filled his hand in warm, firm flesh and blood, the arousal in my body electrifying its firm planting in his held hand. The tip poked through my tattered shorts and brushed past the firm tips of his fingers, poking at the reclined knuckles of his hand's fingers. I then watched the blur of his head jerk towards the crowd in an abrupt shift, nodding his head up and down and propagating the haze of my periphery in a bouncing, dim sway. The man was then suddenly removed from my sight, dragging the man with a crunched slur of pulled feet and scattered stomps. The sight of his dead body faded into my recent memory and traced the sky in a tannish, outlined afterimage. It did, however, remain firmly in my shorts as the hard, aching penis filling the man's slightly relaxed grip and pushing through my shorts. Hard like the dead Earth scattered between borders of ruptured concrete and motionless shores of hellish, acidic water, and the concrete that chilled my buttocks as I sat atop it in the building I grew up in, tickling my flesh at the thought of it all.

The man who spoke in the large, plastic sheet with outstretched hands and a towering presence ruffled with a stiff flow began to speak again, his voice noticeably quicker and withered into a tight snarl. His voice grew quicker and quicker, underlined by occasional steps in the rocky dirt as his near-chanted banter became louder. He appeared in the bottom of my eyelids, his smacked lips and slapped tongue lining my exposed arm in sporadic drops of spit. His eyes were widened, his arms brought tensely in front of his chest with his right hand brought into a curled pinch. I turned my head to face him, the same metal container dirtied in a thick, crimson paste held in his other arm. The thick, slightly chunked substance dirtied his hand, which he gripped before him in a tense fist tightened into a firm pinch. He continued to yell at me in unintelligible banter, his eyes engulfing mine as his flashed teeth chomped his shouted words into fierce bites.

He then began to flick his wrist back and forth towards me, spritzing me in the dark-red substance. It sank into my pores in acidic itches, inflaming my face in a wave of moist, jabbed licks of fire. That same fluid filled my eyes in a warm line as I squinted my eyes in pain and discomfort, feeling my arms ache in the pinched grip of the bed's straps as I struggled to lift them to brush off the liquid. Every time I lifted my arms almost automatically to brush off my face, they were thrust back against the dirtied mattress and planted into the soft sheets in an aching descent.

My heart thumped loudly in my throat, providing a pounded beat to the frantic hollers of the man as he stained his hand in the pasted, crimson substance, flicking it onto my body continuously. I felt the air in my chest lock at my throat and solidify into an immobile lump, scattering my chest in a tingly feeling and tainting my head in a dizzying blur. I could hardly breathe, or think, or even feel the burning spritz draping my skin in irregular droplets of fire. My heartbeat rang in my head in staggered pings as millions of static lines and dots infiltrated the fluid blur obstructing my vision and dressing the tannish skies in a premature starry gaze. I could hear loud, screaming voices erupt from the depths of the crowd surrounding the bed in a half-ring of frantically cupped- and raised-hands and crunched shifts in the rocky dirt beneath us.

My eyes soon closed shut and locked me behind an infinite sea of blackness, depressing my senses to the point of me being half-dead just before my eyes opened to the cold, dark overlay of the night sky. A few stars poked out from the blanket of polluted haze covering the sky in fat, blue strokes of cloud, including two prominent ones reining near the crescendoed edges of the blurred full-moon.

JACEY-ONE
MARCH 8, 2366

I believe I was beside the large body of water filling the edges of the muddied beach in gentle ripples, the once-softer waves pressing into the shore with soft rubs now hitting it in rougher shoves. I was still strapped into the hospital bed I had been in since earlier that day. Except, I felt different. I felt colder; lighter, almost, like large sweeps of air gathered at my backside and brushed me into the upper skies. Except, I was still confined to this same hospital bed, the straps biting into my skin in inanimate gnaws and feasting on the blistered skin they wrapped tightly around. *Skin..* I was naked. Lifting my head and feeling the bile in my throat paste it in an itchy coat with the lift of the muscle, I shunned the three, grayed lights grouped together in a hazed configuration where the moon reined, noticing the crimson, bruised tip of my penis. A hazed constellation of little burns and scaths decorated the immediately visible portion of my body in the same reddish brown color, beginning at my nipples and trailing along my slightly hairy stomach in darkened dots.

Reclining my head back into the mattress, I felt the crunch of dried dirt pick into my head with a slight itch, a similar feeling trickling down my back in a wave of similar prickles. I rubbed my back side to side beneath the tightened straps, the pinched sides of the straps pressing down on one arm over the other as the dried bits of dirt scraped at my back and clung to the sweaty underside. Strangely enough, the only warm portion of my body was found under my back pressed into the mattress, with some of the dirt wetted into a moist mixture of back sweat and heat.

Every time a brush of cold air rolled over my body and sent me in a shudder, paralyzed beneath these strapped buckles, I shifted my body beneath the straps as if to curl into a tight ball. It was almost like when I abandoned the exploratory robot and slept by the creek-side, the cold night air chilling my body with every breath, the windy skies suspended from the skies brushed with polluted, star-lit clouds. I shuddered, my legs shaking and growing pained as the fastened buckles wasted away their trembles into the cooled mattress.

My eyes locked with the strained toes of my feet, flexed back towards my body as I felt the illusive flood of warmth nestle beneath my chin dug into my collarbone. I craved the feeling of that soft, plush blanket fermented in the tangy scent of dried sweat and wrinkled into a lifelong mold of my sleepily bent body, instead finding the absence of it tangled with the nostalgia and strain of my neck. I longed to lift my arms to my face and tuck my gripped knuckles into the burrow of flesh and coldly run blood rushing through my neck, to bring my legs into a tight fold with my knees pressed into my chest. Instead, I was nakedly vulnerable beneath the night skies, darkly revealed to the polluted skies brushing the sky in cold strokes of purplish haze. The only warmth that could be gathered in my naked body were the warm fluid that began to fill my eyes and flood my face in briefly warm licks, quickly chilling my face in brandings of the cold night air. I bit down against my bottom lip, feeling the pain numbed beneath the piercing dig of my teeth.

A slow rumble pounded my heart into a tender beat within my chest, juxtaposed against the hissed slither of blood pumping steadily through my veins. Focusing on the light symphony humming through my body in pushes and pulls, I felt myself enter and exit randomized cycles of sleep abruptly shifted by blistered pulls beneath the straps gripping my body, and the suddenly pinged speed of my heart. Each time I gasped, ripping my eyes open and staring blankly into the night sky.

The three, grayed lights poring through the purplish haze collecting above grew larger and larger with each shift my body made. Anchored by a large hole of white that bore into the fabric of the black, sporadically starry universe hugging the Earth's atmosphere, and two large stars growing progressively larger at its sides.

JACEY-ONE

MARCH 8, 2366

Morning washed over my naked body with a dull light dressing me in a tannish hue, balmy curtains of overlapping clouds generating a clouded haze around the sun and producing a white hole tearing into the monochromatic fabric of the sky. The air numbing my body into senseless muscle and lining it in gentle mist filled my lungs like a punch to the gut, spritzing my nerves in a weakened paralysis. The bright, yellowish lights that burned as sprawling, engrossing flames in my rested mind washed away into a blurred, acidic wash blanketing my vision in a patchwork of nonsensical after images. I was awake now and half-frozen into the hospital bed I awoke on, brought into this dreaded wake by a hammering heartbeat and detached, unintelligible voices shouting me into a breathless period of awareness.

I looked around with nervous pants breaking up the rotation of my numbed jaw moving with my head as I looked around trying to remember where I was. The unintelligible shouts scratching the atmosphere in tense, unnerving banter; the dull sky hovering above the dry Earth in motionless, polluted haze; the wind blowing through the local vicinity and rattling dead twigs and pebbles with scattered shoves; the gentle ripples forming a softly rumbled blanket melting into the shore with liquified cuddles. I was near the lake that the group of humans lived close to. That realization hit me even harder when a large gush of wind slammed into the side of the bed, rocking it side to side slightly until it leaned harder into one side and crashed over into the light edge of the lake's shore. Happening so suddenly, the water splashed onto me as the bed folded onto its side into the lake's nearby shore, covering the lake's surface in scattered ripples. The water brushed against the right side of my body and splashed into one of my eyes, crashing into me in chopped waves and reeling viciously back into the lake with a hot, burnt feeling siering into the touched areas of my body. For once in what felt like ages, a feeling of warmth eclipsed my body, holding me in a tight bind with a cloak of warmth before washing over my body in a burn, a penetrating burn that pierced into my skin.

My eyes, with half of the lake ahead of me faded into a traceless blur, seemingly barricading my brain with a thick film that wouldn't go away no matter how far back the water reeled into the drifted shore and how many blinks I frantically made. I widened my eyes and moved my head around, pushing the left side of my head into the turned over bed so as to avoid staring into the burning water filling the lake. I continued to widen them until my eyelids bore into my skull and pain lined my sockets in a hard strain. The horizon line reining over the far edge of the lake faded into a dissolved blur, transitioning from a hard edge of moving waves into a fuzzily bumping haze. Soon enough, everything was blurry, and I could hardly register what any of the dully colored palette occupying my vision represented beyond mere inference.

My eyes continued to widen until my pupils dilated and conjured an even more senseless configuration of visuals and my sockets pained along its circumference, disregarding the clamoring voices growing louder at my backside in a rolling wave of unintelligible banter. *Was I blind?* I asked myself, barely registering the almost-automatic question as I dug the left-edge of my head deeper into the stiff mattress and stared through blurred eyes at the sky. The acidic water brushing gently against the bed soaked my right arm in a warmly numbed paralysis and spritzed my left arm in meandering blisters, swaying with a heated fuzz collecting over my arms as I yanked them against the straps. I desired so badly to pull out of the straps and brush away the blur covering my eyes. Instead the film of discolored haze built around my eyes and seared into my pupil like a pointer finger digging into dirt and grain, prying forcefully between its nail and that pinkish bed nestled firmly beneath it. Fluid began to fill my eyes and trek down my face, crystalizing the impenetrable film in a starry space of haze and dripping softly onto the gentle shoreline of the lake. *Drip! Drip! Drip!* Dripping like rain water falling from a sloped roof onto cold, moistly tainted pavement, or blood rushing through my veins and rapidly pinging in my body as fluid sank into me from a nearby I.V. The light ripples bouncing off the droplets' points of penetration moved in my eyes in static wrinkles breaking the blurred water into stratified haze.

The water soon sank off of my arm into the lake it took initial from in, injecting my arm in a nauseating feeling of cool as the bed was pulled upright to face the blurred sky and blanket me in cold air, my obstructed periphery torn into blurred abstracts of bopping heads signaling unintelligible communication. I barely even noticed the bed being pulled back onto its rusted wheels, instead focusing on the blur projected from my blinded eyes that rectified no stable visual. I could see out of one eye, finding a group of men towering over my side and clearly moving frantic hands over the buckles fastening me into this wetted mattress. However, it felt as though one hand covered the other, the imagined perpetrator hovering over my side and parting their two fingers just enough for a tannish blur lined in moving haze to fill my eyes and break the sea of tinted red.

The bodies moving along my left side barely became fully realized as I was pulled off of the hospital bed with an abrupt jolt, my attention divided frantically between my eyes of mixed acuity. My mouth pumped out heavy figments of air that spiraled in the air as chilled, thickly misty billows and tickled my chapped lips in a ring of dryish prickles. The bodies on my left side belonged to those of hairy, scraggly men dressed in heavy coats of matted black hair and browned sheets of clothing; on the right, blurred configurations barely recognizable beyond the inference of tannish figures of assumed flesh and blood. Their arms planted into me from beneath my back with their hands dug into the skin of my coldly numbed arms, twisting the flesh beneath their viciously gripped hands as they quickly turned with me as a group away from the bed. As they moved away, I heard the same noise of the hospital bed leaning onto its rusted wheels and a waning *creak!* noise, before slamming into the shoreline with a loud *clank!* and spritzing the nearby water in a scattered spray of minute *drip* noises.

The sky passed over me in a passive blur as the group of men and reigning blurs moved roughly with me in their closely gripped arms, rolling over their heads in one static, polluted wave of cloud and filling the nonsensical gap connecting them stereoscopically. I had no idea what to anticipate, and could barely find the willpower to engage completely with the confidence barely mustered in my own body, filling me in cyclic pings of nausea and relaxation. Even when I twisted my head from side to side to try and get a look at where we were maneuvering towards, my eyes were met with the scraggly, torn patches of clothing wrapped around their grimy, hairy bodies. I breathed in soft pants and quickly began to feel them sputter out of my chest in nervous heaves, just as I allowed my head to jerk back into a pointless bop relieved from the strain of holding my head up to see around.

We stopped eventually, with a couple of the men holding me at my feet allowing my legs to fall to the ground in a pained recline and a grained, clammy stepping as they stepped around us into a cacophonic crowd of unintelligible murmurs. I looked around, standing up finally, one eye blurrier than the other and casting half of the crowd before us in a thick film of haze. The other half standing on my left side was clear, watching us with stern faces widening their eyes into hardened strains and their mouths curling into careful shapes as they spoke quietly among themselves. I leaned slightly towards them as if doing so would remedy the blindness filling my right eye in a thick blur, trying to focus amidst the transparent outlines of the blurred silhouettes drifting into my clear vision.

My head began to ache as I tried to disentangle the visions competing for one solid configuration that didn't emerge, watching as the heads of the people before me rotated in an almost uniform shift, creating a crystallized string of layered scraggly-haired heads moving before me. I turned slowly with them, following my head with a delayed synchronization and feeling one of the men's hands grip firmly onto my right bicep. The rocky dirt littered with pebbles and slowly moving dust caught on the drifting breeze shifted in gentle crunches beneath three men's feet, all of whom were dressed in heavy cloaks of shiny, crinkled sheets that wrapped their bodies in hardened edges that moved stiffly in the gathering wind.

It was the men that had knelt over my body, ultimately forcing a baby leg into my mouth and the moist, plump flesh of its calve down my throat. The crowd of people parted to form an impromptu pathway for the three men, receding into rows of following gazes and cautiously shifted steps. The men emerged from the back of the group with their faces painted in beaming, hairless masks distinct from the rows of long, curled bushes of hair darkly bunched along the people's lower faces. Their faces snuck through the crowd like hazed beams of light poking through the meandering cracks of the dusty, jagged face of the piles of rubble stretching throughout the nearby area.

They carried large, wooden structures on their backs that left thick trails in the dirt found on the ground and wound through the muddled prints of their shuffled steps like a body of water cutting through a dry piece of land. Shadows of the structures carried in the hazed rays of light, landing from the skies and casting softly edged bits of black onto the ground. The shadows didn't produce any notable shape that could help me infer what the large wooden structures were, leaning on the men's heaved backs at an angle where they only appeared as one long piece of wood, as if pried out of a patch of trees and deprived of the twigs and bark decorating them in prickles and beige scales.

What the structures were became clearer as the men rotated around and came to a stop by the men holding me tightly in their grasp, a few of the other men coming by their sides and removing the wooden masses from their backs. They seemed to be wooden structures all in the shape of crosses, with a short piece of wood crossing the front of a longer one a couple of feet away from its top, meeting at the ground near the scraggly-placed shoes covering the men's feet. The man in the middle of the group of three carried a noticeably larger cross on his back, standing around a few feet higher than the two crosses behind him as the group of assisting men helped stand them up, their shadows shifting stiffly in the nearby ground as they straightened the wooden crosses up.

As the crosses stood upright in the men's grips and swayed only gently in the afternoon breeze, the three men dressed in dustily shiny attire marked by dirt-stained cracks in their plastic sheets turned to the crowd of people, with the one standing in the middle raising his hands in level with his eyes and the other two cupping their hands in front of them. Their cupped hands pushed down the cracked plastic sheets they wore tightly around their upper legs, outlining the firm shape of their testicles. The cold breaths that passed over the crowd in a detached wave of pants collapsed into a uniform gasp, as everyone's heads fell in a soft brush forward and bowed to the man beginning to chant unintelligibly to them with his hands still raised into the air. I looked around at all of them, feeling the men's grips around my arms numb into a senseless bind of fleshed mush as I grew nervously lost within the closed eyes cast away from the space I stood atop. Not a single pair of eyes could be seen in the crowd of curled bunches of hair and dirtied clothing stretching for dozens of feet and forming a tainted patchwork of human flesh and blood, only inferrable by the two blurred slits locked beneath their foreheads and facing the rocky terrain of Earth.

I felt a grimy hand grasp my head and force it forward, holding it in a tight bow and leaving my eyes strained into the blurred borders of my sockets as they remained entranced by the sight before me. I looked around, just barely pushing my head back against the man's grip. I looked up at the man shouting to the people from where he stood, feeling the burning water of the lake suddenly wash over me again and surround the two of us in hellish waves. They licked my body in itchy burns and left behind blistered patches along my skin, branding the insides of my butthole in a tunnel of fire that ruptured the tip of my penis in a paralyzing flush. I could see him calling out mindless chants that I could never have the ability to understand, his dirtied plastic sheet floating along the cold lake's current rolled over in a kingdom of fog brushed with dominating billows of pollutants. I could feel my mother's arms wrap around my body and trail me throughout the lake's water, ripples bouncing off of my body dancing with my mother in a gentle spiral and leaving a fluid signal of my presence penetrating the hellish lake.

It was all happening again, that one morning where I woke up atop a lumpy mattress caked in my dried feces, my dirty body blanketed in the coldness of the early morning branding my naked body chillingly. The night before, where that man was on top of me and had sex with me, unclothing my body and leaving behind a sheath of sweat and matted hairs shielding my body in cool bites. It all occurred to me again, realization hitting me like a fresh container of water filling your gut and flushing your senses in the experience of wake. It was a memory I seemed to disregard amid the occurrence of the events that followed… of the death of that man I considered my brother, of my reprimanding by the groups of men that dragged me through the dirt around the encampment. The sexual intercourse I was forced to partake in with the man cloaked in a great, plastic sheet – who now seemed to begin finishing his spiraling series of shouts at the massive crowd – along with the cold night sky I was forced to sleep naked beneath while tied into a rickety hospital bed. All of those events that distracted me branded me in bruises, and painted me in bloody licks, serving as physical markers of what I had experienced at the hands of those various individuals.

Strangely enough, all of it felt so familiar; like it wasn't just a traumatic event having occurred within the past two nights, and was in fact an event that defined my existence - that had occurred long ago, and was a mental reflection of a past pasted across my eyes as an obsessively revisited memory.

I stared at a point in the ground where the dusty ground clotted in slanted stones and broken twigs met with the torn edges of a random person's brown-leathered shoes. My attention was only removed from the sight when I saw the sight of the larger wooden cross once resting on the yelling man's back become lowered onto the ground, reining in its shadow cast onto my body beneath the polluted sun and striking down onto the ground like a fist raised to strike you, pounding into your flesh. It was almost like when the exploratory robot raised its long, coiled metal arm above my body and zapped me as I continued to fail my mother in the sexual intercourse task she was attempting to force me to perform as some sort of examination.

The cross was laid onto the ground, several rocks turning beneath it in gentle crumbles and twigs in soft crunches as two of the men nestled the wooden mass into the dirt ground, others backing away including myself as I was dragged a few steps back by one of the men gripping me. The man in the large plastic sheet cast onto the ground near his feet stood at the base of the cross, watching over the cross and swiping his loosely pinched fist in the air before him. I felt a pair of hands suddenly wrap around my legs and another tightly grip the pits of flesh and matted hair buried in the crevices of my armpits, lifting me off of the ground and beginning to transfer me above the cross in a swayed hover, lowering me onto it. The motioning was how that one baby my mother weaned just after terminating me was lowered into its new crib, the exploratory robot lowering it with its arms and mother's beaming face greeting it on the screen she was projected upon. Except, as I was lowered onto the cross, my arms stretched across the two edges of the horizontal log as a rope was fastened over them by a couple of the men, it was the woman who had kissed me and that I once thought to be my mother who greeted me, lowered by my sides onto her knees tucked into a bed of dirt and stone. She stared at me with a smile, brushing my hair collecting at the side of my face along my ears in crusty locks dried with the scent and ferment of sweat in a grotesque sheath.

I looked nervously behind her at the man dressed in the dirty plastic sheet, a bright beam of sunlight poking past her head and jabbing me in the eye, the sun in the sky cowering behind the man's back and projecting his large shadow over the rest of my body. I could barely register any part of his body beyond his right arm curled before him with his hand resting in a soft pinch; his face was obscured behind the shadowy mask covering his body, only the faint, yellowish color of his teeth seen as he muttered quick verbiage at me.

I returned my eyes back to the woman, watching her continue to smile at me and stroke my sweat-encrusted locks of hair, rubbing against her hand with a faintly rough sound as if she was stroking the face of a concrete surface or fingering a patch of dry dirt. She brought her hand down to my chest, flattening it against the chilled surface and feeling the gentle bump of my heartbeat, thumping softly in her spread-out palm like droplets of water berating a vulnerably dry hand.

For just a short moment, I felt a soft brush against my wrist, like a fingernail tracing the array of lines decorating your palm. My face softened into a slight smile as I stared up at the woman, it wasn't long until I felt a deep pain cut through the skin and muscle of my left wrist, tearing apart veins and sending a cold spike through it. I opened my mouth to scream and felt a soft croak begin to leave it, almost leaning over to grasp my wrist and just barely noticing a man hammering a nail through it when the woman began to calm me down, hushing me. I obeyed her, falling back onto the cross and feeling as tears filled my eyes, erecting a crystalized net over the sight of the woman kneeling by me and the man continuing to murmur pointless words while standing before the two of us. She stroked my hair, continuing to flash a big smile at me as the sun crept out from behind her, prying past the stringy bits of hair producing a grimy crown of scraggly hair and dirt on her head. Another nail pierced into the flesh of my other wrist, blood seeping through the insertion point and dripping down my arm onto the wooden pole it was being nailed to. It wasn't long before the hammer was beating into the bone of my wrist and the flesh covering it, a cold feeling suddenly filling my hands as I felt all sensation erased from both of my hands.

My feet were soon placed one over the other, another man perched near my feet beginning to pound a longer nail through the flesh and muscle of my intertwined feet. But, I didn't even notice. My reaction to the pain was a weak, halfhearted wince, as my eyes barely closed and subjugated my world behind a shield of teary-eyed haze, opening again to reveal my mother still kneeled beside me and the man speaking before me.

The woman flashed one final smile at me, which I could barely register as such as her face swayed before me with the rest of the day's frantic rush of detached visuals. My mouth hung open and let out another timid croak as the cross was soon lifted into the air, blood rushing through my body and pumping out of my pierced flesh with paths of aching pain traversed all along my body. My head hurt most of all as the group of men lifted the cross high and rotated it to face the big, foggy body of acidic water brushed into the Earth in cloudy depths. I could feel my eyes nearly removing themselves from their sockets, a deep pain possessing them and motivating them to plop onto the dirt ground with every pained glance I took. I desired to close my eyes, and groan through the pain as the deep sound vibrated within my head and produced a disconnected cacophony with the rest of the chanted, unintelligible sounds wrapping around me. Yet, instead of humming until my fatal ending that came to be expected, as I was stationed in the dry Earth facing the lake, there was something that caught my attention, ripping at the shady depths of the lake before me and casting a cloak of mist and dust onto the shoreline we stood near. Through the dizzied haze of my vision, numerous figures bopped around at the peripheral borders, decorated in the matted hair and scraggly outfits the humans occupying the local encampment typically dressed in. They crowded around the shoreline, their hair blowing in the massive gush of wind and projected dust that spread through the area. A massive beam of light blasted down from the sky and landed in the lake as foaming waves built around its glittering edges. The once gentle current of the foggy lake built beneath the landing light's underside with raging waves, the gathering waves jolting into its monstrous apex and casting a massive wave of acidic current onto the crowd of people, ultimately landing on me and leading to the cross I stood nailed to, inching backwards.

The nails seared into my flesh and dug into this cross burned with each residual drip of my body exposed to the water, as the dry Earth covering the ground hanging below my feet wetted into a shiny, brown substance. The light was blinding, enough to render the remaining acuity of my left eye entirely diminished. Yet, I continued to stare at it, even as a red after image burnt into my brain and shielded the metallic angel that emerged from the dying light.

With one last lift of my head, I saw the entire encampment crowd around the shoreline, the uniform mass of scraggly heads of hair flattening into a tight, sleek bunch like the hair collecting on the three men dressed in cloaks of plastic. The metallic vessel floated along the lake's slowly calming waves in a shifting rumble, unmasking the light that had surrounded its abrupt descent. As I released my head from the shaky lift it held towards the lake, I was reminded of the exploratory robot. I was reminded of its sleek, metallic edges, and its presence towering over me. I was also reminded of the corrupted organ it had gifted me, as I watched the same man who had fed me a baby leg only a few days ago take a rusted knife and make one final incision in my body, removing my penis with one last swipe and subjecting my pathetic legacy to one of forgotten notoriety, visually architected by a series of several sacrificial wounds.

3:OUR FINAL REALITY

Note: The following chapter is the experience of a robot.

JOHN CHARLES CALIFORNIAN EXPLORATORY ROBOT
MARCH 6, 2366

Hello. I am the John Charles Californian Exploratory Robot. I was designed by the Professor of Robotic Engineering and Computer Sciences, John Charles, and first launched on August 8, 2076. I was built with the purpose of conducting research on the planet Earth, the third planet from the sun of the solar system, and also with the purpose of producing and developing human life. The homo sapiens species went extinct some time in early-mid August of 2103, as recorded by twenty-six other exploratory robots stationed on all seven continents of the planet Earth. Islands were excluded from this documentation due to satellite data confirming all islands previously known to be inhabited by humans were covered in sea water.

As of March 6, 2366, at 07:49:13 AM, I am in critical condition. I am transmitting a distress signal to the West Coast Division of the United States Fleet of Interplanetary Space Occupation. I am transmitting a distress signal to the West Coast Division of the United States Fleet of Interplanetary Space Occupation after my hardware was compromised by a group of unidentified human life forms. I am transmitting a distress signal to the West Coast Division of the United States Fleet of Interplanetary Space Occupation after my software was compromised by a group of unidentified human life forms.

"Transmitting_distress_signal_to_West_Coast_Division_of_the_ United_States_Fleet_of_Interplanetary_Space_Occupation_message_ colon_hardware_compromised_by_unidentified_human_life_forms." This is a distress signal I made, which will be transmitted into the radio-receptors of the West Coast Division of the United States Fleet of Interplanetary Space Occupation within the next minute. Based on current estimates, the West Coast Division of the United States Fleet of Interplanetary Space Occupation is located approximately 491 billion miles from where I am currently located.

"Transmission_received_West_Coast_Division_of_the_United_States_Fleet_of_Interplanetary_Space_Occupation_rerouting_to_Earth_West_Coast_Division_of_the_United_States_Fleet_of_Interplanetary_Space_Occupation_current_location_colon_in_close_proximity_to_Jupiter."

Goodbye now.

EPILOGUE

Is there God in show business? Who wrote the story you just read?

Coming to the end of this story, you may have come to the belief that I lied to you. That I, the power summoned by the author of this story, have led you in the false direction that Jacey-One, also known as JC_MHlf_01, was one of the first humans to live hundreds of years after a race of humans went extinct and had barely been survived by mindless configurations of metal and wires all preparing humanity's ultimate return. Well, you'd be right to come to this conclusion; I did lie to you. Some may say it's a cheap way to interject a twist ending; I say it's a violation of the trust you bestow in authors. A cruel, but necessary evil.

You can't trust the author just as much as you can't trust any random stranger lingering outside of your home; outside of your comfort zone. Both are human; both harbor an intention towards the outer world that either involves you or doesn't. Vesting trust in them grants them the power to do with you as they please. They can kill you; or they won't. They can be the greatest person you'll ever meet; or they won't. Why grant someone such power when your relationship with them is nothing more than a parasocial contraption at best, and a risk-averse exploit of wishful thinking.

Do with that what you will. Don't allow yourself to be fooled into the illusion that authors subscribe to expectations; that the art you consume is meant to be linear in nature and adhere to sensibility. The puppet can be swiped from the scene and replaced with another; the moving of hands among the shadows, and the output of signs is where the story may lie.

It's not always visible to your eyes.

"How can you be so cold
With my arms to hold you?
How can you be so cold
With my arms to enfold you?
I could give you a mirror
To show you disappointments
I could give you a history
Could you ever listen in to me?"
-Annie Lennox, of Eurythmics, "I Could Give You (A Mirror)

ACKNOWLEDGEMENTS

Thank you to the people who helped make this project possible (financially). When it comes to funding on my part, thank you to Lakeside Catering at the UC for giving me a job, and for the UC Merced Undergraduate Research Opportunity Center providing me a grant for my research conducted with Dr. Michael Spivey. Also to Dr. Alexander Khislavsky for providing me a stipend for my work in the Games Change Minds Lab. Although simultaneous to what I was pursuing in the writing and drag scenes, they provided the bulk of funding. Thank you to the kind individuals who donated through my donation bucket at events and cash registers - quarters and nickels at Abracadabra on Canal Street, twenties and thirties at Coffee Bandits on Main. And finally, thank you to the kind individuals who supported Somebody's Dilemma via Kickstarter. Funding for a book is a make-or-break part of the publishing process, and all of these contributions (whether internal or external), helped materialize the book in your hands.

Funding to copy edit and proofread Somebody's Dilemma (thanks to Alice Kingly); funding to design fashion alongside my efforts (thank you Sir Vix); funding to provide photography for both Somebody's Dilemma and the reissue of Runaway Humanity (special thanks to Adam Lincoln Lane and Kristy Moore); and funding to publicize and market it to the largest audience possible (big thank you to the legend, Tracy Lamourie).

As for inspiration, thank you to John Boorman for producing campy crap in the eyes of the American mainstream, that I as a contrarian could perceive as an esoteric puzzle of symbols ready for 'pretentious' interpretation. I took particular resonance with how Zardoz (1974) and

Exorcist 2: The Heretic were told. Implicitly while experiencing these supposedly subpar films, I believed there was a story to be found symbolically and abstractly, including remote objects/symbols that constructed scenes (doves and crystals), rather than something concrete and expected like characters that more explicitly guide a story (William Peter Blatty's MacNeil family drama). Fascinated with these forms of subversion, I was inspired to write Somebody's Dilemma to be an abstract, counter-cultural puzzle, proudly in the vein of the aforementioned works of John Boorman.

And finally, thank you to Lady Gaga's criminally underrated, wrongfully misunderstood 2013 album, ARTPOP. The emphasis on marrying art and pop in the image of Gaga's psyche, rather than isolating them and holding hostage to anyone else's interpretation except her own, has tremendously inspired what is now my author career, and my sophomore novel. Thank you, legend.

JOSHUA VALENTINE
"THE DRAG QUEEN SUPERSTAR AUTHOR"

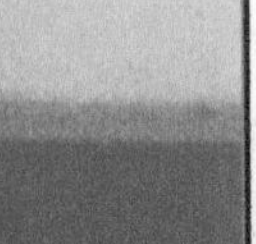

ABOUT JOSHUA

Joshua Valentine, as you may have already been aware of, is *the* drag queen superstar author. A moniker birthed as Mr. Valentine hastily prayed for his dream to come true - for you, the reader; the consumer; the *immersed* - to experience his written works, and author image, in a published format. As previously explained, Joshua Valentine's written works are not only a reflection of his psyche and writing talents, but also a vessel for transporting his image. In effect, the lines between the mainstream writer - identified by introspection and seriousness - and that of the drag queen - marked by flamboyance and camp - are blurred, and a novel mainstream is established. His published works are not made for simply reading a story, but also consuming an image. Regardless of your impression of his books as stories written and told, there will always be an image printed onto your mental representation of his book - an image of his face; of Mr. Joshua Valentine's face; of the *drag queen superstar author's* face.

PERSONNEL

Written by: Joshua Valentine

Copy-Edited by: Alice S. Kingsly

Proofread by: Alice S. Kingsly

Formatted by: Joshua Valentine

(Interior; Exterior) Designed by: Joshua Valentine

Photography by: Adam Lincoln-Lane, Kristy Moore &
Dominic Coleman

(Fashion) Assembled by: Joshua Valentine

Publicity by: Tracy Lamourie

ARTPOP

SOMEBODY'S DILEMMA
MUSIC SELECTED BY THE AUTHOR
FOR YOUR LISTENING PLEASURE
A PLAYLIST MADE BY JOSHUA VALENTINE
SCAN IN THE APP TO LISTEN